EDITED BY
BETH MEACHAM

TERRY'S
UNIVERSE

TOR

A TOM DOHERTY ASSOCIATES BOOK
NEW YORK

TERRY'S UNIVERSE

Copyright © 1988 by Carol Carr
Afterword copyright © 1988 by The Kilimanjaro Corporation

A TOR Book

Published by Tom Doherty Associates
49 West 24 Street
New York, N.Y. 10010

Cover art by M. Presley, from the collection of Harlan Ellison

ISBN: 0-812-54592-3   Can. ISBN: 0-812-54593-1

Library of Congress Catalog Card Number: 87-50871

First edition: June 1988
First mass market edition: March 1989

Printed in the United States of America

0 9 8 7 6 5 4 3 2 1

Contents

Introduction

It's been almost a year since Terry Carr passed out of our lives, and it is no easier to write about it now than it was just after that sad day in April 1987. Terry was an important person in my life, but he was more important to science fiction. Most people knew Terry as an anthologist, as a writer, as a fan, or, sometimes, as their own editor. But a few of us knew him as a member of our profession, editors, and it is astonishing to realize how influential he was. In a very real sense, Terry shaped sf as we know it today. He did that by discovering and fostering new writers, and by setting a standard of editorial professionalism. You'll know the names of the writers, even if you don't associate them with Terry—many of them (but by no means all) have contributed to this book; take a look at the table of contents, and try to imagine science fiction without them.

The standards he set for book editors are taken for granted these days in sf, although writers who sell novels in other genres soon discover that they aren't universal. Terry was one of the first editors to insist that sf be treated just like literature, that an editor and writer work together to develop a book. Terry originated the idea of getting blurbs for paperback originals. Today, the paperback original is the backbone of science fiction and fantasy, and it is where most editorial work is done. But not too long ago, "real" sf was published only in magazines or in hardcover—and it is due to Terry Carr that things are different now.

I first encountered Terry in the pages of *Universe,* his annual anthology of innovative short stories, and in his Best of the Year volumes. Actually, I was avidly reading the books he published from the late sixties on (especially those amazing Ace Specials), but of course I didn't know it; I only knew that there was some really great sf being published in those years. But gradually I became aware that there was such an entity as Terry Carr. He was listed as the editor of those anthologies I liked so much. He wrote some amazingly good short stories. He wrote novels, one of which was very good indeed (*Cirque*—the others, well Terry himself once threatened me with bodily harm if I ever mentioned them). I began to pay attention, and by the late seventies had developed an acute case of hero-worship.

I first met Terry on the telephone. I had been fortunate enough to be hired as the editorial assistant in the Ace sf department. One day, during my first week on the job, I answered the phone and an unidentified voice asked for Susan Allison (my new boss). When I said she wasn't in, the voice responded with the most disgusted "well SHIT" I'd ever heard. Sensing that there was a problem, I asked if maybe I could help, or at least take a message. He said he was Terry Carr, and that he needed some information about the contract for the new Specials; I don't remember what I said after that—I only hope it made sense. Susan told me to call Terry back that afternoon with the answers, and from that day on I was his assistant too.

Over the next few years, Terry taught me how to be an editor. He did it by example, and by telling me how and why he did things; he told me about his successes and his mistakes, and why he thought each was each. And he listened to me. Terry was the person I could always call to share the good news or commiserate about the bad. He helped me solve a lot of problems, but I think I was most grateful for the way he made me see the funny side of almost everything. By and by the hero-worship became a friendship, and the problem to be talked out was as likely to be his as mine. Terry's friendship was one of the treasures of my life, and it endured through a lot of changes, through collaboration and competition, and through the difficult last year of his life. He was good at a lot of things, but taking care of himself was not one of them.

I knew for months that he could die at any moment, but it was still a shock to get that phone call. When someone that important to your life passes out of it, it becomes vital to say or do something about it. People send flowers, they bring food to the living, they donate to charities. In this case, many people wrote essays and appreciations: Terry's friends were writers, after all. Some publishers took out black-bordered advertisements, a practice that Terry had made some pretty wicked jokes about to me in the past. It was clear to me that all *I* could do that would be appropriate was what Terry himself had taught me to do: make good books. Then I found out that Terry's wife, Carol, had been left in some financial difficulties, and my desire to "do something" became overwhelming. So this book was born, with the help of a lot of friends and an understanding publisher.

The stories in this anthology have all been donated by the authors, and *all* the proceeds are going to Carol Carr. One of the nicest thing about Terry's universe is the generosity of the people in it. But then, the urge to "do something for Terry" is awfully strong. Most of these stories were written especially for the book, and you won't find any of them published anywhere else for quite a while. And it isn't just the people whose words are here who helped out; I especially want to thank Lucius Shepard, Karen Haber, Richard Curtis, Damon Knight, Tom Doherty, Virginia Kidd, Pat LoBrutto, Tappan King, Debbie Notkin and Malcolm Edwards for their help, suggestions, cooperation and support.

Terry's Universe is a snapshot of the universe of science fiction that would not have existed without Terry Carr. It is dedicated by all of us to his memory, and it is my own way of saying a public thank you to the person who taught me everything I know about being a good editor. I hope you'll enjoy it.

—BETH MEACHAM

House of Bones

Robert Silverberg

After the evening meal Paul starts tapping on his drum and chanting quietly to himself, and Marty picks up the rhythm, chanting too. And then the two of them launch into that night's installment of the tribal epic, which is what happens, sooner or later, every evening.

It all sounds very intense but I don't have a clue to the meaning. They sing the epic in the religious language, which I've never been allowed to learn. It has the same relation to the everyday language, I guess, as Latin does to French or Spanish. But it's private, sacred, for insiders only. Not for the likes of me.

"Tell it, man!" B.J. yells. "Let it roll!" Danny shouts.

Paul and Marty are really getting into it. Then a gust of fierce stinging cold whistles through the house as the reindeer-hide flap over the doorway is lifted, and Zeus comes stomping in.

Zeus is the chieftain. Big burly man, starting to run to fat a little. Mean-looking, just as you'd expect. Heavy black beard streaked with gray and hard, glittering eyes that glow like rubies in a face wrinkled and carved by windburn and time. Despite the Paleolithic cold, all he's wearing is a cloak of black fur, loosely draped. The thick hair on his heavy chest is turning gray too. Festoons of jewelry announce his power and status: necklaces of sea-shells, bone beads, and amber, a pendant of yellow wolf teeth, an ivory headband, bracelets carved from bone, five or six rings.

Sudden silence. Ordinarily when Zeus drops in at B.J.'s house it's for a little roistering and tale-telling and butt-pinching, but tonight he has come without either of his wives, and he looks troubled, grim. Jabs a finger toward Jeanne.

"You saw the stranger today? What's he like?"

There's been a stranger lurking near the village all week, leaving traces everywhere—footprints in the permafrost, hastily covered-over campsites, broken flints, scraps of charred meat. The whole tribe's keyed. Strangers aren't common. I was the last one, a year and a half ago. God only knows why they took me in: because I seemed so pitiful to them, maybe. But the way they've been talking, they'll kill this one on sight if they can. Paul and Marty composed a Song of the Stranger last week and Marty sang it by the campfire two different nights. It was in the religious language so I couldn't understand a word of it. But it sounded terrifying.

Jeanne is Marty's wife. She got a good look at the stranger this afternoon, down by the river while netting fish for dinner. "He's short," she tells Zeus. "Shorter than any of you, but with big muscles, like Gebravar." Gebravar is Jeanne's name for me. The people of the tribe are strong, but they didn't pump iron when they were kids. My muscles fascinate them. "His hair is yellow and his eyes are gray. And he's ugly. Nasty. Big head, big flat nose. Walks with his shoulders hunched and his head down." Jeanne shudders. "He's like a pig. A real beast. A goblin. Trying to steal fish from the net, he was. But he ran away when he saw me."

Zeus listens, glowering, asking a question now and then—did he say anything, how was he dressed, was his skin painted in any way. Then he turns to Paul.

"What do you think he is?"

"A ghost," Paul says. These people see ghosts everywhere. And Paul, who is the bard of the tribe, thinks about them all the time. His poems are full of ghosts. He feels the world of ghosts pressing in, pressing in. "Ghosts have gray eyes," he says. "This man has gray eyes."

"A ghost, maybe, yes. But what kind of ghost?"

"What *kind*?"

Zeus glares. "You should listen to your own poems," he snaps. "Can't you see it? This is a Scavenger Folk man prowling around. Or the ghost of one."

General uproar and hubbub at that.

I turn to Sally. Sally's my woman. I still have trouble saying that she's my wife, but that's what she really is. I call her Sally because there once was a girl back home who I thought I might marry, and that was her name, far from here in another geological epoch.

I ask Sally who the Scavenger Folk are.

"From the old times," she says. "Lived here when we first came. But they're all dead now. They—"

That's all she gets a chance to tell me. Zeus is suddenly looming over me. He's always regarded me with a mixture of amusement and tolerant contempt, but now there's something new in his eye. "Here is something you will do for us," he says to me. "It takes a stranger to find a stranger. This will be your task. Whether he is a ghost or a man, we must know the truth. So you, tomorrow: you will go out and you will find him and you will

3

take him. Do you understand? At first light you will go to search for him, and you will not come back until you have him."

I try to say something, but my lips don't want to move. My silence seems good enough for Zeus, though. He smiles and nods fiercely and swings around, and goes stalking off into the night.

They all gather around me, excited in that kind of animated edgy way that comes over you when someone you know is picked for some big distinction. I can't tell whether they envy me or feel sorry for me. B.J. hugs me, Danny punches me in the arm, Paul runs up a jubilant-sounding number on his drum. Marty pulls a wickedly sharp stone blade about nine inches long out of his kit-bag and presses it into my hand.

"Here. You take this. You may need it."

I stare at it as if he had handed me a live grenade.

"Look," I say. "I don't know anything about stalking and capturing people."

"Come *on*," B.J. says. "What's the problem?"

B.J. is an architect. Paul's a poet. Marty sings, better than Pavarotti. Danny paints and sculpts. I think of them as my special buddies. They're all what you could loosely call Cro-Magnon men. I'm not. They treat me just like one of the gang, though. We five, we're some bunch. Without them I'd have gone crazy here. Lost as I am, cut off as I am from everything I used to be and know.

"You're strong and quick," Marty says. "You can do it."

"And you're pretty smart, in your crazy way," says Paul. "Smarter than *he* is. We aren't worried at all."

If they're a little condescending sometimes, I suppose I deserve it. They're highly skilled individuals, after all, proud of the things they can do. To them I'm a kind of retard. That's a novelty for me. I used to be considered highly skilled too, back where I came from.

4

"You go with me," I say to Marty. "You and Paul both. I'll do whatever has to be done but I want you to back me up."

"No," Marty says. "You do this alone."

"B.J.? Danny?"

"No," they say. And their smiles harden, their eyes grow chilly. Suddenly it doesn't look so chummy around here. We may be buddies but I have to go out there by myself. Or I may have misread the whole situation and we aren't such big buddies at all. Either way this is some kind of test, some rite of passage maybe, an initiation. I don't know. Just when I think these people are exactly like us except for a few piddling differences of customs and languages, I realize how alien they really are. Not savages, far from it. But they aren't even remotely like modern people. They're something entirely else. Their bodies and their minds are pure *Homo sapiens* but their souls are different from ours by 20,000 years.

To Sally I say, "Tell me more about the Scavenger Folk."

"Like animals, they were," she says. "They could speak but only in grunts and belches. They were bad hunters and they ate dead things that they found on the ground, or stole the kills of others."

"They smelled like garbage," says Danny. "Like an old dump where everything was rotten. And they didn't know how to paint or sculpt."

"This was how they screwed," says Marty, grabbing the nearest woman, pushing her down, pretending to hump her from behind. Everyone laughs, cheers, stamps his feet.

"And they walked like this," says B.J., doing an ape-shuffle, banging his chest with his fists.

There's a lot more, a lot of locker-room stuff about the ugly shaggy stupid smelly disgusting Scavenger Folk. How dirty they were, how barbaric. How the pregnant women kept the babies in their bellies twelve or thirteen months and they came out already hairy, with a full mouth of teeth. All ancient history, handed down through the generations by bards like Paul in the epics. None of them has ever actually seen a Scavenger. But they sure seem to detest them.

"They're all dead," Paul says. "They were killed in the migration wars long ago. That has to be a ghost out there."

Of course I've guessed what's up. I'm no archaeologist at all—West Point, fourth generation. My skills are in electronics, computers, time-shift physics. There was such horrible political infighting among the archaeology boys about who was going to get to go to the past that in the end none of them went and the gig wound up going to the military. Still, they sent me here with enough crash-course archaeology to be able to see that the Scavengers must have been what we call the Neanderthals, that shambling race of also-rans that got left behind in the evolutionary sweepstakes.

So there really had been a war of extermination between the slow-witted Scavengers and clever *Homo sapiens* here in Ice Age Europe. But there must have been a few survivors left on the losing side, and one of them, God knows why, is wandering around near this village.

Now I'm supposed to find the ugly stranger and capture him. Or kill him, I guess. Is that what Zeus wants from me? To take the stranger's blood on my head? A very civilized tribe, they are, even if they do hunt huge woolly elephants and build houses out of their whitened bones. Too civilized to do their own murdering, and they figure they can send me out to do it for them.

"I don't think he's a Scavenger," Danny says. "I think he's from Naz Glesim. The Naz Glesim people have gray eyes. Besides, what would a ghost want with fish?"

Naz Glesim is a land far to the northeast, perhaps near

eolithic the world is divided into a thousand little nations. Danny once went on a great solo journey through all the neighboring lands: he's a kind of tribal Marco Polo.

"You better not let the chief hear that," B.J. tells him. "He'll break your balls. Anyway, the Naz Glesim people aren't ugly. They look just like us except for their eyes."

"Well, there's that," Danny concedes. "But I still think—"

Paul shakes his head. That gesture goes way back, too. "A Scavenger ghost," he insists.

B.J. looks at me. "What do you think, Pumangiup?" That's his name for me.

"Me?" I say. "What do I know about these things?"

"You come from far away. You ever see a man like that?"

"I've seen plenty of ugly men, yes." The people of the tribe are tall and lean, brown hair and dark shining eyes, wide faces, bold cheekbones. If they had better teeth they'd be gorgeous. "But I don't know about this one. I'd have to see him."

Sally brings a new platter of grilled fish over. I run my hand fondly over her bare haunch. Inside this house made of mammoth bones nobody wears very much clothing, because the structure is well insulated and the heat builds up even in the dead of winter. To me Sally is far and away the best-looking woman in the tribe, high firm breasts, long supple legs, alert, inquisitive face. She was the mate of a man who had to be killed last summer because he became infested with ghosts. Danny and B.J. and a couple of the others bashed his head in, by way of a mercy killing, and then there was a wild six-day wake, dancing and wailing around the clock. Because she needed a change of luck they gave Sally to me, or me to her, figuring a holy fool like me must carry the charm of the gods. We have a fine time, Sally and I. We were two lost souls when we came together, and together we've kept each other from tumbling even deeper into the darkness.

7

"You'll be all right," B.J. says. "You can handle it. The gods love you."

"I hope that's true," I tell him.

Much later in the night Sally and I hold each other as though we both know that this could be our last time. She's all over me, hot, eager. There's no privacy in the bone-house and the others can hear us, four couples and I don't know how many kids, but that doesn't matter. It's dark. Our little bed of fox pelts is our own little world.

There's nothing esoteric, by the way, about these people's style of lovemaking. There are only so many ways that a male human body and a female human body can be joined together, and all of them, it seems, had already been invented by the time the glaciers came.

At dawn, by first light, I am on my way, alone, to hunt the Scavenger man. I rub the rough strange wall of the house of bones for luck, and off I go.

The village stretches for a couple of hundred yards along the bank of a cold, swiftly flowing river. The three round bone-houses where most of us live are arranged in a row, and the fourth one, the long house that is the residence of Zeus and his family and also serves as the temple and house of parliament, is just beyond them. On the far side of it is the new fifth house that we've been building this past week. Farther down, there's a workshop where tools are made and hides are scraped, and then a butchering area, and just past that there's an immense garbage dump and a towering heap of mammoth bones for future construction projects.

A sparse pine forest lies east of the village, and beyond it are the rolling hills and open plains where the mammoths and rhinos graze. No one ever goes into the river, because it's too cold and the current is too strong, and so it hems us in like a wall on our western border. I want to teach the tribesfolk how to build kayaks one of these days. I should also try to teach them how to swim, I

8

guess. And maybe a few years further along I'd like to see if we can chop down some trees and build a bridge. Will it shock the pants off them when I come out with all this useful stuff? They think I'm an idiot, because I don't know about the different grades of mud and frozen ground, the colors of charcoal, the uses and qualities of antler, bone, fat, hide, and stone. They feel sorry for me because I'm so limited. But they like me all the same. And the gods *love* me. At least B.J. thinks so.

I start my search down by the riverfront, since that's where Jeanne saw the Scavenger yesterday. The sun, at dawn on this Ice Age autumn morning, is small and pale, a sad little lemon far away. But the wind is quiet now. The ground is still soft from the summer thaw, and I look for tracks. There's permafrost five feet down, but the topsoil, at least, turns spongy in May and gets downright muddy by July. Then it hardens again and by October it's like steel, but by October we live mostly indoors.

There are footprints all over the place. We wear leather sandals, but a lot of us go barefoot much of the time, even now, in forty-degree weather. The people of the tribe have long, narrow feet with high arches. But down by the water near the fishnets I pick up a different spoor, the mark of a short, thick, low-arched foot with curled-under toes. It must be my Neanderthal. I smile. I feel like Sherlock Holmes. "Hey, look, Marty," I say to the sleeping village. "I've got the ugly bugger's track. B.J.? Paul? Danny? You just watch me. I'm going to find him faster than you could believe."

Those aren't their actual names. I just call them that, Marty, Paul, B.J., Danny. Around here everyone gives everyone else his own private set of names. Marty's name for B.J. is Ungklava. He calls Danny Tisbalalak and Paul is Shibgamon. Paul calls Marty Dolibog. His name for B.J. is Kalamok. And so on all around the tribe, a ton of names, hundreds and hundreds of names for just forty or fifty people. It's a confusing system. They have reasons for it that satisfy them. You learn to live with it.

A man never reveals his true name, the one his mother whispered when he was born. Not even his father knows that, or his wife. You could put hot stones between his legs and he still wouldn't tell you that true name of his, because that'd bring every ghost from Cornwall to Vladivostok down on his ass to haunt him. The world is full of angry ghosts, resentful of the living, ready to jump on anyone who'll give them an opening and plague him like leeches, like bedbugs, like every malign and perverse bloodsucking pest rolled into one.

We are somewhere in western Russia, or maybe Poland. The landscape suggests that: flat, bleak, a cold grassy steppe with a few oaks and birches and pines here and there. Of course a lot of Europe must look like that in this glacial epoch. But the clincher is the fact that these people build mammoth-bone houses. The only place that was ever done was Eastern Europe, so far as anybody down the line knows. Possibly they're the oldest true houses in the world.

What gets me is the immensity of this prehistoric age, the spans of time. It goes back and back and back and all of it is alive for these people. We think it's a big deal to go to England and see a cathedral a thousand years old. They've been hunting on this steppe thirty times as long. Can you visualize 30,000 years? To you, George Washington lived an incredibly long time ago. George is going to have his 300th birthday very soon. Make a stack of books a foot high and tell yourself that that stands for all the time that has gone by since George was born in 1732. Now go on stacking up the books. When you've got a pile as high as a ten-story building, that's 30,000 years.

A stack of years almost as high as that separates me from you, right this minute. In my bad moments, when the loneliness and the fear and the pain and the remembrance of all that I have lost start to operate on me, I feel that stack of years pressing on me with the weight of a mountain. I try not to let it get me down. But that's a hell of a weight to carry. Now and then it grinds me right into the frozen ground.

The flat-footed track leads me up to the north, around the garbage dump, and toward the forest. Then I lose it. The prints go round and round, double back to the garbage dump, then to the butchering area, then toward the forest again, then all the way over to the river. I can't make sense of the pattern. The poor dumb bastard just seems to have been milling around, foraging in the garbage for anything edible, then taking off again but not going far, checking back to see if anything's been caught in the fishnet, and so on. Where's he sleeping? Out in the open, I guess. Well, if what I heard last night is true, he's as hairy as a gorilla; maybe the cold doesn't bother him much.

Now that I've lost the trail, I have some time to think about the nature of the mission, and I start getting uncomfortable.

I'm carrying a long stone knife. I'm out here to kill. I picked the military for my profession a long time ago, but it wasn't with the idea of killing anyone, and certainly not in hand-to-hand combat. I guess I see myself as a representative of civilization, somebody trying to hold back the night, not as anyone who would go creeping around planning to stick a sharp flint blade into some miserable solitary tramp.

But I might well be the one that gets killed. He's wild, he's hungry, he's scared, he's primitive. He may not be very smart, but at least he's shrewd enough to have made it to adulthood, and he's out here earning his living by his wits and his strength. This is his world, not mine. He may be stalking me even while I'm stalking him, and when we catch up with each other he won't be fighting by any rules I ever learned. A good argument for turning back right now.

11

On the other hand if I come home in one piece with the Scavenger still at large, Zeus will hang my hide on the bone-house wall for disobeying him. We may all be great buddies here but when the chief gives the word, you hop to it or else. That's the way it's been since history began and I have no reason to think it's any different back here.

I simply have to kill the Scavenger. That's all there is to it.

I don't want to get killed by a wild man in this forest, and I don't want to be nailed up by a tribal court-martial either. I want to live to get back to my own time. I still hang on to the faint chance that the rainbow will come back for me and take me down the line to tell my tale in what I have already started to think of as the future. I want to make my report.

The news I'd like to bring you people up there in the world of the future is that these Ice Age folk don't see themselves as primitive. They know, they absolutely *know*, that they're the crown of creation. They have a language—two of them, in fact—they have history, they have music, they have poetry, they have technology, they have art, they have architecture. They have religion. They have laws. They have a way of life that has worked for thousands of years, that will go on working for thousands more. You may think it's all grunts and war clubs back here, but you're wrong. I can make this world real to you, if I could only get back there to you.

But even if I can't ever get back, there's a lot I want to do here. I want to learn that epic of theirs and write it down for you to read. I want to teach them about kayaks and bridges, and maybe more. I want to finish building the bone-house we started last week. I want to go on horsing around with my buddies B.J. and Danny and Marty and Paul. I want Sally. Christ, I might even have kids by her, and inject my own futuristic genes into the Ice Age gene pool.

I don't want to die today trying to fulfill a dumb murderous mission in this cold bleak prehistoric forest.

The morning grows warmer, though not warm. I pick up the trail again, or think I do, and start off toward the east and north, into the forest. Behind me I hear the sounds of laughter and shouting and song as work gets going on the new house, but soon I'm out of earshot. Now I hold the knife in my hand, ready for anything. There are wolves in here, as well as a frightened half man who may try to kill me before I can kill him.

I wonder how likely it is that I'll find him. I wonder how long I'm supposed to stay out here, too—a couple of hours, a day, a week?—and what I'm supposed to use for food, and how I keep my ass from freezing after dark, and what Zeus will say or do if I come back empty-handed.

I'm wandering around randomly now. I don't feel like Sherlock Holmes any longer.

Working on the bone-house, that's what I'd rather be doing now. Winter is coming on and the tribe has grown too big for the existing four houses. B.J. directs the job and Marty and Paul sing and chant and play the drum and flute, and about seven of us do the heavy labor.

"Pile those jawbones chin down," B.J. will yell, as I try to slip one into the foundation the wrong way around. *"Chin down,* bozo! That's better." Paul bangs out a terrific riff on the drum to applaud me for getting it right the second time. Marty starts making up a ballad about how dumb I am, and everyone laughs. But it's loving laughter. "Now that backbone over there," B.J. yells to me. I pull a long string of mammoth vertebrae from the huge pile. The bones are white, old bones that have been lying around a long time. They're dense and heavy. "Wedge it down in there good! Tighter! Tighter!" I huff and puff under the immense weight of the thing, and stagger a little, and somehow get it where it belongs, and jump out of the way just in time as Danny and two other men come tottering toward me carrying a gigantic skull.

The winter-houses are intricate and elaborate structures that require real ingenuity of design and construction. At this point in time B.J. may well be the best architect the world has ever known. He carries around a piece of ivory on which he has carved a blueprint for the house, and makes sure everybody weaves the bones and skulls and tusks into the structure just the right way. There's no shortage of construction materials. After 30,000 years of hunting mammoths in this territory, these people have enough bones lying around to build a city the size of Los Angeles.

The houses are warm and snug. They're round and domed, like big igloos made out of bones. The foundation is a circle of mammoth skulls with maybe a hundred mammoth jawbones stacked up over them in fancy herringbone patterns to form the wall. The roof is made of hides stretched over enormous tusks mounted overhead as arches. The whole thing is supported by a wooden frame and smaller bones are chinked in to seal the openings in the walls, plus a plastering of red clay. There's an entranceway made up of gigantic thighbones set up on end. It may all sound bizarre but there's a weird kind of beauty to it and you have no idea, once you're inside, that the bitter winds of the Pleistocene are howling all around you.

The tribe is seminomadic and lives by hunting and gathering. In the summer, which is about two months long, they roam the steppe, killing mammoths and rhinos and musk oxen, and bagging up berries and nuts to get them through the winter. Toward what I would guess is August the weather turns cold and they start to head for their village of bone-houses, hunting reindeer along the way. By the time the really bad weather arrives— think Minnesota-and-a-half—they're settled in for the winter with six months' worth of meat stored in deep-freeze pits in the permafrost. It's an orderly, rhythmic life. There's a real community here. I'd be willing to call it a civilization. But—as I stalk my human prey out here in the cold—I remind myself that life here is harsh and strange. Alien. Maybe I'm doing all this buddy-buddy nickname stuff simply to save my own sanity, you think? I don't know.

If I get killed out here today the thing I'll regret most is never learning their secret religious language and not being able to understand the big historical epic that they sing every night. They just don't want to teach it to me. Evidently it's something outsiders aren't meant to understand.

The epic, Sally tells me, is an immense account of everything that's ever happened: the *Iliad* and the *Odyssey* and the *Encyclopaedia Britannica* all rolled into one, a vast tale of gods and kings and men and warfare and migrations and vanished empires and great calamities. The text is so big and Sally's recounting of it is so sketchy that I have only the foggiest idea of what it's about, but when I hear it I want desperately to understand it. It's the actual history of a forgotten world, the tribal annals of thirty millennia, told in a forgotten language, all of it as lost to us as last year's dreams.

If I could learn it and translate it I would set it all down in writing so that maybe it would be found by archaeologists thousands of years from now. I've been taking notes on these people already, an account of what they're like and how I happen to be living among them. I've made twenty tablets so far, using the same clay that the tribe uses to make its pots and sculptures, and firing it in the same beehive-shaped kiln. It's a godawful slow job writing on slabs of clay with my little bone knife. I bake my tablets and bury them in the cobblestone floor of the house. Somewhere in the twenty-first or twenty-second century a Russian archaeologist will dig them up and they'll give him one hell of a jolt. But of their history, their myths, their poetry, I don't have a thing, because of the language problem. Not a damned thing.

Noon has come and gone. I find some white berries on a glossy-leaved bush and, after only a moment's hesitation, gobble them down. There's a faint sweetness there. I'm still hungry even after I pick the bush clean.

If I were back in the village now, we'd have knocked off work at noon for a lunch of dried fruit and strips of preserved reindeer meat, washed down with mugs of mildly fermented fruit juice. The fermentation is accidental, I think, an artifact of their storage methods. But obviously there are yeasts here and I'd like to try to invent wine and beer. Maybe they'll make me a god for that. This year I invented writing, but I did it for my sake and not for theirs and they aren't much interested in it. I think they'll be more impressed with beer.

A hard, nasty wind has started up out of the east. It's September now and the long winter is clamping down. In half an hour the temperature has dropped fifteen degrees, and I'm freezing. I'm wearing a fur parka and trousers, but that thin icy wind cuts right through. And it scours up the fine dry loose topsoil and flings it in our faces. Someday that light yellow dust will lie thirty feet deep over this village, and over B.J. and Marty and Danny and Paul, and probably over me as well.

Soon they'll be quitting for the day. The house will take eight or ten more days to finish, if early-season snowstorms don't interrupt. I can imagine Paul hitting the drum six good raps to wind things up and everybody making a run for indoors, whooping and hollering. These are high-spirited guys. They jump and shout and sing, punch each other playfully on the arms, brag about the goddesses they've screwed and the holy rhinos they've killed. Not that they're kids. My guess is that they're twenty-five, thirty years old, senior men of the tribe. The life expectancy here seems to be about forty-five. I'm thirty-four. I have a grandmother alive back in Illinois. Nobody here could possibly believe that. The one I call Zeus, the oldest and richest man in town, looks to be about fifty-three, probably is younger than that, and is generally regarded as favored by the gods because he's lived so long. He's a wild old bastard, still full of bounce and vigor. He lets you know that he keeps those two wives of his busy all night long, even at his age. These are robust people. They lead a tough life, but they don't know that, and so their souls are buoyant. I definitely will try to turn them on to beer next summer, if I last that long and if I can figure out the technology. This could be one hell of a party town.

Sometimes I can't help feeling abandoned by my own time. I know it's irrational. It has to be just an accident that I'm marooned here. But there are times when I think the people up there in 2013 simply shrugged and forgot about me when things went wrong, and it pisses me off tremendously until I get it under control. I'm a professionally trained hard-ass. But I'm 20,000 years from home and there are times when it hurts more than I can stand.

Maybe beer isn't the answer. Maybe what I need is a still. Brew up some stronger stuff than beer, a little moonshine to get me through those very black moments when the anger and the really heavy resentment start breaking through.

In the beginning the tribe looked on me, I guess, as a moron. Of course I was in shock. The time trip was a lot more traumatic than the experiments with rabbits and turtles had led us to think.

There I was, naked, dizzy, stunned, blinking and gaping, retching and puking. The air had a bitter acid smell to it—who expected that, that the air would smell differ-

ent in the past?—and it was so cold it burned my
nostrils. I knew at once that I hadn't landed in the pleas-
ant France of the Cro-Magnons but in some harsher,
bleaker land far to the east. I could still see the rainbow
glow of the Zeller ring, but it was vanishing fast, and
then it was gone.

The tribe found me ten minutes later. That was an
absolute fluke. I could have wandered for months, en-
countering nothing but reindeer and bison. I could have
frozen; I could have starved. But no, the men I would
come to call B.J. and Danny and Marty and Paul were
hunting near the place where I dropped out of the sky
and they stumbled on me right away. Thank God they
didn't see me arrive. They'd have decided that I was a
supernatural being and would have expected miracles
from me, and I can't do miracles. Instead they simply
took me for some poor dope who had wandered so far
from home that he didn't know where he was, which
after all was essentially the truth.

I must have seemed like one sad case. I couldn't speak
their language or any other language they knew. I carried no weapons. I didn't know how to make tools out of
flints or sew a fur parka or set up a snare for a wolf or
stampede a herd of mammoths into a trap. I didn't know
anything, in fact, not a single useful thing. But instead of
spearing me on the spot they took me to their village, fed
me, clothed me, taught me their language. Threw their
arms around me and told me what a great guy I was.
They made me one of them. That was a year and a half
ago. I'm a kind of holy fool for them, a sacred idiot.

I was supposed to be here just four days and then the
Zeller Effect rainbow would come for me and carry me
home. Of course within a few weeks I realized that something had gone wonky at the uptime end, that the experi-
ment had malfunctioned and that I probably wasn't ever
going to get home. There was that risk all along. Well,
here I am, here I stay. First came stinging pain and an-

ger and I suppose grief when the truth finally caught up with me. Now there's just a dull ache that won't go away.

In early afternoon I stumble across the Scavenger Man. It's pure dumb luck. The trail has long since given out—the forest floor is covered with soft pine duff here, and I'm not enough of a hunter to distinguish one spoor from another in that—and I'm simply moving aimlessly when I see some broken branches, and then I get a whiff of burning wood, and I follow that scent twenty or thirty yards over a low rise and there he is, hunkered down by a hastily thrown-together little hearth roasting a couple of ptarmigans on a green spit. A scavenger he may be, but he's a better man than I am when it comes to skulling ptarmigans.

He's really ugly. Jeanne wasn't exaggerating at all.

His head is huge and juts back a long way. His mouth is like a muzzle and his chin is hardly there at all and his forehead slopes down to huge brow ridges like an ape's. His hair is like straw, and it's all over him, though he isn't really shaggy, no hairier than a lot of men I've known. His eyes are gray, yes, and small, deep-set. He's built low and thick, like an Olympic weight lifter. He's wearing a strip of fur around his middle and nothing else. He's an honest-to-God Neanderthal, straight out of the textbooks, and when I see him a chill runs down my spine as though up till this minute I had never really believed that I had traveled 20,000 years in time and now, holy shit, the whole concept has finally become real to me.

He sniffs and gets my wind, and his big brows knit and his whole body goes tense. He stares at me, checking me out, sizing me up. It's very quiet here and we are primordial enemies, face to face with no one else around. I've never felt anything like that before.

We are maybe twenty feet from each other. I can smell

him and he can smell me, and it's the smell of fear on both sides. I can't begin to anticipate his move. He rocks back and forth a little, as if getting ready to spring up and come charging, or maybe bolt off into the forest.

But he doesn't do that. The first moment of tension passes and he eases back. He doesn't try to attack, and he doesn't get up to run. He just sits there in a kind of patient, tired way, staring at me, waiting to see what I'm going to do. I wonder if I'm being suckered, set up for a sudden onslaught.

I'm so cold and hungry and tired that I wonder if I'll be able to kill him when he comes at me. For a moment I almost don't care.

Then I laugh at myself for expecting shrewdness and trickery from a Neanderthal man. Between one moment and the next all the menace goes out of him for me. He isn't pretty but he doesn't seem like a goblin, or a demon, just an ugly thick-bodied man sitting alone in a chilly forest.

And I know that sure as anything I'm not going to try to kill him, not because he's so terrifying but because he isn't.

"They sent me out here to kill you," I say, showing him the flint knife.

He goes on staring. I might just as well be speaking English, or Sanskrit.

"I'm not going to do it," I tell him. "That's the first thing you ought to know. I've never killed anyone before and I'm not going to begin with a complete stranger. Okay? Is that understood?"

He says something now. His voice is soft and indistinct, but I can tell that he's speaking some entirely other language.

"I can't understand what you're telling me," I say, "and you don't understand me. So we're even."

I take a couple of steps toward him. The blade is still in my hand. He doesn't move. I see now that he's got no weapons and even though he's powerfully built and could probably rip my arms off in two seconds, I'd be able to put the blade into him first. I point to the north, away from the village, and make a broad sweeping gesture. "You'd be wise to head off that way," I say, speaking very slowly and loudly, as if that would matter. "Get yourself out of the neighborhood. They'll kill you otherwise. You understand? *Capisce? Verstehen Sie?* Go. Scat. Scram. I won't kill you, but they will."

I gesture some more, vociferously pantomiming his route to the north. He looks at me. He looks at the knife. His enormous cavernous nostrils widen and flicker. For a moment I think I've misread him in the most idiotically naive way, that he's been simply biding his time getting ready to jump me as soon as I stop making speeches.

Then he pulls a chunk of meat from the bird he's been roasting, and offers it to me.

"I come here to kill you, and you give me lunch?"

He holds it out. A bribe? Begging for his life?

"I can't," I say. "I came here to kill you. Look, I'm just going to turn around and go back, all right? If anybody asks, I never saw you." He waves the meat at me and I begin to salivate as though it's pheasant under glass. But no, no, I can't take his lunch. I point to him, and again to the north, and once more indicate that he ought not to let the sun set on him in this town. Then I turn and start to walk away, wondering if this is the moment when he'll leap up and spring on me from behind and choke the life out of me.

I take five steps, ten, and then I hear him moving behind me.

So this is it. We really are going to fight.

I turn, my knife at the ready. He looks down at it sadly. He's standing there with the piece of meat still in his hand, coming after me to give it to me anyway.

"Jesus," I say. "You're just lonely."

He says something in that soft blurred language of his

and holds out the meat. I take it and bolt it down fast, even though it's only half-cooked—dumb Neanderthal!—and I almost gag. He smiles. I don't care what he looks like, if he smiles and shares his food then he's human by me. I smile too. Zeus is going to murder me. We sit down together and watch the other ptarmigan cook, and when it's ready we share it, neither of us saying a word. He has trouble getting a wing off, and I hand him my knife, which he uses in a clumsy way and hands back to me.

After lunch I get up and say, "I'm going back now. I wish to hell you'd head off to the hills before they catch you."

And I turn, and go.

And he follows me like a lost dog who has just adopted a new owner.

So I bring him back to the village with me. There's simply no way to get rid of him short of physically attacking him, and I'm not going to do that. As we emerge from the forest a sickening wave of fear sweeps over me. I think at first it's the roast ptarmigan trying to come back up, but no, it's downright terror, because the Scavenger is obviously planning to stick with me right to the end, and the end is not going to be good. I can see Zeus' blazing eyes, his furious scowl. The thwarted Ice Age chieftain in a storm of wrath. Since I didn't do the job, they will. They'll kill him and maybe they'll kill me too, since I've revealed myself to be a dangerous moron who will bring home the very enemy he was sent out to eliminate.

"This is dumb," I tell the Neanderthal. "You shouldn't be doing this."

He smiles again. You don't understand shit, do you, fellow?

We are past the garbage dump now, past the butchering area. B.J. and his crew are at work on the new house.

B.J. looks up when he sees me and his eyes are bright with surprise.

He nudges Marty and Marty nudges Paul, and Paul taps Danny on the shoulder. They point to me and to the Neanderthal. They look at each other. They open their mouths but they don't say anything. They whisper, they shake their heads. They back off a little, and circle around us, gaping, staring.

Christ. Here it comes.

I can imagine what they're thinking. They're thinking that I have really screwed up. That I've brought a ghost home for dinner. Or else an enemy that I was supposed to kill. They're thinking that I'm an absolute lunatic, that I'm an idiot, and now they've got to do the dirty work that I was too dumb to do. And I wonder if I'll try to defend the Neanderthal against them, and what it'll be like if I do. What am I going to do, take them all on at once? And go down swinging as my four sweet buddies close in on me and flatten me into the permafrost? I will. If they force me to it, by God I will. I'll go for their guts with Marty's long stone blade if they try anything on the Neanderthal, or on me.

I don't want to think about it. I don't want to think about any of this.

Then Marty points and claps his hands and jumps about three feet in the air.

"Hey!" he yells. "Look at that! He brought the ghost back with him!"

And then they move in on me, just like that, the four of them, swarming all around me, pressing close, pummelling hard. There's no room to use the knife. They come on too fast. I do what I can with elbows, knees, even teeth. But they pound me from every side, open fists against my ribs, sides of hands crashing against the meat of my back. The breath goes from me and I come close to toppling as pain breaks out all over me at once. I need all of my strength, and then some, to keep from

23

going down under their onslaught, and I think, this is a dumb way to die, beaten to death by a bunch of berserk cave men in 20,000 B.C.

But after the first few wild moments things become a bit quieter and I get myself together and manage to push them back from me a little way, and I land a good one that sends Paul reeling backward with blood spouting from his lip, and I whirl toward B.J. and start to take him out, figuring I'll deal with Marty on the rebound. And then I realize that they aren't really fighting with me any more, and in fact that they never were.

It dawns on me that they were smiling and laughing as they worked me over, that their eyes were full of laughter and love, that if they had truly wanted to work me over it would have taken the four of them about seven and a half seconds to do it.

They're just having fun. They're playing with me in a jolly roughhouse way.

They step back from me. We all stand there quietly for a moment, breathing hard, rubbing our cuts and bruises. The thought of throwing up crosses my mind and I push it away.

"You brought the ghost back," Marty says again.

"Not a ghost," I say. "He's real."

"Not a ghost?"

"Not a ghost, no. He's live. He followed me back here."

"Can you believe it?" B.J. cries. "Live! Followed him back here! Just came marching right in here with him!" He turns to Paul. His eyes are gleaming and for a second I think they're going to jump me all over again. If they do I don't think I'm going to be able to deal with it. But he says simply, "This has to be a song by tonight. This is something special."

"I'm going to get the chief," says Danny, and runs off.

"Look, I'm sorry," I say. "I know what the chief wanted. I just couldn't do it."

"Do what?" B.J. asks. "What are you talking about?" says Paul.

"Kill him," I say. "He was just sitting there by his fire, roasting a couple of birds, and he offered me a chunk, and—"

"*Kill* him?" B.J. says. "You were going to kill him?"

"Wasn't that what I was supposed—"

He goggles at me and starts to answer, but just then Zeus comes running up, and pretty much everyone else in the tribe, the women and the kids too, and they sweep up around us like the tide. Cheering, yelling, dancing, pummeling me in that cheerful bone-smashing way of theirs, laughing, shouting. Forming a ring around the Scavenger Man and throwing their hands in the air. It's a jubilee. Even Zeus is grinning. Marty begins to sing and Paul gets going on the drum. And Zeus comes over to me and embraces me like the big old bear that he is.

"I had it all wrong, didn't I?" I say later to B.J. "You were all just testing me, sure. But not to see how good a hunter I am."

He looks at me without any comprehension at all and doesn't answer. B.J., with that crafty architect's mind of his that takes in everything.

"You wanted to see if I was really human, right? If I had compassion, if I could treat a lost stranger the way I was treated myself."

Blank stares. Deadpan faces.

"Marty? Paul?"

They shrug. Tap their foreheads: the timeless gesture, ages old.

Are they putting me on? I don't know. But I'm certain that I'm right. If I had killed the Neanderthal they almost certainly would have killed me. That must have been it. I need to believe that that was it. All the time that I was congratulating them for not being the savages I had expected them to be, they were wondering how

25

much of a savage *I* was. They had tested the depth of my humanity; and I had passed. And they finally see that I'm civilized too.

At any rate the Scavenger Man lives with us now. Not as a member of the tribe, of course, but as a sacred pet of some sort, a tame chimpanzee, perhaps. He may very well be the last of his kind, or close to it; and though the tribe looks upon him as something dopey and filthy and pathetic, they're not going to do him any harm. To them he's a pitiful bedraggled savage who'll bring good luck if he's treated well. He'll keep the ghosts away. Hell, maybe that's why they took me in, too.

As for me, I've given up what little hope I had of going home. The Zeller rainbow will never return for me, of that I'm altogether sure. But that's all right. I've been through some changes. I've come to terms with it.

We finished the new house yesterday and B.J. let me put the last tusk in place, the one they call the ghost-bone, that keeps dark spirits outside. It's apparently a big honor to be the one who sets up the ghost-bone. Afterward the four of them sang the Song of the House, which is a sort of dedication. Like all their other songs, it's in the old language, the secret one, the sacred one. I couldn't sing it with them, not having the words, but I came in with oom-pahs on the choruses and that seemed to go down pretty well.

I told them that by the next time we need to build a house, I will have invented beer, so that we can all go out when it's finished and get drunk to celebrate properly.

Of course they didn't know what the hell I was talking about, but they looked pleased anyway.

And tomorrow, Paul says, he's going to begin teaching me the other language. The secret one. The one that only the members of the tribe may know.

Kore 87

Ursula K. Le Guin

Did he take me away from her or did she make me leave him? I don't know if what came first was the light. I don't know where my home was. I remember the dark car. Long, and large, and so fast that the road broke like a wave. There was the smell of the car and the smell of the sod, a cleft, an opening. The road went down, I know. What flowers smell like sometimes I remember. In the name of the hyacinth I find the colors purple, pink, red, and the color of pomegranate. But there is a forbidden color. If I say its name the punishment will come upon me, the breaking, the terrible calling; if I say the name of milk the earth will ache. The earth will ache and reach for me again, white arms and brown arms groping and grasping, seeking, choking. If I was there, under his roof, was it wrong that I was there? Was I not wanted there? I was chosen, I was queen. The arms reached out but they couldn't catch me. I didn't look up as we drove by the long, black rivers. The car went so fast by the rivers! But we would stop for me to name the rivers: Memory that carries remembering away, and Anger that runs so gently smoothing the pebbles round, and Terror that we swam in fearlessly. And then the waterfalls! I gave them no names. They are still falling down and down from deep to deeper dark till the last glimmering is lost and only the long voice of water comes back from below saying what we cannot say. Sound is a slower traveler than light, and so more sure. It was the calling that came to me from the high places, never the light. How could the light come here within? This is no place for light. It's too heavy here. But in the calling came the hyacinth, the colors that come before the light. O Mother! Mother! Mother! Who called? Who called her? me?

He's rich, Mother. He lives there in the basement of the old house with old things, dried things, roots and coins and chests and shadows and closets. He lives down in the cellar, but he's rich. He could buy anything.

No, he didn't hurt me only once. When I was frightened when he came when I was there alone. He took me away then he made me go down inside. We went inside where I had never been and I was there then. Yes, when my mother's working I always stay alone. I stay in the house and garden, where else is there to go? No, I don't know my daddy. Yes, no, I don't know. I don't know what it means. He made me come with him in the car. I went with him. Yes he touched me there. Yes he did that. Yes he did that. Yes we did that. Yes I said no I didn't say. He said I was his wife. He said everything he had was mine. Can I see my mother now?

Yes he gave me jewelry. I took it yes. I wore it yes. It was beautiful, the stones, amethyst, rose amethyst, ruby. He gave me the crown of hyacinth, of pomegranate stone. He gave me the ring of gold I wear. We never left the basement no. He said it was dangerous outside. He said there was a war. He said there were enemies. He never hurt me only at the start. He needed me. We did that yes I am his wife. With him I rule that place. With him I judge you all. To whom do you think you come?

She came to me and came back to me, the musician's wife, my friend. I knew she would come back. She came back crying. I knew she would. I was waiting for her by the road, and cried with her when she came back alone, but not for long. Here tears dry away. Here in the dark no mourning is. A few tears, like pomegranate seeds, five or six little half-transparent seeds that look like uncut rubies, that's enough, enough to eat, enough.

O Mother don't cry, I was only playing hide and seek! I only hid! I was joking, Mother, I didn't mean to stay so long. I didn't know it was so late. I didn't notice it was dark. We were playing kings and queens and hide and seek and I didn't know, I didn't know, I didn't know. Do I live there? Is this my home? This is outside the earth and I have lived inside. This is inside the earth and I have lived outside. This is dark and I come from the light, from the dark into this light. He loves me well. He waits for me. Why is your love winter, Mother? Why are his hands so cold?

What does my mother do? She keeps the house.

There is no river long enough to wear her anger down. She will never forget and will always be afraid. You have made an enemy indeed, my lord.

Mother, be comforted. Don't cry and make me cry. Come winter I'll come back and spring is my return. I'll bring the hyacinths. You can depend on me, you know, I'm not a child now. But if I am your daughter how can I be his wife? How can I be your wife when I am her daughter? What do you want of me, who sleep in my arms? These are her arms around me rocking me, rocking me. I wear the ring of gold he gave me as I walk in the garden she grew for me, the red flowers, the purple flowers, the pomegranate trees with roots of white and brown that reach down deep. To be sought forever, but shall I be found and never seek myself and never find? To be one body root and flower, to break the sod, to drive the dark car home, to turn, return, where is my home? Shall I bear no daughter?

Slack Lankhmar Afternoon
Featuring Hisvet

Fritz Leiber

When the Gray Mouser under Lok's curse involuntarily slipped deep down into the grainy earth during the full moon ceremony (Satyrs) on Hangman's Hill (Rime Isle) and—most unwillingly!—became somewhat acclimatized to his somewhat dark and dismal, close-fitting surroundings, the first civilized place he visited in the course of his journeyings underground throughout Netherworld was the buried rat city of Lankhmar Below.

As consciousness glimmered, glowed, and then shone noontide bright in the Gray Mouser's skull, he would have been certain he was dreaming, for in his nostrils was the smell of Lankhmar earth, richly redolent of the grainfields, and Great Salt Marsh, the river Hlal, and the ashes of innumerable fires, and the decay of myriad entities, a unique melange of odors, and he was ensconced

31

in one of the secretmost rooms of all Lankhmar city, one
he knew well although he had visited it only once, and
how could his underground journeying possibly have
carried him so far, two thousand leagues or more, one-
tenth the way at least around all Nehwon world?—except that he had never in his life had a dream in which
the furniture and actors were so clearly distinct and open
to scrutiny in all their details.

But as we know, it was the Mouser's custom on waking
anywhere not to move more than an eye muscle or make
the least sound, even that of a deeper breath, until he
had taken in and thoroughly mastered the nature of his
surroundings and his own circumstances amongst them.

He was comfortably seated cross-legged about a
Lankhmar cubit (a forearm's length) behind a narrow low
table beside the foot of the wide bed, sheeted in white
silk curiously coarse of weave, in the combined underground bedroom and boudoir of the rat princess Hisvet,
his tormentingest onetime paramour, daughter of the
wealthy grain merchant Hisvin, in the buried city of
Lankhmar Below. He knew it was that room and no
other by its pale violet hangings, silver fittings, and a half
hundred more apposite details, chiefest perhaps two
painted panels in the far wall depicting an unclad maiden
and crocodile erotically intertwined and a youth and
leopardess similarly entangled. As had been the case
some five years ago, the room was lit by narrow tanks of
glowworms at the foot of the walls, but now also by silver
cages hanging cornice high and imprisoning flashing fire-
beetles, glowwasps, nightbees, and diamondflies big as
robins or starlings. While on the low table before him
rested a silver water clock with visible pool, upon the
center of which a large drop fell every third breath or
dozenth heartbeat, making circular ripples and a cut
crystal carafe of pale golden wine, reminding him he was
abominably thirsty.

So much for the furniture of his dream, vision, or true

sighting. The actors included slim Hisvet herself wearing a violet wrap whose color matched the hangings and her lips. She was seated on the bed's foot, looking as merry and schoolgirl innocent (and devilishly attractive) as always, her fine silver-blonde hair drawn through a small ring of that metal behind her head; while standing at dutiful attention close before her were two barefoot maids with hair cropped short and wearing identical closely fitting hip-length black and white tunics. Hisvet was lecturing them, laying out rules of some sort, apparently, and they were listening most earnestly, although they showed it in different ways, the brunette nodding her head, smiling her understandings, and darting her gaze with sharp intelligence, while the blonde maintained a sober and distant—yet wide-eyed—expression, as though memorizing Hisvet's every word, inscribing each one in a compartment of her brain reserved for that purpose alone.

But although Hisvet worked her violet lips and the tip of her mottled blue and pink tongue continuously in the movements of speech and lifted an admonitory right forefinger from time to time and once touched it successively on the tips of the outspread fingertips of her supine left hand to emphasize points one, two, three, and four, not a single word could the Gray Mouser hear. Nor did any one of the three ever look once in his direction, even the saucy dark-haired wench whose gaze went everywhere else.

Since superficially both maids were in their servile wise and very short tunics quite as attractive as their ravishing mistress, their disregard of him began to wound the Mouser's vanity not a little.

Since there seemed nothing for the moment to do but watch them, the Mouser soon developed a hankering to see their naked shapes. So far as the maids were concerned, he might get his wish simply by waiting. Hisvet had a remarkable instinct for such matters and was perfectly willing to let other women entertain for her—distribute her favors, as it were.

But as to her own secret person, it still remained a mystery to the Mouser whether under the robes, wraps, and armor she affected there was a normal maiden form or a slender rat tail and eight tits, which his imagination pictured as converging pairs of large-nippled and large-aureoled bud-breasts, the third pair to either side of her umbilicus and the fourth close together upon her pubis.

It also was a mystery to him whether the three females and he were all now of rat size or human size—ten inches or five feet high. Certainly he'd had none of the shape-changing elixir that was used in moving between Lankhmar Above and the rat city of Lankhmar Below.

His hankerings continued. Surely he deserved some reward for all the underground perils he'd braved. Women could do men so much good so easily.

There remained the problem of the three women's perfect inaudibility.

Either, he guessed, they were engaged in an elaborate pantomime (plotted by Hisvet to tease him?) or it *was* a dream despite its realism, or else there was some hermetic barrier (most likely magical) between his ears and them.

Supporting this last possibility was the point that while he could see the giant luminescent insects move about in their cages, striking the silver bars with wing and limb while making their bright shinings and flashes, no angry buzzings or sounds of any sort came down from them. While (most telling of all in its way) only silence accompanied the infrequent but regular plashes of the singular crystalline drops into the shimmering pool of the water clock so close at hand.

One final circumstance suggestive of magic at work and matching the strange quiet of the scene otherwise so real: miraculously suspended in the air above the near edge of the low table, in a vertical attitude with ring-pommeled small silver grip uppermost, was a tapering whip of white snow-serpent hide scarcely a cubit long, so close at hand he could perceive its finely rugose surface, yet spy no thread or other explanation of its quiet suspension.

Well, that was the scene, he told himself. Now to decide on how to enter it, assert himself as one of the actors. He would lean suddenly forward, he told himself, reach out his right hand, seize with his three bottom fingers the neck of the carafe, unstopper it with forefinger and thumb preparatory to putting it to his parched lips, saying meanwhile something to the effect of, "Greetings, dearest delightful demoiselle, do me the kindnesss of interrupting this charade to give an old friend notice. Don't be alarmed, girls," that last being for the two maids, of course.

No sooner thought than done!

But, from the start, things went most grievously agley. On his first move he felt himself gripped by a general paralysis that struck like lightning. His whole front was bruised, his right hand and arm scraped, from every side dark brown grainy walls rushed in upon him, his "Greetings" became on the first syllable a strangled growl that stabbed his ears, pained his whole skull, and changed to a fit of coughing that left him with what seemed a mouthful of raw dirt.

He was *still* in the same horrid buried predicament he'd been in ever since he'd slipped down out of the full moon ceremony on Gallows Hill into the cold cruel ground that was at once so strangely permeable to his involuntary passage through it and so adamantly resistant to his attempts to escape it. This time he'd been fooled by the perfection of the occult vision, that let him see through solid earth for a distance around him, into thinking he was free, disregarding the evidence of all his other avenues of awareness. Evidently he *had* somehow been brought to Lankhmar's under environs and nothing now remained to do but begin anew the slow game of regularizing his breathing, calming his pounding heart, and freeing his mouth grain by grain of the dirt that had entered it during his spasm, carefully working his tongue to best advantage, in order to assure bare survival. For after the pain in his skull subsided he became aware of a general weakness and a wavering of consciousness that told him he was very near the edge between being and not being and must work most cunningly to draw back from it.

During this endeavor he was assisted by the fact that he never quite altogether lost sight of a larger white and violet visual reality around him, there were patchy flashes and glimpses of it alternating with the grainy dark dirt, and he was also helped by the faint yellow glow continuing to emanate from his upper face.

When the Mouser finally rewon all the territory he'd lost by his incautious sally, he was surprised to see fair Hisvet still going through all the motions of talking, and the winsome maids through those of attending her every word, as animatedly as before. Whatever was she saying?

While carefully maintaining all underground breathing routines, he concentrated his attention on other channels of sensation than the visual, seeking to widen and deepen and bringing to bear all his inner powers, and after a time his efforts were rewarded.

The next heavy drop fell into the pool of the water clock with an audible dulcet *plash!* He almost, but not quite, gave a start.

Almost immediately a glowwasp *buzzed* and a diamondfly *whirred* its transparent wings against the wire-thin pale bars.

Hisvet leaned back on her elbows and said in silver tones, "At ease, girls."

They appeared to relax their attention—a little, at any rate.

She tapped three fingers against the ruby rondure of her lips as she yawned prettily. "My, that was a most lengthy and boring lecture," she commented. "Yet you endured it most commendably, dear Threesie," she addressed the dark-haired maid. "And you too, Foursie," she told the fair-haired one. She picked up from beside her a long emerald-headed pin and flourished it playfully. "There was not once the need for me to make use of *this* upon either of you," she said, laughing, "to recall to attention the willful wandering mind and wake the lazy dreamer."

Both girls shaped their lips to appreciative smiles, while giving the pin most sour looks.

Hisvet handed it to Foursie, who bore it somewhat gingerly across the room to a drawered chest topped with cosmetics and mirrors, and inserted it into a spherical black cushion that held jewel-headed others such compassing all the hues of the rainbow.

Meanwhile Hisvet addressed Threesie, whose eyes widened as she listened, "During my talk I twice got the distinct impression that we were being spied on by an evil intelligence, one of the criminous sort my father deals with, or one of our own enemies, or a cast-off lover perchance," and she searched her gaze around the walls, lingering somewhat overlong, the Mouser felt, in his direction.

"I will meditate on it," she continued. "Dear Threesie, fetch me my silver-inlaid black opal figure of the world of Nehwon which I call The Opener of the Way."

Threesie nodded dutifully and went to the same chest Foursie had just visited, passing her midway.

"Dear Foursie," Hisvet greeted the blonde, "fetch me a beaker of white wine. My throat has grown quite dry with all that stupid talking."

Foursie bowed her fair-thatched head and came to the low table set against the wall behind which the Mouser was embedded in earth invisible to him. He studied her appreciatively as she unstoppered the carafe he'd so disastrously snatched at and neatly filled a shining glass so tall and narrow it looked like a measuring tube. Her white uniform tunic was secured down the front with large circular jet buttons.

Returning to her mistress, she went down on her knees without bending her slender body in any other way and proffered the refreshment.

"Taste it first," Hisvet instructed.

Getting this instruction, not uncommonly given servants by aristocrats, Foursie threw back her head and poured a short gush of the fluid between her parted lips without touching them to the glass, which she next held out to show its level was perceptibly decreased.

Hisvet accepted it, saying, "That was well executed, Foursie. Next time don't wait for instruction. And you might lick your lips and smile to show that you enjoyed."

Foursie bobbed her head.

"Dear demoiselle," Threesie called from where she knelt at the chest of drawers, "I cannot find The Opener."

"Have you searched carefully for it?" Hisvet called back, her voice becoming slightly thin. "It is an oblate sphere big as two thumbs, inset with silver bounding the continents and flat diamonds for the cities and a larger amethyst and turquoise making the death and life poles."

"Dear demoiselle, I know The Opener," Threesie called respectfully.

Hisvet, who was looking at Foursie again, shrugged her shoulders, then set the narrow glass to her lips and downed its contents in three swallows. "That was refreshing." Again the lip pats.

A rutching sound turned her attention back to Threesie. "No, do not open the other drawers," she directed, "it would not be there. Just search the top one thoroughly and *find it*. Set out the contents one by one on top of the chest if necessary."

"Yes, demoiselle."

Hisvet caught Foursie's eye again, rolled hers toward busy Threesie, sketched another shrug, and commented confidingly, "This could become a tiresome annoyance, you know, a true weariness. No, girl, don't bob your head. That's all right on Threesie, but it's not your style. Incline it once, demurely."

"Yes, mistress." Her single nod was shy as a virgin princess'.

"How are you doing, Threesie?"

The brunette turned to face them. Her reply was barely loud enough to cross the room. "Demoiselle, I must confess myself defeated."

After a rather long pause, Hisvet said reflectively, "That could be quite bothersome for you, Threesie, you know. As senior maid present you would be wholly responsible for any deficiencies, disappearances, or thefts. Think about it."

After another pause, she sighed and said, holding out the empty glass, "Foursie, fetch me the springy implement of correction."

The blonde inclined her head, took the glass, and, walking somewhat more slowly, returned to the low table, set down the glass, refilled it, and reached across to seize the magically suspended white whip, which she lifted with a little twist and bore off with the glass thereby solving a minor mystery for the Mouser. The whip had simply been hanging on a hook on the wall. But since the wall had been and was again invisible to him, so was the hook protruding from it.

He felt a stirring of interest in the scene he spied on from his confining point of vantage, and was duly grateful to have his mind taken a little off his own troubles. He knew something of Hisvet's ways and could guess the next developments, or at least speculate rewardingly. Dark-haired Threesie seemed well cast as the villain or culprit of this triangular piece. Leaning back against the chest of drawers and scowling, she looked a bird of ill omen in her uniform black tunic, though the large circular alabaster buttons going down the front added a comic note. Foursie did her kneeling trick a second time. Hisvet accepted the whip and replenished drink, saying graciously, "Thank you, my dear. I feel much better with these both by me. Well, Threesie?"

"I am thinking, demoiselle," that one said, "and it comes to me that when I entered this room Foursie was crouched where I stand now with the drawer I have just searched thoroughly open, and she was rummaging around in it. She pushed it shut at once, but may well have taken somewhat from it, I realize now, and hid about her person."

"Demoiselle, that's not true!" Foursie protested, turning pale. "The drawer was never open, nor I at it."

"She is a vicious little liar, dear mistress," Threesie shot back. "Mark how she blanches!"

"Hush, girls," Hisvet reproved. "I have thought of a simple way to settle this most unseemly dispute. Threesie dear, had Foursie opportunity to hide The Opener elswewhere in the room after she took it, if she did? As I recall, I entered shortly after you did."

"No, mistress, she had not."

"Well, then," Hisvet said, smiling. "Threesie, come here. Foursie dear, strip off your tunic, so she may search you thoroughly."

"Demoiselle!" the blonde uttered reproachfully, "You would not shame me so."

"No shame at all," Hisvet assured her ingenuously, lifting her silver eyebrows. "Why, child, suppose I were entertaining a lover, I might very well—probably would—have you and Threesie disrobe, so as not to embarrass him, or at all events make us both feel conspicuous. Or we might have the whim to ask one of you or both to join in our play under direction. Frix understood these things, as I hope Threesie does. Frix was incomparable. Not even Twosie comes close to matching her. But as you know, Frix managed to work out her term of service, discharge the geas my father set upon her. There's never been another Onesie, and that's why."

Both maids nodded agreement, though somewhat grimly, in their two different styles. They'd each heard somewhat too much about the Incomparable Onesie.

The Mouser was beginning to enjoy himself. Why, look, the piece was barely begun and Hisvet had managed to switch around the roles of the two other characters! He wished Fafhrd were here, he'd enjoy hearing Frix praised so. He'd been quite gone on the princess of Arilia, especially when she'd been Hisvet's imperturbable slave-maid. Though the large loon wouldn't appreciate being entombed, that was certain. Probably too big to survive by scavenging air in any case. Which reminded him, he'd best keep in mind his own breathing. And not lose sight of the ever-present possibility of the intrusion into the scene of some third force from either the under- or overworld. Talk about having to watch two ways—!

In response to Hisvet's "And so, no nonsense, child. Strip, I said!" Foursie had been arguing, "Have compassion, demoiselle. To disrobe for a lover would be one thing. But to strip to be searched by a fellow servant is simply too humiliating. I couldn't bear it!"

Hisvet sprang up off the bed. "I've quite lost patience with you, you prudish little bitch. Who are you to say what you'll bear—or bare, for that matter? Threesie, grip her arms! If she struggles, pinion them behind her."

The dark maid, who was already back of Foursie, seized and tightly held her elbows down at her sides, meanwhile smiling somewhat evilly at her mistress across the fair maid's shoulder. Hisvet reached out a straight right arm, chucked the girl's chin up until they were looking each other straight in the eye, and then proceeded very deliberately to unbutton the top black button.

Foursie said, with as much dignity as she could muster, "I would have submitted to you, demoiselle, without my arms held."

But Hisvet said only, very deliberately also, "You are a silly schoolgirl, Foursie dear, needing considerable teaching, which you're going to get. You would submit to me? But not to my maid acting on my orders? To begin with, Threesie is not your equal fellow servant. She outranks you and is empowered to correct you in my absence."

As she spoke she went on undoing the buttons, taking her time and digging her knuckles and pressing the large buttons into the girl's flesh edgewise as she did so. At the undoing of the third button the maid's small, firm, pink-nippled breasts popped out. Hisvet continued, "But as it is you're getting your way, aren't you, Foursie? I am disrobing you and not dear Threesie here though she is witnessing. In fact, I'm 'maiding' you, how's that for topsy-turvy? You're getting the deluxe treatment, one might say, though I much doubt you will get much pleasure from it."

She finished with the buttons, looked the girl up and down, lightly flicked her breasts with the back of her hand, and said with a cheery laugh, "There, that wasn't so bad now, was it, dear? Threesie, finish."

Grinning, the dark maid slid the white tunic down Foursie's arms and off them. "Why, you are blushing, Foursie," Hisvet observed, chuckling. "On Whore Street that's a specialty, I'm told, and ups the price. Inspect the garment carefully," she warned Threesie. "Feel along each seam and hem. She may have pilfered something smaller than The Opener. And now, dear child, prepare yourself to be searched from head to toe by a maid who is your superior, whilst I direct and witness." Taking up the silver-handled whip of white snowserpent hide from the bed and gesturing with it, she directed Foursie, "Lift out your arms a little from your sides. There, that's enough. And stand so that your entire anatomy is more accessible. A little wider stance, please. Yes, that will do."

The Mouser noted that all the maid's body hair had been shaven or plucked. So that practice, favored by witless Glipkerio, the Scarecrow Overlord, was still followed in Lankhmar. A seemly and most attractive one, the Mouser thought. "There's nothing hidden in the garment, Threesie? You're sure? Well, toss it by the far wall and then you might begin by running your fingers through Foursie's hair. Bend forward, child! Slowly and carefully, Threesie. I know her mop's quite short, but you'd be shocked to learn how much a little hair can sometimes hide. And don't forget the ears. We're looking for tiny things."

Hisvet yawned and took a long swallow of wine. Foursie glared at her nearer tormentor. There is something peculiarly degrading about being handled by the ears, having them spread and bent this way and that. But Threesie, learning from her mistress, only smiled sweetly back.

"And now the mouth," Hisvet directed. "Open wide, Foursie, as for the barber-surgeon. Feel in each cheek, Threesie. I don't suppose Foursie's been playing the little squirrel, but there's no telling. And now . . . Surely you're not at a loss, Threesie? Perhaps I should have expressed it, search her from top to bottom. You may lubricate your fingers with my pomade. But use it sparingly, its basis is the essential oil with which they anoint the Emperor of the East. Don't agonize so, Foursie! Imagine it's your lover exploring you, dextrously demonstrating his tender regard. Who is your lover, Foursie? You do have one, I trust? Come to recall, I've caught the fair page Hari looking at you in that certain way. I wonder what he'd think if he could see you as you're presently occupied. Droll. I've half a mind to summon him. Well, that's half done. And now, Threesie, her darker avenue of amatory bliss. Bend over, Foursie. Treat her gently, Threesie. Some of these matters appear to be quite new to our little girl, advanced subjects for our student, though I know that's hard to credit. What, Foursie, tears? Cheer up, child! You're not proved guilty yet; in fact you're well on the way to being cleared. Life has all sorts of surprises."

The Mouser smiled cynically from his weird invisible prison. Around Hisvet surprises were invariably disastrous, he knew from experiences. He was thoroughly enjoying himself, so far as his limited circumstances permitted. He thought of how all of his greatest loves and infatuations had been for short and slim girls like these. Lilyblack came to mind, back when he'd bravoed and racketeered for Pulg and Fafhrd had found god in Issek. Reetha, who'd been Glipkerio's silver-chained maid. Ivivis of Quarmall, supple as a snake. Innocent tragic Ivrian, his first love, whose princess-dreams he'd fed. Cif, of course. The nightfilly Ivmiss Ovartamortes. That made seven, counting Hisvet. And there was one other, an eighth, whose name and identity evaded him, who was also a maid by profession and particularly delectable because somehow forbidden. Who *had* she been? What *was* her name? If he could recall one more detail he'd remember all. Maddening! Of course, he'd had all manner of larger women, but this elusive memory involved all smaller than himself, his special pantheon of little darlings. You'd think a man in his grave (and that was truly his situation, face it) would be able to concentrate his mind upon one subject, but no, even here there were details to distract you, self-responsibilities that had to be taken care of, as keeping up an even rhythm of shallow breathing, pushing back intrusive dirt off of his lips, keeping constant watch before and behind— It occurred to him that Foursie too must be telling herself that last thing, though much good it would do her— which reminded him to return to the enjoyment of the three-girl comedy which destiny had provided for his secret viewing.

Hisvet was saying, "Now, Foursie, go to the far wall and stand facing it while I hear Threesie's report and confer with her. And stop blubbering, girl! Use your discarded tunic to wipe the tears and snot off your face."

Hisvet led Threesie back to the foot of the bed, set her empty glass on the low table, and said in a voice that The Mouser could barely hear, despite the advantages of nearness and occult audition, "I take it, Threesie, you didn't find The Opener, or anything else?"

"No, dear demoiselle, I did not," the dark maid replied and then went on in a voice that was more like a stage whisper, "I'm certain she's swallowed it. I suggest she be given a strong emetic and if that fails a powerful cathartic. Or both together, to save time."

Foursie too heard that, the Mouser judged by the way her shoulders drew together as she faced the wall.

Hisvet shook her head and said in the same low tones as before, "No, that won't be necessary, I think, though it could be amusing under other circumstances. Now it suits my design to have her think she's been completely cleared of any suspicion of theft." She faced around and changed to her ringingest silver voice, "Congratulations, Foursie, you'll be glad to hear that your fellow maid has given you a clean bill of health. Isn't that wonderful? And now come here at once. No, don't try to put on your tunic. Leave that soiled rag. You need a lot more practice in serving naked, which you ought to be able to do every bit as efficiently, coolly, and nicely without the reassurance of a frock. And perhaps practice in other activities one generally carries out best in one's skin. Beginning now."

The Lankhmar demoiselle in the violet wrap yawned again and stretched. "That wretched session has quite wearied me. Foursie, you may begin your nude reapprenticeship (that's a joke, girl) by fetching me a fat pillow from the head of the bed."

When Foursie came around with her plump lemon-hued burden, her eyes asking a question, Hisvet indicated with her whip the bottom corner of the bed and, when the fair maid had placed the pillow there, gave her the whip, saying, "Hold this for me," and stretched herself out with her head on the pillow. But after murmuring, "Ah, that's better," and wriggling her toes, she lifted up on an elbow, looked toward Threesie, and pointed with her other hand down at the carpet by the foot of the bed, saying, "Threesie, come here. I want to show you something privately."

When the dark maid came eagerly, all agog for more secrets, Hisvet laid her silver-tressed head back again upon the pillow, whose hue contrasted nicely with her violet wrap, and said, "Lean down, so your head is close to mine. I want this to be quite private. Foursie, stand clear."

But when Threesie stooped down, her lips working with high excitement, Hisvet began at once to criticize. "No, don't bend your knees! I did not bid you crouch over me like an animal. Keep your legs straight."

By bending her waist more, pushing her buttocks back, and also throwing her arms out behind her, the dark maid managed to comply with her instructions without overbalancing. Her and her mistress' faces were upside down to each other.

"But, demoiselle," Threesie pointed out humbly, "when I bend over like this in this short tunic, I expose myself behind. Especially with your rule against undergarments."

Hisvet smiled up at her. "That's very true," she observed, "and I designed them partly with that in mind, so that when told to pick up something from the floor, for instance, a maid would stoop gracefully, as in a curtsy, keeping her head and shoulders erect. It's far more seemly and civilized."

Threesie said uncertainly, "But when you go down like that you have to bend your knees, you squat. You told me not to bend—"

"That's quite a different matter," Hisvet interrupted, impatience gathering in her voice. "I told you to lean down your head."

"But, demoiselle," Threesie faltered.

Hisvet reached up and caught an earlobe between forefinger and thumb, dug in the nails, twisted sharply, and gave a downward tug. Threesie squealed. Hisvet let go and, patting her cheek, told her, "That's all right. I just wanted to rivet your attention and make you stop your silly babble. Now, listen carefully. While you did the body search on Foursie passably well, it became frightfully obvious that you, as well as Foursie, needless to say, were in sore need of instruction in the amatory arts, which, it falls on me to give you, since you're my own dear maid and no one else's." And reaching her hand higher, she hooked her fingers around the back of Threesie's neck and pulled her head down briskly but thoughtfully, leaning her own head to the left at the last moment, so that her lips met at an angle those of Threesie, who managed to keep her balance by farther and somewhat desperate rearward outthrustings.

The Mouser thought, I knew that this was coming. But one certainly cannot fault the little darlings for their occasional itch for each other, since their taste is so exactly like my own. Strange, come to think of it, that Fafhrd and I have never seemed to experience this like-sex urge. Is it a deficiency in us? I must discuss the question with him, sometime. And with Cif too, for that matter, ask her if she and Afreyt ever played games . . . no, maybe not ask, I could understand Afreyt lusting for Cif, but not dear Ciffy for that beanpole Venus.

Hisvet shifted her fingers behind Threesie's head to the short hairs there, lifted her head to its original position as briskly as she'd lowered it, and said, "That was passable, also. Next time, if such should be, employ your tongue somewhat more freely. Be adventurous, girl."

Wide-eyed Threesie gasped, "Excuse me, demoiselle, but was that kiss, for which I thank you most humbly, the something you said you wished to show me privately?"

"No, it was not," Hisvet informed her, thrusting a hand deep into a side pocket of her wrap. "That is a different matter, rather sadder for you." Pulling Threesie's head down again, this time by the neck of her black tunic, she brought a fist out of the pocket, opened it under Threesie's eyes, displaying on her cupped palm a globular black opal traveled with silver lines and pocked here and there with small pale glittering dots. "What do you suppose this is?" she asked.

"It appears to be The Opener of the Way, dear demoiselle," Threesie faltered, "But how—"

"Quite right, girl. I took it earlier from the chest myself and just now remembered. So Foursie could hardly have swallowed it, could she? Or even taken it from the chest, for that matter."

"No, demoiselle," the dark maid agreed reluctantly. "But Foursie's only a servant of the lowest rank, little better than a slave. It was natural to suspect her. Moreover, you yourself must have known—"

"I told you I only now remembered!" Hisvet reminded her in dangerous tones. She raised her voice. "Foursie!"

"Yes, demoiselle?" came the swift reply.

"Threesie is to be punished for bearing false witness against a fellow servant. Since you're the party who would have been injured, I think it's most appropriate that you administer the chastisement. Moreover, you are conveniently at hand and have my whip. Do you know how to use it?"

"I think I do, demoiselle," Foursie answered evenly. "When I was a child down on the farm I used to ride a mule."

"That's nice to know," Hisvet called. "Wait for directions."

As Threesie quite involuntarily started to move away, Hisvet rotated the fist grasping her tunic, so that it tightened around Threesie's neck and Hisvet's knuckles dug into the maid's throat.

"Listen," she hissed, "if you so much as move a step or flex your knees during what's coming, I'll have my father put a geas on you. And not a relatively nice and easy one like Frix. She merely had to serve me faithfully and cheerfully as slave until she'd thrice saved my life at risk of her own. Straighten those knees now!"

Threesie complied. She had seen old Hisvin send a berserk cook into mortal convulsions, so he died in his tracks with mouth exuding greenish foam, merely by staring at him fixedly.

Hisvet eased her grip on the top of Threesie's tunic. She scowled in thought. Then her face broke into a smile. She called, "Foursie, here's how. Time your blows to the plashes of the water clock, one for one, nothing in between—don't let yourself get carried away. Start with the third plash after the next. I'll call the first of those so you get it right."

Hisvet's hand on the neck of the black tunic became busy, undoing the three top big white buttons rapidly.

The water clock plashed, sounding unnaturally loud. Hisvet called "Ready!" Tension took hold.

Though pendant, the dark maid's breasts were quite as small and firm as the fair one's with thicker nipples the rosy hue of fresh-scrubbed copper. Hisvet fondled them.

"How many blows, demoiselle?" Threesie asked in a small, fearfully anxious voice. "In all?"

"Hush! I haven't decided yet. You're supposed to be enjoying this. And you really are, I can tell, for your nipples are hardening despite your tremors. And your aureoles are all goose bumps. You should indicate pleasure at my squeezings and finger dancing across your tits by sighing and moaning."

The water clock *plashed*. "One!" Hisvet called, then ominously for Threesie's benefit, "You've started to bend your legs again," and, taking the hand away from the maid's bosom, reached out and gave each of her knees a firm shove.

In his retreat the Mouser spared a glance for the ripples spreading and reflecting in the clock's pool. A shiver of genuine fear surprised him at the thought that he seemed to be just too well placed for watching for it all to be a matter of chance. Had Hisvet arranged it so? Did she somehow know that he, or at least some spirit, was watching invisibly? Was it all to get him off guard?

No, he told himself, I'm starting to think too tricky. This was just one of those glorious guilty visions that, it was to be hoped, lightened the last moments of buried men less fortunate or resourceful than he. His eyes feasted on Foursie as the girl positioned herself to the far side of Threesie's quivering rear, measuring distances with her eyes and the white whip, her pink-nippled breasts jouncing a bit as she danced with excitement. She was flushed all over and not with embarrassment, he was sure.

Plash went the water clock. "Two!" Hisvet called. She shifted her hand to the back of Threesie's neck, pulled down until the maid's blanched tight face was a handbreadth above her own, said rapidly, "We're doing another kiss. It'll help you bear the pain and I want to feel you getting it, taste your reaction. Keep your knees straight," and she pulled the maid's face down all the way and kissed her fiercely. Her free hand played with Threesie's maiden breasts.

The third *plash* was tailed with a narrow *thwack* and muffled squeal. Threesie bucked. And all for me, the little darlings, the Mouser thought. Foursie's blue eyes flashed like a fury's in ecstasy. She was breathing hard. She drew back the white whip to begin another blow, remembered in time to wait. Hisvet let up Threesie's head to breathe. "Lovely," she told her. "Your scream came down my throat. It tasted like divine spice." Then, "Excellent, Foursie," she called. "Stay on your toes, girl."

Threesie cried, "Hesset help me," invoking the Lankhmar moon goddess. "Make her stop, demoiselle, I'll do anything."

Hisvet said, "Hush, girl. Hesset give you courage," and pulled down her head again, stifling her cries against her waiting lips. Her other hand pressed back on the maid's knees.

The three sounds were much the same. Threesie's buck was more of a caper. The Mouser was surprised by his arousal, felt a flicker of shame, recalled in time to breathe shallowly, et cetera. The moment Hisvet let up Threesie's head to take a breath, the maid pleaded, "Make her stop, she'll kill me," then couldn't contain indignation, "Demoiselle, you knew she hadn't stolen the jewel. You led me on." Hisvet's hand, busy with her breasts, seized up flesh and skin midway between them as though her thumb and forefinger knuckle were pinchers, squeezed, twisted, rubbed together, and jerked down all at once. Threesie squealed.

"Silence, you stupid slut," her mistress hissed. "You enjoyed making her suffer, now you're paying. You little fool! Don't you realize a maid who falsely betrays her fellow maid would just as readily betray her mistress? I expect real loyalty from my maids. Foursie, lay on hard." And she pulled the maid's face against hers just as the drop *plashed* and the third blow fell. This time when Hisvet released her head, there were no instant words, tears spurted down instead. Hisvet shook them off, dipped her free hand again in her wide pocket.

And this time the Mouser was surprised by his impulse to shut his eyes. But nasty fascination and urgent messages from his stiffening member were too strong.

Hisvet lectured, "One other thing I expect of my maid: Love, when the whim is on me. That's the chief reason she must always keep herself clean and attractive." She mopped Threesie's face with a large kerchief, then held it to her nose. "Blow," she commanded. "And then swallow hard. I don't want you blubbering snot on me."

Threesie obeyed, but then the injustice of it all overwhelmed her. "But it isn't *fair*," she bleated woefully. "It's not fair at *all*."

Those words and tones had a strange and unexpected effect upon the earth-embraced Mouser. They recalled to him the name that had eluded him of the eighth little darling. A score and two or three years slipped away and he was lolling dishabille on the wide couch in the private dining chamber of the Silver Eel tavern in Lankhmar, and Ivrian's maid Freg was racing back and forth before him in her delicious young slim nakedness and then she had stopped by him and turned toward him, tears spurting from her eyes, and bleated woefully those identical same trite words.

He knew the circumstances all right, knew them by heart. Barely a fortnight had passed since the fairly satisfactory ending of the affair of Omphal's jewel-crusted skull and other vengeful brown bones from the forgotten burial crypt in the great house of the Thieves Guild. The gems salvaged had been adequate, especially when there was added thereto the person of Ivrian, a lean shifty fox-faced glorious redhead. He'd had her the second night after, though that hadn't been easy, and it was more or less understood between Fafhrd and him that Freg was the Northerner's booty. But then the big oaf had delayed making his move, dawdled over nailing down his conquest, seemed hardly grateful at all to the Mouser for having taken on the more difficult seduction, leaving his comrade the juicier, tenderer prey, to be had for no more exertion than pushing back onto the bed (nine times out of ten the big man was incomprehensibly slower than he about such matters) so that after two or three more nights and nothing forwarder, and feeling impatient and feckless and at war with all Nehwon—and with Fafhrd too, for the nonce—and opportunity presenting, he'd yielded to temptation and bedded the silly chit, which hadn't been all that easy either. And then on their third or fourth assignation she turned stormy and accused him of getting her drunk and forcing her the first time and claimed to have been deeply in love with Fafhrd and he with her, she knew, only they'd been moving slowly so as to savor fully their romance before declaring and enjoying it, and the Mouser had cut in with his nasty lust and wily ways and managed to root a child in her, she was certain of that, and so spoiled everything. And although he was still deeply infatuated with Freg, that had angered him and he'd told the little fool that he always tried out the virtue of girls who set their cap for Fafhrd and tried to romance him, to see if they were worthy of him and would stay faithful, and none of them had passed the test so far, but she'd done worst. And she had spouted tears and whimpered those nine words Threesie'd just voiced. And the next day Freg had been gone from Lankhmar, no one knew where, and Fafhrd had fallen into a melancholy fit, and Ivrian'd turned nasty, and he'd not breathed a word then or ever about the part he'd played.

All of which went to show, he told himself, how a suddenly triggered lost memory, like a ghost from the grave, could be so real as to blot out completely a poignantly interesting, nastily fascinating present, almost create another present, as it were, for several heartbeats till it had run its course inside his eyes.

They were between blows in Hisvet's boudoir. The violet wrap was undone just far enough to bare her own small palely violet-nippled breasts and she was holding down to them the tousled head of the dark maid, who was tonguing them industriously under instruction. The fair maid was doing a rapid little dance in place to contain her pent excitement and rotating the poised white whip in a little circle in time with her flashing toes. Hisvet called gayly to incite her on, "Remember, Foursie, the slut had her fingers up you prying around, not gently, I'll warrant," and the clock *plashed* and the whip whistled and *thwacked* and Threesie joined in the dance.

When Hisvet let up her head, the dark maid said rapidly. "If you'll have her stop just for a while, demoiselle, I'll lick your ass most lovingly, I promise," and Hisvet replied, "All in good time, girl," and reaching back in an excess of arousal caught hold with thumb and forefinger knuckle of her by the midst of her maiden mound and gave it the same sort of pinchers tweak as she had the maid's flesh midway between her breasts, where a blue bruise now showed; and the dark maid squealed muffledly.

But then, just as Foursie stayed her dance to strike and the Mouser's erection grew almost unbearably hard, Hisvet cried sharply, "Break off the whipping, Foursie! Don't strike again!" and the maid obeyed with a spasmodic effort, and Hisvet ducked her head and shoulders out from under Threesie's arched front and stared searchingly at the wall by the water clock just where the whip had hung, her nostrils flaring and with blue-and-pink-mottled tongue showing in her open mouth. She announced raptly and anxiously, "I sense the near presence of Death or a close relative, some murderous demon lord or deadly demoness. It must have scented your ecstasy of torment, Threesie, and come hunting."

The Mouser felt they were all staring straight at him, then noted that their gazes went in slightly different directions: Hisvet's intense but cool, Foursie's shocked and terrified as she backed away, dropping the pristine white whip, Threesie's somewhat not yet grasping her good fortune, as she stood in bent position in her sagging and worked-up black tunic stretched back toward her rear crisscrossed with red welts and with her knees still straight.

Hisvet continued, "Run, Foursie, and warn my father of this menace. Bid him haste here, bringing his wand and sigils. Nay, do not stay to dress or hunt a towel, as if you were a simpering virgin. Go as you are. And speed! There's *danger* here, you witlet!"

Then, turning her furious attention to Threesie, "Quit standing there so docilely bent over with legs invitingly spread, lame brain, all ready for the slavering hounds of death to mount you. Spring to and defend *my* rear, mind cripple!"

Just then the Mouser felt what seemed a large centipede crawl across his left thigh, somehow insinuating itself between his flesh and the grainy earth encasing him, and then march down his rigid, like embedded, cock, and settle itself in a ring 'round his tumescent glans. And there swung in 'round his head from the other side, moving through the earth effortlessly, a face like a beautiful skull tightly covered by blue-pied, chalky white skin with eyes that were intent red embers and pressed itself against his own face closely from forehead to chin, so he felt through her blue lips mashing his/her individual two ranks of teeth. He realized that the centipede was the bone tips of her skeletal hand (the other pressed the back of his neck at the base of his own skull) and whose bony fingertips now moved slightly upon his stiff member, inducing it to spend one drop, but one drop only, of its load, giving him a sickening, joyless jolt of heavy black pain that left him weak and gasping. But no sooner had that pain begun to fade down when the slim bone fingers moved and the second jolt came equal the first, and after agonizing pauses the third and fourth.

The stangury! The worst pain that a man can suffer, he'd once heard, when urine must be voided drop by drop—this was the same, except it was his seed.

And it kept on.

His wavering mind confused it with the plashes of the water clock. But Threesie had suffered only eight or nine stripes at most. How many drops would it take to discharge his heavy load? And render his member flaccid? Two score hundred?

The violet-hung boudoir and Hisvet and her crew were gone. All that remained for vision was the vermilion volume lit by pain's hot ember eyes and his phosphorescent mask, hell in a very small place.

In a voice that was rough, rasping, infinitely dry, sardonic-tender, Death's Sister whispered throatily, "My very own dear love. My dearest one."

As his torment continued, his wavering consciousness and gasping and trembling general weakness warned him the end was near. Despite the continuing jolts of agony, he concentrated regularing his breathing, making it shallow, pushing back with his tongue the grains his gasps had drawn. With the roaring in his ears, it became a surf of boulders he had to keep at bay.

Isosceles

Kate Wilhelm

I came wide awake all at once, certain Todd had called me. I strained to hear before the second thought came, that it had been a dream. It was exactly how he used to sound. On the other twin bed Brandon made a sleep noise, but did not stir. I slipped out of bed and groped for my dressing gown and slippers in the dark, but I had no cause for worry; Brandon's sleep was profound, and the beds were separate. Close together, but apart.

I left the bedroom and wandered through the hall to the living room where the darkness was not so intense. Sky light, a glow from a switch on the VCR, a reflection from a clock on an end table made the room seem bright after the stygian cave of the bedroom. It was three-thirty. I continued through the apartment, the entire seventh floor of the building, on my way to the breakfast room that opened to a balcony. And there I sat looking out over the Gulf of Mexico, a vast pit of blackness with lights like lonely stars coursing their orbits at the edge of the universe. The air had cooled and felt better than the manufactured air inside. Dawn would bring back the heat, and by afternoon this balcony would be uninhabitable. I opened my dressing gown to let the air dry my skin, and I tried to bring the dream to mind.

There was nothing more than the one word, my name, spoken in Todd's voice. I had mellowed many things about him over the past few years, created an imaginary Todd. During my waking dreams when we talked, his voice was softer, a bit huskier, a more tentative voice, and very seductive, but the voice that had drawn me from sleep was unchanged, his own.

I was five or six when my grandmother died, and the loss had been devastating. I had wept bitterly day after day. First my mother had left, not died, just left; then my grandmother had left. Father had comforted me as best he could. He cuddled and rocked me and soothed me with utter nonsense. On the balcony that night, preoccupied as I was by the way voices could be re-created with such exactitude, I remembered Father's words.

"Honey," he had said to ease my grief, "she isn't gone. She's a little tiny lady who lives in your head now. She'll never go away from you."

After that I spoke to her, and listened hard; sometimes she responded. I had put my mother in there, too, and often the three of us had conversations, even arguments. I always won. Before Grandmother became ill, I told her once that when I got big and she was little, I would take care of her. Everyone had thought that was very precocious. But it had come to pass; she was very little, and Mother, and Todd, too. When he left, I worked on shrinking him down to fit into his place, and added him; Mother refused to speak to him, but Grandmother was kind.

I had not yet decided if I would ever put Father in there, or Brandon. They would know all my dreams and fantasies, and Father had never been patient with ideas he had not originated. It might be amusing, I sometimes thought, considering Father, to put him in a closed space with his mother, and mine. What conversations we might all have then! Father was married to his fifth wife, and I wondered if he put his women in his head and fought with them, if they fought with each other.

The next time I woke up, Brandon's hand was on my shoulder. "You're as cold as a fish," he said.

I sat up, blinking at daylight. "What time is it?"

"Six-thirty. I'll go make coffee. You all right?"

"Fine. Sure. It was hot in the bedroom." I stood up, sore all over, and hated it being six-thirty. Suddenly I laughed, startling both of us.

"Now what?" Brandon asked, eyeing me narrowly.

"A dream. I promised I wouldn't ever tell you another dream, remember?" He hated my dreams, thought I was obsessed with them, with all kinds of unreality.

"You might as well tell me," he said.

"All right. I must have been getting stiff out here. I dreamed I stood up and stretched one wing, then the other, and hopped on the railing." I stretched my arms wide and turned, looking at the gulf below, dazzling with sunlight at a slant; a faint breeze played with miniature whitecaps, tossing them here and there apparently at random. "It was dawn in my dream," I went on, not looking at him. "I lifted off the balcony and rode an air current higher and higher; when I looked down you were here, yelling at me. You yelled, 'You don't do anything right!' And I realized that I had dreamed myself into a blue-footed booby. There were my great blue feet dangling in the air, and you were furious."

I began to laugh again; when I turned, he was gone. I followed him to the kitchen where he was measuring water for coffee. "Brandon, I'm not blaming you for yelling at me, or anything else. It was a silly dream. My feet were funny."

"Right," he said.

He finished with the coffee materials and went to shower. Brandon was still the most handsome man I had ever seen. He could have posed for Michelangelo's "David." We were the same age, thirty-two. Todd was thirty-two also. The three of us had been braided together all our lives. In elementary school, high school, as undergraduates, always the three of us. We used to laugh at the same things, weep at the same things. Now Brandon did not laugh at things I thought funny.

I used to tell them both my dreams and we had long, discursive talks about dream analysis, full of Freudian significance, full of misinformation and nonsense. Then we would fall into helpless laughter. Todd and I became lovers. Todd left. Brandon and I became married. But it was Todd's voice that called me from sleep, Todd who lived in my head, Todd who listened to my dreams now and laughed with me at them, in the changed voice I had given the Todd who lived in my head.

The coffee was done. I poured myself a cup and took it with me to my bathroom. When Brandon and I were both dressed and proper, ready for our usual toast and coffee and juice, neither of us mentioned the dream again. We were very civil and polite. He would be late. I would do a little shopping after I left my own job. Dinner as usual at seven-thirty. Of course. Remember the Neilsons' dinner party tomorrow night. Of course. It would be a scorcher. Stay in where it's cool. Of course. Have a good day. And you. Of course.

Brandon worked for a very prestigious brokerage firm. He managed estates, set up trust funds, helped his clients find tax dodges, helped the wealthy become very wealthy. My job was of a different sort altogether. I made seven fifty an hour as a museum archivist at the university in Tampa, a thirty-four-mile drive each way. It was more money than I had ever made in my life. The last time Father had come to visit, in June, with his newest bride, he asked indignantly why I still held that stinking job. Because, I did not answer him, if I didn't hold it, I would have to stay home all day, go to luncheons, charity events, be on committees, and generally pretend to be a rich bitch. I had not yet become accustomed to the idea of being rich, much less the actuality. I worked five days a week, got filthy dirty day after day, and liked my job. If anyone lost a painting, I found it. Dates of certain shows, who was featured, what was hung; I found the information. Trace the meandering path of a particular print. I did it. In August everything at school was virtually comatose, but I went in daily at ten. I had little to do, and was spending most of my time on record keeping, adding data to the computer files, getting ready for the new students in September. In September Brandon and I would be gone. Hurricane season. We both knew and never mentioned that we suspected our tower of concrete and glass was a temptation to the god of winds who ruled during hurricane season. Of course, the season started in July, picked up a bit of steam in August, peaked in September, and dragged on into October. But everyone knew September was the month of greatest danger. We would be in New York and London.

Traffic was normal that morning, heavy, erratic, too fast, or too slow. Tampa Bay looked postcard pretty, the pollution invisible. The sky was cloudless, and would be siphoning moisture for hours yet, to be dumped again around four-thirty or five, when I would be driving home. Another thing I could not have told my father when he asked why I continued to work was that I welcomed the long drive.

—Todd?

—I'm here.

—I know. Have you come up with a good analysis yet?

—Nope. not a good one, but one that might do. Want to hear?

—Oh yes.

I had been mulling over this one dream for weeks and finally had turned it over to Todd-in-my-head. In the dream a small child caught a fish, a sheepshead, except that instead of black and gray/white, this one was orange and yellow, but still a sheepshead. He put it in a bucket of water to show me when I arrived. By the time I got there, the fish was very sad-looking, deflated. In fact, it was dead. I picked it up, draped it over my arm like a dish towel, and walked to the edge of the water with it. The waves were very gentle, hardly reaching my ankles. I put the fish in the water and it started to scream. Startled, the little boy and I backed away and stared at it, speechless. The fish began to inflate, to twitch, to flick its tail as it came to life. It swam out to a groin and climbed on top of it. It looked back at me and called, "Stay, Claire!" Then it vanished into the water.

—Well, the Todd voice started—the little boy is you, obviously, in disguise. The fish is you, and the gulf, everything is you. You caught yourself and killed yourself in the bucket, and the only part of you that can swim to freedom is the part that you already killed.

"Shut up!" I reached over and turned on the radio.

That morning in the southbound lanes of the interstate there was an RV, a Busch truck, and half a dozen cars in a muddle. Since I was heading north, my motion was not interrupted. Police officers were detouring traffic off the freeway onto the outlying streets of north Pinellas County where the tourists could see at close hand the ice-cream-colored houses of endless subdivisions. I drove on, listening to a breathless radio voice describe the chaos on the interstate.

When Todd was accepted for his doctoral studies in marine biology here, I had come with him, and then Brandon had been transferred to St. Petersburg from the New York office of his company. We were together again. At first, Todd and I lived in a trailer court not far from the university. Twice the winds came in from the gulf, and flung our trailer high up in a live oak tree. Both times we happened to be at school; we returned home to find home gone. The wind and water gods scorned trailers; they always hurled them into trees. We lived on fish and crabs and, when we did not have time to go fishing, on black beans and rice, Cuban style. We learned to drink the thick, black Cuban coffee. When it was mango season, we gorged on them; at avocado time we fattened on avocadoes. I knew memories were gushing like lava only because Todd had called me from sleep, but the memories were erupting furiously, explosively, and I could not stem them any more than a geologist could plug a volcano.

I changed the radio station and listened to a different announcer describe the newest sinkhole that had appeared in south St. Petersburg. I nodded; the monster was feeding again. Once I told Brandon about the monster that took a bite now and then; he looked at me as if I had gone mad. "I won't talk about it when we have company," I had reassured him to his evident relief.

At the museum, I waved to two men in the shop framing prints and went on to my own office, a clutter I had inherited when I was hired, and had never been able to disentangle. I had seen people wandering about with a vase, or a sculpture, or a painting, looking forlorn, undecided, then, coming to a decision, head for my office and deposit whatever object they had and leave again, satisfied at a job well done. In the beginning I had protested feebly, but I gave that up early on. If they put things somewhere else I would be called upon to find them eventually anyway. That day there were some Peruvian wall hangings, half a dozen Netsuke jades, a stack of photographs, two Ming dogs, and a miscellany of shell sculptures that belonged in a tourist-trap shop, not a museum, and a couple of cameras: I made a visual record of everything we exhibited. And there were piles of papers here and there.

I had started to relax a little in the car, and now the process completed itself; I drew in a long breath as my chest loosened and the tension in my shoulders vanished. And that, of course, was why I kept my job. I was happy in that cluttered office, in that insignificant museum, doing work that no one on earth cared a damn about.

I was looking forward to having lunch with Felice Lapata that day. She was sixty, the head of the psychology department, finishing some research she had been engaged in for many years. She was as brown as a nut, with wiry gray hair, snapping black eyes, and nicotine stains on her fingers and teeth.

When Todd left, Felice had come searching for me. "Let's go," she had said. "We're going out to get drunk."

She did not believe in dream analysis. "It's leftover junk, stuff you didn't file away properly yet," she maintained. "Like all that junk in your office."

We argued a little about that; I usually told her the funny dreams, but we had never talked about the dream that had opened one of the deepest chasms between Brandon and me.

"In this dream," I had told him, "we're at a party given by one of your clients, a very rich oil sheik. There are floating hands bearing trays of champagne, canapes, just white-gloved hands, no bodies. I sort of float over to you and the sheik, yet I can see myself across the room talking to some other people at the same time. You and the sheik are watching the other me, and he asks how much. At first you don't know what he means, but he repeats it, How much? And then you realize he wants to buy me, that he'll pay your price. And I wake up."

Brandon had exploded. "Is that what you think? That I'm a monster of some kind? My God, Claire, you blame me for your dreams! What do you want from me? What am I supposed to do? See a shrink, for God's sake!"

"I didn't say I blamed you for anything. I thought it was funny. It has pieces from *Beauty and the Beast,* and pieces from the headlines . . . I thought it was funny."

He looked at me bitterly. "Don't tell me your dreams anymore. Okay? If there's something on your mind, just say it. Don't dress it up in dream garbage."

He had turned to stamp out of the living room. A blazing sunset filled the windows, torched the whole world behind him. "How much?" I asked his back. "I couldn't provide the answer in my dream. How much?"

He stopped, but did not face me again, and after a second he left.

"How much?" I whispered to myself, and really wished I knew the answer.

I had not sought a psychiatrist, but I had talked about dreams to Felice, who did not believe they had any significance. This morning was the first time in months that I had mentioned a dream to Brandon, and I wouldn't have brought it up if it had not been funny. It was Todd's fault, I thought then. He had called me from sleep and the day had started off strange, and continued strange.

"Felice," I asked at lunch that day, "what happens when you hear a voice in your head, just like a voice in the room with you, that clear?"

She shrugged. "Can be a lot of things. Epilepsy is one. Some people hear music and can't tell it isn't real. A little tremor in the brain triggers an audio memory. A tumor can do it. Drugs. High fever."

She talked about it several minutes, but I had stopped listening. Did the earth shake? No, but there was this little brain tremor. I poked at my salad.

That night, over dinner at the marina, Brandon said, "Sorry about this morning. I was scared when I got up and couldn't find you. The balcony's the last place I thought to look."

I had not even considered that my absence might have alarmed him; instantly I felt guilt rise. "I'm sorry, too. I broke our bargain, talking about my dreams."

He took my hand. "It was a funny thing to dream. Remember when we saw the flock of blue-footed boobies that time? How excited we were?"

And it was over. Our arguments always dissolved in memories of other times, times when we played and laughed openly and did not look for slights behind words and glances.

We had taken Father out in the boat in June, and that, the condo, our cars, all had impressed him deeply. He had found a new respect for me, and I didn't disillusion him about any of it. We did not own the condo, I had thought back at him wordlessly. We owned a piece of paper that said we could live in the building that was built on leased land that could be recalled by the land-holding company at their pleasure. But probably the sea would reclaim the land before the company got around to it. The condo came with housekeeping service and yard maintenance. We could live there only if we did not have children or pets, and if we made our payments regularly. The boat was not paid for, nor was Brandon's newest car, a Mercedes. We were rich. We had rich people's obligations. Because Brandon liked to eat in restaurants I cooked meals at the condo only once or twice a week. When we entertained, the food was catered because he was certain that was more impressive than having a wife in the kitchen. He did not object to my job because it was neat having a wife involved with the arts in any way. He liked to mention it casually.

He had drawn up our life plan more than three years ago, when we were married. We would live in the condo for a few years, then buy one of the big houses fronting the bay and start a family when we were both thirty-five. That was early enough. It would give him time to get well established, to let us travel, make connections, and still have our family.

But I could not tell him about the little people who lived in my head, that one of them was Todd. I could no longer tell him my dreams. He held my hand in the restaurant and talked about his day, the way he liked to do. He always told me the good things he did, and the bad things. If he had dreams, I would have listened to them; I would have liked hearing his dreams.

When we returned to our tower, the sky was violet, the air was still hot, but starting to cool off finally. Brandon had an hour or two of work to take care of, as usual, and I decided to take a walk. Our schedules were unvariable. Up at six-thirty, off to the salt mines, dinner at seven-thirty, Brandon to work another hour or two, and bed at eleven-thirty. That gave us half an hour to make love or not, and still go to sleep by twelve. Weekends I refused to get up by the clock, or Brandon's internal clock either. He thought I was lazy.

I walked in the sand near the edge of the whispering water. The water temperature was eighty-six; the air was eighty-six also. The water felt warmer now than the air.

—Todd?

—I'm here.

—I know. Why did you wake me up in the night?

—Maybe I was lonely?

I scowled at a meeting of sandpipers that made way for me. A family of father, mother, boy overtook me, laughing, the boy darting this way and that, into the warm water, up to the warmer sand, back to the water. A couple came from the other way, holding hands. The waves crested and glowed with the phosphorescent photoplankton that always came in August. I thought of the tiny creatures blooming, glowing, exploding with new life, then vanishing again, their cycle done. But what ecstasy it must have been while it lasted!

Far off in the west the clouds had formed themselves into mountains, and they too glowed, faded, with lightning so distant there was no sound of thunder. The storm might move inland during the night and shake the buildings, whip the palm trees, throw a trailer or two into a live oak . . .

—We were happy, weren't we? Before Brandon came?

—We were always happy.

—Why did you go away then, you bastard?

In my head he laughed, and I stood still with fists clenched, wanting to throw something hard all the way across the world. Todd used to say that we never ask ourselves questions we can't answer. "You don't have to know the answer," he had said patiently, "but you have to know the question is answerable. You can't even ask about things you know nothing of. And most of the time, you already know the answer. You just have to reorganize your knowledge to make it accessible. Asking a good question attests to a tremendous amount of knowledge."

Todd had had three more years of post-graduate work, then research at Woods Hole to complete, and finally he would have received his doctorate in marine biology, with teaching and research ever after. In those days there were giants, and people could foretell the future. The future had looked marvelous, and although we had to scrounge for crabs and fish, or make beans and rice serve, we believed ourselves to be rich. When Brandon arrived, he had more money than either of us had ever imagined. He rented a beach house with a room for Todd and me to use when we could, for as long as we wanted. He got his first boat and we went diving now and then. We went to the Keys. I wanted it never to end, the three of us happy together.

Then the offer came to Todd; he could cut short his graduate work by putting in time on a vessel bound for the South American coast, on a research project that would take a year. It was too expensive for him to consider; he turned it down with regrets. There was a second, even better, offer that he accepted. We said such inane things to each other.

I'll wait.

I don't want you to.

But I love you.

I love you too, but I won't be coming back. It's over. Can't you see that?

Todd in my head takes the part sometimes; he sounds much more mournful than Todd out there sounded at the moment. *He* had been excited and happy. I had said to him, "You don't have to make the choice, your work or me. You can have both!"

"I love you too much," he had said. "You get in the way because I love you. You'd be a constant worry."

Stupid! I unclenched my fists and turned to walk back the way I had come on the beach. The moon rode the flat water now, made a trail that broke only when it neared the shore, keeping people like me from treading it. Stupid, I repeated to myself. And now he was calling me because he was lonely? "Fat chance, kiddo," I said under my breath. "You made your bed, dummy. Be lonely. See if I care." Besides, I didn't believe my own facile explanation of the voice that had called me. Todd would never be lonely as long as he had his work.

Back in high school we had created a dilemma over the senior prom. I had two dates. We argued what to do about it for months; it did not seem fair for me to have two when some girls did not even have one escort.

"Face it," Todd had said finally. "We're an isosceles triangle. Brandon and I both love you and you love both of us. We go as a trio."

"Not isosceles," I objected after sorting out triangles. "If I'm going to be part of a triangle, I want it to be equilateral."

"Can't do it," Todd said. "You're bigger than both of us. We two can be equal, but you can't be. It has to be isosceles."

"If Todd would get himself a different girl, we could be a square," Brandon had suggested helpfully. At Todd's snort, he had shrugged. "Isosceles it is then."

Brandon and I had become an acute angle after Todd left. We married and became a very proper right angle, and now we were settling into an oblique angle. Then a straight line? I tried to picture it, his toes and mine together, our bodies stretched out away from each other. Or maybe joined crown to crown. I had reached the condo that reared up ten stories, lighted so brightly that the moon dimmed in comparison. Rapunzel, are you there, I wanted to call out, but I didn't. Too many people were still wandering up and down the beach. I remembered reading about a tidal wave after the Krakatoa eruption; it had been one hundred fifteen feet high. The tower must have been about that. One good tsunami, I thought, gazing at it. That was all it would take. And I thought: you don't need two to make a straight line. One person alone can do that.

I reminded myself that I had loved Brandon and Todd equally from the time I was twelve; I hosed sand off my feet and went inside.

Tomorrow night we would have dinner with the Neilsons, very nice people, both of them. They had a very nice house. The food would be very nice; the other guests would be very nice. Brandon would be nice and I would be very, very nice. Nicer than anyone else. Nicer than I had been in months.

"Evening, Mrs. Kyle," the security man said.

"Good evening," I said, practicing my very nicest smile and voice. The effort made my eyes burn.

I glanced in on Brandon, muttering incantations to his computer, but did not interrupt him. Instead, I showered and put on a short robe. Walking on the beach always made me sticky. It was the combination of salt and humidity and gasoline fumes, I was certain. I used to mourn for the coquinas, the half-inch rainbow-hued shell creatures so thick on the beach they made a carpet that sank and rose with the coming and going of the waves. Lead poisoning, I whispered to them, lifting handfuls to wash in the surf, mercury poisoning, carcinogenic petrochemicals . . . Todd said that whatever was in the air was also in the shallows, and I stopped trying to clean them, but I still showered after walking on the beach.

Because I did not want to pick a fight with Brandon, or hurt him, or be anything but nice, I did not go to bed first, although I was very tired and sleepy. I sat on the linen-covered couch in the living room with every intention of clicking on the TV, or the VCR, or music. In a minute, I thought, and closed my eyes.

We were out in the gulf on our boat that shifted from a racing yacht to a tug to a ferry to the Queen Elizabeth. I did not object to the changing fortunes the boat expressed. Todd was scooping a net into the water, each time bringing in a new treasure, something never before seen by human eyes. When I tried to see his catches, he and Brandon guarded the plastic pail jealously. Whenever Todd landed a new rarity, Brandon raced below to bring up another bucket. The buckets were all yellow and quite small, ten-cent-store equipment. I thought both of them were being silly, but I was hurt because they did not let me see what they had. Then I went to the stern and leaned against the rail. At my turn to stoke the fire, I went below without argument and shoveled more and more coal into the furnace. That was the kind of boat it was then. "You're making it too hot," one of the crew said and dived over the side.

·It had grown dark. I was still at the rail when there was a tremendous explosion and I was thrown into the water. A fire erupted; people screamed, and a child was calling me plaintively. "I'm here," I called back, clinging to a door. I knew it was a door because I was holding a smooth glass knob and water bubbled up through the keyhole. The child called again; I paddled to the sound of his voice, groped in the inky waters until my fingers closed on his arm, and I hauled him aboard my door.

We drifted for hours, days, months, endlessly. When I dozed, the little boy vanished; I jumped into the water to find him again and bring him back to safety. I let down my long hair and tied him to me securely; then I held and rocked him, soothed him, and was soothed in turn. We told each other stories as we drifted together. When I admitted I was lost, he looked at the stars and pointed our way; finally we reached a wild and dangerous shore, swampy and snake-infested, with savage beasts lurking in the impenetrable woods beyond the sand. I hoisted the child onto my shoulders and started to walk, hip deep in the swamp, dreading alligators, snakes, leeches, things I could not imagine, things Todd would welcome catching. With every step the mangrove jungle deepened behind me, a tree sent down roots, new trunks rose, the leafy canopy filled in. I yearned to slip beneath the black waters, become one with the roots and creatures who lived there, but always the child's warm breath on my neck, his firm hands on my shoulders, his sighs and yawns and snatches of nonsense words drove me on, weeping and terrified, up to my chin in water, on dry sands, back in the swamp, on and on.

Then someone was taking him away; I fought with the invisible person, who tugged at the child, forced him off my back, yanked my hair out with him. I yelled.

"My God," Brandon was saying, holding my arm, shaking me. "Wake up, Claire! It's a dream!"

I pulled free and felt my hair, cut very short, and then pressed my hands hard over my eyes.

Brandon made certain I was awake before he left to get us both a drink, wine for me, bourbon for him. His eyes were troubled when he came back.

"What is it, Claire? What's wrong?"

I touched the wine to my lips, put it down. What I really wanted was a cup of thick, black Cuban coffee. I shook my head and started to get up. He held me with his hand hard on my arm.

"Tell me your dream," he said.

I shook my head again.

"Please. I'm sorry I ever said for you not to talk about them. You've always had wonderful dreams. Please."

So I told him. Already it seemed distant and much shorter than I had thought. In relief Brandon picked up his drink and sipped it.

"You always were far ahead of both of us," he said after a moment. "That's what the dream is about, you know. You leave both of us playing with sea urchins while you're off saving a real kid. Let's do it now. Let's have the baby."

This time I did stand up. "I want coffee," I said and hurried to the kitchen. Was that what the dream meant, that I wanted to have a child now? Brandon followed and watched with a tender smile as I fussed with coffee beans and filters.

"Things have eased up quite a bit," he said. "I wanted to wait until I made vice president, but that will come. I doubt they'll want to transfer me again. I have too many good contacts here. I know damn well there's no problem with the condo. We can be out from under in a week if we want to."

He talked on, thinking out loud, the way he liked to do, examining the pros and cons deliberately, and I thought again, wildly, was that what the dream meant? I wanted to talk to Felice, and I knew what she would say about the meaning—there wasn't any. Bits and pieces of unfiled junk cluttering up your brain. Why wasn't it filed away properly then, I demanded of myself angrily. Why leave out junk to combine and recombine in ever new patterns that seem to have meaning?

—You never ask a question until you have the answer also, or until you know the answer is available. Except when the question deals with pure information, like how far away is the sun, or what is the chemical makeup of the various bodies of water. And those are answerable, if not by you, or a book, then by someone with the proper equipment to find—

—Todd, shut up! I don't want to talk philosophy now. ". . . on our way to Neilson's tomorrow night. I think it might be too small, but it's on high ground, one of the highest lots facing the bay, I bet . . ."

I ignored Brandon.

—Todd, why did you leave like that? I would have waited!

—I told you. Chance of a lifetime, rare opportunity, dream research voyage. Then two years of hard grind.

—I never saw the second letter, or heard the phone call you said you got. There wasn't a second letter or call, was there?

—First something is inconceivable, and that means exactly that. You can't think of it, can't say yes or no because it is altogether taboo. Then there is the conceivable but deniable. At that point the inconceivable becomes just impossible, you see. Although you still deny it, now you can think of it, and it may return again and again, each time eroding the denial a little bit more until impossible becomes possible, something you can consider. That's how the system works, Claire. Science, economics, love—

"Brandon," I said, no doubt interrupting his flow of

words, unhearing, uncaring, "has Todd paid you back in full yet?"

I watched the coffee pot that was making sputtering noises, almost ready. There was no motion from Brandon for a time that seemed much too long, but I did not turn to look at him.

"You know?"

"Of course." And I knew. From inconceivable to that moment had taken nearly four years.

He talked about it, naturally. He talked about everything he did all the time, and now that this one secret was no longer between us, he had no more worry about saying the one wrong thing, making the one slip he had always feared. His relief was touching. He looked years younger, boyish even.

Todd did not sell me, and Brandon did not buy me. I nodded to myself. Of course. People didn't do things like that, not in real life. Todd simply had needed money to go on his dream research cruise, and Brandon had provided it. A loan. Business. How much? I would never ask. It was answerable, and that night Brandon would have told me if I had asked.

"It's twelve," I said when Brandon paused. "Go on to bed."

"Let's both go to bed and think about the best way to take care of that other little matter," he said with a smile.

I thought of the litle boy in my dream. I had not saved him at all; he had saved me. Without him, I would have drowned along with Todd and Brandon. He was out there in the world somewhere waiting for me to find him, and I was thirty-two. I knew I had better get on with it.

"Brandon," I said then, "did you get a warranty? In writing? I think the merchandise has just gone bad."

While he explained and then yelled and then explained some more, I summoned Todd in my head.

—And you! Out!

—I could have told you about him, my mother said,
—but you never ask me anything.

It was true, I never asked her anything. I was not certain there would be answers if I did. It wasn't too late to
find out, I thought vaguely at her, but not like this, not
with her a speck in my brain.

—You too, out!

That left only my grandmother, whom I decided to
keep. She had talked very little over the past twenty
years, after all.

"Claire, have you heard a thing I've said? I'm sorry. It
was a terrible mistake. We should have talked about it
years ago, all three of us. I didn't impose conditions. It
just seemed better for everyone that way. What more
can I say now?"

He asked the question; he knew the answer. Nothing.
Three years with Todd, three with Brandon; the symme-
try was unbroken. Isosceles. A tremor in the brain had
shaken my whole world apart and tomorrow I would start
building a new world, one that included a little boy to
guide me from the swamps.

Transients

Carter Scholz

so came to this pass, where time and space turn back upon themselves, where only by miming the voices, even my own, might I reconstruct that remote and untouchable past. I found these fragments one rainy night after the repetitions had commenced, and transcribed them, trying again to make the voices live, and again failing. For memory offers sequence unlike any sequence out of life, and words are yet a further remove. No art or wish can recall them as they were. These are only words, I say them out of habit, expecting nothing of them but an approach to the origins of my present state.

Chad. After my mother's father died, his presence in the house became more pronounced. In her madness she would think me him. After his death I had moved into his room, and so inherited his importance to her. My father shut it all out, until he could no more, and a month before the divorce was to be settled, in April, he drove his car into a tree. Leaving me alone with. Too soon to speak of this.

Nights we went driving. Gray and I would take a car, past midnight, and cruise through dark towns. We had no aim. It pleased us to drive while all slept. We drove at random, away from the city, losing ourselves and then trying to find our way back. Each time out we went farther. When, rarely, my parents would deny me their car we would take Gray's. The odometer was broken and we put odd amounts of gas in the tank so his parents could never tell, by reading the gauge, how far we had gone. We went once into Canada. Gray's mother sometimes waited up and questioned him, but he evaded her. She worried about the city, thought we were going there. She thought I was corrupting Gray. She was right. I see her from outside, in the living room, a cup of cold forgotten coffee on the sofa arm, as Gray goes past, head down, upstairs, unable to tell her. Because whatever she might imagine, how could he tell her the truth? That we went nowhere, nowhere at all.

Those nights of gliding over long roads, through the dark towns, with the headlights bringing a small sphere of night close, and the windows up to keep out the dark, the radio softly playing music, or static, those nights prepared us.

Cheryl. We're in Minnesota now. I think it's late August. We've been to Washington and Illinois and Arizona and some places we couldn't tell where we were before we were gone again.

We're by a lake now. John is swimming. I'm writing this card because I have ideas of mailing it, to Chad I guess, hi Chad, but I don't really believe the mails will work for us now. Not when the roads don't. John jokes that the road's a conveyor belt taking us backward. I wish he wouldn't joke when he's frightened.

We seem to change places whenever we're not thinking about where we are.

We came down through evergreens from the highway, about a mile in all. The trees were wet from rain right to the lake, although it was clear when we arrived, and we took off our clothes and swam far out. The water seemed very cold at first, then it seemed almost warm. The sun was, is, very bright. I swam on my stomach, then my back, then in a kind of corkscrew, rolling with each stroke, until John grabbed my legs.

Chad, if you somehow get this, please don't mind about John. I don't know what to say. I want you to be happy.

Chad. The sign flashed a brief pattern in the night rain in front of the small hotel where we had landed. TRAN-SIENTS it said, in sharp erratic flashes, revelations they seemed, like those I used to have when I was younger and just beginning to suspect the nature of things. Precise and clear and fading with time, like a struck bell or a piano note. And it seemed that in those flashes, or between them, I could make sense of it, of our state, and so I said to the others, "It's all right now," as if saying it would make it so.

These are the scenes, sharp and precise, even in their fading, that I remember from the weeks after we first realized that we were no longer fixed in the world.

George. When we went shooting in the Pine Barrens it was overcast, a slate cold day near the shore, with a sea wind blowing. We drove two hours in the van to reach the dirt road I remembered that ended in scrub. The hard ground where we stopped was littered with small triangles of fired clay, and spent shells stamped flat.

Gray and John got the trap and birds while I tore open the carton of shells. Chad watched me. He makes me nervous. The cylinders spilled over the vinyl seat, an inch of flanged brass at the hammer end, the red cardboard folded into itself like an unopened flower at the other.

I can still hear the sound of the spring launching the clay birds, and the cough of the shotgun. I shot a hundred birds in groups of twenty-five. In the first group I hit ten, in the second twelve. I was out of practice. But then I found my rhythm, and hit twenty in the third group and all of the last, yelling "Pull!", tracking, squeezing till the gun kicked and the clay burst in the pallid sky.

In strange towns. In the center of town was a cemetery where the stones thrust unevenly from the dry ground like playing cards, skewed and riding the roll of the terrain. The oldest we found read JOS BROWN 1665. We were surrounded by a constant roar of traffic and the stench of factories. There were thousands of graves under a spongy turf that made you walk gingerly.

Farther on we found a Holiday Inn, where we spent the night. Gray used his credit card, knowing he was close to its limit, fearful that some bank computer was tracking its unnatural travels.

There were three people near us in the bar, a fortyish blowzy redhead, a fat fiftyish businessman, and a thin guy about our age. The redhead was laughing and the man was not. The young thin guy was gazing off into infinities.

In our room, after Gray was asleep, I went to the window and watched cars pass on the elevated highway. The night was close and warm, with the smell of petroleum thick in the air. I went away from the window and lay down and stayed awake another hour. I woke once and looked outside. All the city lights were gone. It was raining.

In the morning I woke with Gray beside me, so I knew it was no personal damnation, or if it was I had somehow carried him along. On the dresser was a poem I'd written the night before. I read it through, tore it to sixteenths, and burned it in the ashtray. Then I lit a cigarette and stared out the motel window at an unfamiliar landscape, waiting for Gray to waken.

It was a bright snowy day, and an empty two-lane highway stretched away from us into white hills. Single cars passed, singing on the asphalt; and most carried skis on top. The light dusting of powder on the road skirled in arabesques in their wakes. Gray stirred and opened his eyes.

"Welcome to Vermont, I believe."

He sat up suddenly. "Oh Jesus. Again?"

"What did you expect, old buddy?"

"I thought this only happened when we were moving."

"We're moving all the time."

He pushed back his hair and rubbed his eyes. Our clothes were strewn over the bedspread. I went over to check our wallets. I had ten dollars, Gray had fifteen.

"We better get out soon."

"Why?"

"The maids will be coming around. We're not registered, obviously."

He sat silently for a minute. "So let them arrest us. I could go for it."

But we moved out, and started hitchhiking. After a while a blue Toyota stopped for us. I settled into the back seat and shut my eyes, knowing that soon enough, when I opened them again, the car and the landscape would be changed. I reached out and squeezed Gray's shoulder in the front seat, praying not to lose him as well.

John. When I first came to the farm I couldn't sleep for the quiet, some nights not till dawn, when I could hear the others already up, running water and frying eggs on the big black stove. At last I would doze and then have as much trouble waking. My eyes would be gritty, my head heavy, and I would burrow under the sheets until the cool morning air grew warm and I started to sweat under the light cotton. I would get up, sit blank-eyed on the edge of the bed for minutes before I was ready to go downstairs. By then everyone would be outside working. They were very tolerant of me. Most went to bed by ten and were up by six or seven, and I never knew what they thought of me with my lights on so late, reading. Sometimes I could hear couples giggling or making love, and that made me think of how alone I was, how long it would be before Diane would arrive when her job ended.

During the hottest part of the day, while everyone else was sensibly lounging, I worked in the garden, bending and sweating, nearly naked, to make up for my sleeping in. I got very dark in that summer sun. Later on Cheryl liked that. I had the idea that I was sweating out some dire poison, some poison of the town we had all come from, but by the time we had been scattered and traveling a few autumn months, through all the windy rainy states, my tan was gone, the backs of my hands were as light as my palms, and Cheryl was gone from me, and I didn't care about the rest, and it was damnation, mine alone.

Chad. So we had what we wanted, for a summer at least, the eight of us. It was not a long walk to the Delaware River, and there was a small tourist town ten miles away, into which we drove once a week in all our splendid disarray. Of course we knew it couldn't last; in September we would be back on the roads, to jobs or schools or to the other edge of the country. If I'd known that in my passion to escape that I would drag the others, those I loved, with me into this terrible state, I would have gone away from them. But I thought love could save me.

One night, very warm, I couldn't sleep, so I went out, stepping over two people tangled in sleeping bags on the living-room floor. They were passing through; I didn't know them. I woke no one. When I stepped out of the house I heard the forge going in the barn, and went over to watch. The road was still warm on my feet as I crossed it. The night was still except for the punctuations of a hammer on hot iron. Gray was swinging a twenty-pound sledge at a red bar. Three afternoons a week he played the village blacksmith for tourists in the nearby town, and sold little pieces of crafted junk for outlandish prices. He hit the bar a few times, then held it in water. The barn was hot and damp. Gray didn't see me. I sleepily admired his body, his movements, his involvement with his task. I'd been in very good shape myself that summer, and every morning was surprised by myself in the bathroom mirror. It was the best I'd ever looked.

Afer a while he saw me, and started.

"You been there long?"

I nodded. "Couldn't sleep."

He went back to work, and about then started the feeling. Ridiculous. Stop. Stop! I picked up a pad I'd left there the day before, and began to draw him. A mistake. After five minutes I had a tremendous erection. About then he came over to see what I'd been doing. He was very sharp. Looking only at the drawing he took a breath. I was shaking; it was all new to me.

"Let's go outside," he said at last.

We walked to the stream. Long, long silence.

He sat down and drew a deep breath. "I don't know. Shit, I'm tired."

I probed into my mind a bit deeper and saw how long

this thing had been there. Oh, Jesus. We sat for a long time, under stars and silence. I never suffered so much. Suddenly he stood and kicked his pants off. "Hell," he said. The word exorcised something. All my muscles loosened; I almost laughed. Gray squatted naked and shivering by the stream. I felt almost maternal then. I went to him and touched his chest; it was hard, and gritty with hair and sweat and ash. I kissed it. And him. And at last I took him in my mouth and he me in his.

There was an uneasy time afterward. Flushed, I listened to his breathing wind down to normal. After a while he went to the stream. I heard him pissing, then splashing about. I went after, to wash myself. A breeze had come up. While I was bent over he splashed me. I looked up, stunned. He was grinning through his beard; his body glistened, wet, dark, and white in the moonlight. He lunged at me. We went down in two feet of water, wrestling. He pinned my shoulders to the bottom for a few long seconds, then let me up. I grinned fiercely. "Come on," I said. We splashed each other, directing hard, flat, stinging sprays with our palms. Then laughed like loons, back on shore, and let the wind dry us, and dressed. I went back to the house, and he to the forge. And I told Diane nothing.

Diane. He told me: three early springs of his mother's madness, after her father's death. Her threats and deceptions at home, and more horrible those outside. The running and screaming through midnight streets, the scenes in the market, the police, the asylum. His father's drift to lassitude and despair, and the suicide attempts. Each day a hell of boxes nested one in the next, and him thinking in his innocence that this was eternity, and in his susceptibility thereby making it so. He signed her commission papers on his eighteenth birthday.

And I told him that I had been raped by my father, and that made the bond. Secret wounds we all shared, in the farmhouse that summer. How did he put it? All suburbs the same, and we were all of us from suburbs, and under twenty-one, except Molly who's thirty and Gray who seems older than he is. All suburbs the same. George and the guilty secret of his sister. Gray's damned Italian blood ties; his smile like a threat of murder. Dave's cop father, who (his mother told him) needed a gun by the bed to get off. John, who'd tried to kill himself his first year at the seminary, and he told no one but us. Cheryl, who thought herself stupid and was saner than any of us. And me with my father who survived the camps and raped his daughter. All of us wanted to escape our roots, to start anew.

Chad had lost Cheryl to John. I'd lost Cheryl to John. We were together for no reason but that. I wanted only to be loose, from my own past. And he gave me that, oh yes. He showed me all too well what I wanted, what I needed.

Molly. God's love, what a disastrous crew. How did I land among them? I've eight years on Gray, and at least ten on George. Gray and I were together then, and what it was brought me on to George I don't know, unless it was his willingness to accept the worst in me placidly. Yes, Gray always fought me when I was arbitrary, and ignored me when I hurt; at such times I was simply bad, and he wouldn't have it. I remember letting Gray think it was him who'd arranged the farmhouse, when it was my own trip to that greasy realtor that clinched it. It was enough to make me vomit, and George was the only one I could tell straight out. Gray would have killed the slimy bastard, or possibly me.

Then, just before we moved into the place, George

took us shooting. I remember the way he ignored the lot of us, and I'm sure he'd have made the trip alone, him and his whole bloody arsenal.

He went off to shoot at clay birds. He asked me to pull for him, showing me how to cock the catapult, load the disc, and yank the cord at his shout. Only after he'd hit twenty running did he let the rest of us have a crack.

He showed me how to shoot a pistol, a light long-barreled .22, at cans about fifty feet away. We hadn't brought the cans; this site was a shooter's area. The ground was littered with old casings, some bright, some rusted almost to the color of dirt. After I had the hang of the pistol, he gave me a shot with his .44. I'd expected it to kick, but the recoil nearly took my arm off. "Why, you—" I started to say, but then I saw him smiling. Not a smile exactly. His eyes were a bit lit. Then dumb Molly put her hand to her mouth and said, "Oh." For I realized that the whole trip had been for me. To exorcise my real-tor. I hadn't known that I wanted to kill the bastard till that handgun nearly dislocated my shoulder; and at that moment I realized that I didn't need to kill him. And George had seen that, had drawn it out of me when I didn't yet know it myself, and at that moment, smelling gunpowder, I thought him the gentlest fellow on earth. He'd honestly been angrier about that realtor than I'd been; but his way was to turn anger into a kind of preci-sion. All anger was in the kick of that .44, and instantly discharged, and for a moment I thought I understood him.

"Now," he said, "we'll learn to shoot." And he spilled out the bullets and spent half an hour having me aim and pull the trigger on empty chambers, over and over, while he paced around me correcting my form, even standing directly in front of me, sighting down the barrel and insisting I pull the trigger; which I did with reluc-tance, even knowing the gun was empty.

That was the first and last time I ever held a gun. Later

I realized that his need for such precision was helplessness.

George. After John and Cheryl left us, we loaded the van and I let Gray drive. North. But we didn't make New York. I'd checked the map, and I knew the road was right. But when we crossed the border we saw a sign saying HARRISBURG. I'd grown up in Harrisburg, Pennsylvania. It was about two hundred miles away. So this was obviously some boondock Harrisburg in New York, and as a joke I yelled, "Not there! Not Harrisburg! Get me out of here!" And then we started to see Pennsylvania highway signs. Gray slowed the van and pulled onto the shoulder, to look at a map. I knew where we had to be. And I knew where we were. I was very cold. Because when I left Harrisburg, hating it more than it is healthy to hate anything, I knew, I promised myself, that if I ever came back to it I would die a peculiar and horrible death. So while Gray studied his maps I wondered what that death would be like. The van shuddered in the slipstream of passing trucks. Without a word Gray turned it around. We began to see signs for Wheeling. I'd gone to college, for a year, in West Virginia. But when we crossed the border we were in Maine.

"It's my fault," said Chad, calmly.

"What the hell do you mean?"

"I don't know what I mean. Something's happened. I think I'm the catalyst."

For a week we drove around. We played games of where-are-we-now. Along the way we found campuses with unguarded lounges to sleep in; or more often we just pulled the van to the side of the road, but then at least a couple of us had to sleep outside. We stole some sleeping bags from a sporting goods store.

Soon Molly wanted out. I still felt weird about it, even after Gray and I talked. He said he knew that the two of them couldn't work it out, and he hoped we'd do better.

And even though I'd courted her, when it happened I couldn't believe her intensity. Was I that serious after all? As serious as she was? From the first she was jealous of our time, wanted me alone with her as much as possible. Our dislocation, as Chad called it, brought things to a head.

We were pulled over for lunch on a county road in maybe Iowa, although ten minutes before we'd been stealing groceries from a market in Vermont. She didn't know any more than me what "out" meant at this point, but she was positive, and I had to decide whether or not to go with her. She was pale and frightened and crying. "I'm too old for this!" Maybe I should have. Dammit I should! But a weird exhilaration was growing in me as we traveled; I was inheriting a secret kingdom, and I did not honestly know how much there was between Molly and me, or how long, in this new world we'd entered, it would last. One day we'd landed among mountains. What mountains! As clear and uncompromising as God. Could I give that up for love?

But she didn't wait for my answer. That's what I can't quite forgive: she didn't wait. She started to walk. And I sat too long, feeling miserable and watching her, ready to follow, and I saw her small figure reach the border of the town ahead, and she vanished. I cried out, "Oh, not like that! Not like that!"

Chad was hunched in the back of the van, saying, "Why have I done this? I only wanted . . ." His long slender fingers closing on nothing.

Anywhere. Then we were past caring. We picked up hitchhikers, carelessly, madly, giggling as they climbed in.

"Where you heading?" they might ask.

"Anywhere, everywhere, nowhere."

And so off, in our vortex of night, our unstuck center, through an ambiguous and familiar landscape, past the white-on-green Interstate signs and the noncommittal names like Oakland, Fairlawn, Middleton. We could feel the brief discontinuities, but it took our hitchhikers a while to catch on. They thought only that they had fallen among madmen or drug addicts, Gray running the van up to eighty and waiting for a cop to follow, then pushing to a hundred while behind us the siren screamed and the patrol car ran up on us, and we hoped for a border, and we always made it, suddenly the cop was gone, vanished, and our hitchhiker looked sick. We would drop them later at the side of a road in Oregon, Montana, who knew? and roar off to find another border. Crossing was all we had. We *were* insane. Once Gray screamed up on a slow truck at a hundred, gambling to strike a border before the truck. By then I doubt it mattered to him, he probably saw death as just another border, and wondered what new roads it would bring, but we did strike a border, and we went on at the same speed, and on. And Gray laughed and laughed.

We welcomed it, this our special state.

Dave. We sold the van when we ran out of money, after peddling Gray's ironwork and George's guns. There was no point to keeping the van, I could see that, but, man, George let it go too easy. And his guns. I knew what those meant to him.

Wasn't much left then. Diane gone, and Molly, and Chad and Gray. John and Cheryl gone so long nobody talked about them anymore.

George dickering in the lot with a short fat slob in a mustache a size too big and hair a size too small. I took a walk. At the end of the lot, half-obscured, a sign read, WELCOME TO THE COMMUNITY OF. I walked that way. And never got back. Returning on the same road, there was no van, no lot. I was somewhere else.

I was never afraid for my life, just for my mind. I never thought that someday I'd wake up in the middle of the ocean. We never ended very far from a town. I was only worried that some other kind of transection could occur. I'd seen the couples change. I'd seen how Chad's thoughts could become George's, or Gray's Chad's, or Molly's Diane's. I didn't want my mind invaded.

What is community?

I'll find a place with no relation to my past. I'll settle there and find work, find some land, and plant it: a kind of anchor. I'll stay away from the mailbox and the telephone. Once or twice I'd tried telephoning. I got no answers, or strange electronic sounds mixed in with snatches of voice, high-pitched lonesome cries and furious fast babbling, a frightened mix that left me dizzy and seemed to whip the nexus we moved in to greater violence. I'll live quietly in a neutral place, avoiding anything I feel might snare me again. Was I lost then from the others, whom I loved? Would I be forced into an isolation beyond the redemption of any community? Very well, I was lost.

Gray. We arrived at sunset. We were swinging farther and farther afield, spending scarcely an hour in any one place. Desert, fog, wind, snow. Even day and night seemed to have lost their meaning. We slept in parks, or empty college dormitories, or behind filling stations. The snow worried me; it was the end of autumn, if that meant anything to us.

I couldn't say where we were. But I was alive to his mood, the odd wistfulness he projected. "Nice place," he said dreamily.

"Yeah, I guess." I watched the trees sway and toss against the clear dusk. High white clouds feathered against a deep azure, their edges a faint coral. I picked up my backpack and shrugged it on. "Come on. Let's get to a border."

"I don't know."

"Neither do I. I'm tired. Let's move."

He continued to stand there, leaning on his pack.

"Chad, come on. We can't sleep in a place like this, it's too affluent, we'll get rousted, it's like fucking Tenafly."

"Yes, it is."

Then I saw it. The skin at my nape crawled. "Let's blow. Let's get out of here."

"I'm staying, Gray."

I didn't know what to say. "What is this noise? I thought you hated the place."

"Maybe I'm tired of hating it."

I said in the shittiest voice I owned, "Well cut my leg off and call me Rimbaud. *Pardonnez-moi*. As you once explained it, going to the farm, we were escaping exactly this."

"No. I'm not going on."

I started to sweat. I felt him sinking into his death, and I wanted to slap him awake. Not because I loved him: I did not. But because he had shown me and taught me things, and some of his awareness had entered me, and if he could succumb so could a part of myself. So I tried to pull him out of this trap. Borrowing his art with words, I became reasonable: "We won't stop here. It's not the place, it's how did you say it, the very air of the place that's bad. The very air, as if it were polluted, only it's not your lungs, it's your soul it kills."

"No. I don't know."

"Chad, you'll *die*, man, you know you will! Listen, listen, you got me into all this. You can't cut out on me now. You have to help me through this." I was desperate now, begging.

"You stay too. We can leave if things get bad." His voice was distant, drugged.

"Oh, no. No. How many times did you tell me? That it wasn't your parents, not your mother's craziness or your father's weakness, not disease or death. . . ." I was using things against him, things he had told me in his own weakness. He jerked, just once. "The place, boy. It's the place that trapped them. As it traps everyone, in different ways. You'll stay, and the day will come when you cross a border and nothing happens, and you're only in the next town, and the next, and the towns stretch on and on without change and dead. Maybe we are dead," I said reasonably, "but we have to keep moving. Because there may be someplace for us. But not here. You don't want this."

He wasn't listening to me. To himself he said: "Why must we despise our origins?"

He was going to leave me, and suddenly I was frantic. I blurted: "Are you going to let them *win?*"

Then he screamed. I had never heard him scream, and it froze me. He ran down the street toward the edge of town, and I went after him, the backpack jouncing on my back, slowing me. I should have been able to catch him, he was no runner, but terror was on him and by the time I went through after him I ended somewhere cold and dark and he was somewhere else.

Chad. This place. I know where I am at last. I know the streets and where they lead, the cul-de-sacs and the thoroughfares. They are empty, as if in my final passage I had created the town for myself alone, in perpetual twilight, in perpetual silence, in a last frozen surge of self-hate. I shall not try to cross out.

The house. Of course it would still be here, unchanged, waiting, empty. I know where the furniture is in the dark, and where the ghosts walk. And my room, yes, unchanged, where I grew (his room before) and took in the spiritless air and inevitably changed it into myself, myself into it, bending to the odd gravity of this place.

In the first week of my return my beard and hair receded. I grew shorter. Time was a plaything for the house. An infant, I found myself ancient behind each door. Outside it rained, and in the rain were voices. What patterns with what ignorance, loathing and ill grace would I reenact, reliving everything, not knowing even now what is past and what future, not knowing whether I have lived what I've written here, or imagined it all, not to look for the roots of it in how badly we all had lived, the images we took to be real, how we had collaborated in the pollutions of the spirit that came to be the air of this place, of so many places across America, the fictions we had not courage to forsake, the dreams—nightmares, rather—we shrugged off or let lapse to simple sleep. I remember, or do I foresee, those years when the old man sat and sharpened his pencils and worked his puzzles while awaiting death. Is the old man not myself? Did I not know from the first that I would end like him, in this room, listening to jets move hollowly in the sky, watching the dust transfixed like wasted moments in the fading evening light?

Always in April it came, as though the burgeoning of possibility outside were not bearable sane, as if the warped air pressed down the harder to deny natural possibility and force instead the riot of madness, and I behind the door, behind the shield of the radio playing the blandest music at the softest volume, three in the morning, to cover the sounds from without, never the crashes or screams, but I dared not play it louder. Thinking, in the hollows of those hours, that this was eternity and I damned in it, imagining all the light I could never escape to, yet looking always for the first chance, the smallest crack in the fabric of things through which I could flee, swearing never to return.

All I hate binds me here. They come nightly, the ghosts, these three whose blood I share, to reenact those horrible rituals of pain, guilt, recrimination, to which I was unwilling witness then, so much more so now, for I see that the gravity of hate, for me, as it was for them, is stronger than that of love. They come, and I quail, my only defense the fading memory of the others, lost now, those I loved, whose voices are ever more indistinct, until I feel I have invented them, until I feel I have never had any life but this. Lost: all of us doomed enough to think that bonds of love could outpull those of time and place and blood. By effort of will I had unfixed myself, thinking it the only salvation, and by sympathy those who cared for me became likewise unfixed. But the bond was not strong enough to resist the centrifuge of our histories: we separated. I to return. And them? I wonder what homes they have found, or earned, those few loved ones I persist in inventing or remembering. I wonder what evasions, persisting too long from blood to blood, have weakened the fabric of reality enough to make this our state possible, and I wonder how many there are like us, how many have preceded and how many will follow us out of the world of consequence to end in the gray recesses of the fictive, how many cannot simply cross from New Jersey to New York, how many for whom every border is a leap into dread, and how many will end like me, at last unwilling to make the leap, or unable. For Gray was wrong about that: I am not back in the Cartesian world. When I walk to the edge of Tenafly and go across, I find myself again in Tenafly, and again. And however far I walk within the town, each night finds me again here, in this house.

Night. It begins again. And the voices, those I hate and those I tried to love (which is stronger?), both so tenuous yet so tenacious, and my self helpless in its remembering or imagining, knowing only that I failed and

The Dragon Line

Michael Swanwick

Driving by the mall in King of Prussia that night, I noticed that between the sky and earth where the horizon used to be is now a jagged-edged region, spangled with bright industrial lights. For a long yearning instant, before the car topped the rise and I had to switch lanes or else be shunted onto the expressway, I wished I could enter that dark zone, dissolve into its airless mystery and cold ethereal beauty. But of course that was impossible: Faerie is no more. It can be glimpsed, but no longer grasped.

At the light, Shikra shoved the mirror up under my nose, and held the cut-down fraction of a McDonald's straw while I did up a line. A winter flurry of tinkling white powder stung through my head to freeze up at the base of the skull, and the light changed, and off we went.

"Burn that rubber, Boss-man," Shikra laughed. She drew up her knees, balancing the mirror before her chin, and snorted the rest for herself.

There was an opening to the left, and I switched lanes, injecting the Jaguar like a virus into the stream of traffic, looped around and was headed back toward Germantown. A swirling white pattern of flat crystals grew in my left eye, until it filled my vision. I was only seeing out of the right now. I closed the left and rubbed it, bringing tears, but still the hallucination hovered, floating within the orb of vision. I sniffed, bringing up my mouth to one side. Beside me, Shikra had her butterfly knife out and was chopping more coke.

"Hey, enough of that, okay? We've got work to do."

Shikra turned an angry face my way. Then she hit the window controls and threw the mirror, powder and all, into the wind. Three grams of purest Peruvian offered to the Goddess.

"Happy now, shithead?" Her eyes and teeth flashed, all sinister smile in mulatto skin, and for a second she was beautiful, this petite teenaged monstrosity, in the same way that a copperhead can be beautiful, or a wasp, even as it injects the poison under your skin. I felt a flash of desire and of tender, paternal love, and then we were at the Chemical Road turnoff, and I drifted the Jag through three lanes of traffic to make the turn. Shikra was laughing and excited, and I was too.

It was going to be a dangerous night.

Applied Standard Technologies stood away from the road, a compound of low, sprawling buildings afloat on oceanic lawns. The guard waved us through and I drove up to the Lab B lot. There were few cars there; one had British plates. I looked at that one for a long moment, then stepped out onto the tarmac desert. The sky was close, stained a dull red by reflected halogen lights. Suspended between vastnesses, I was touched by a cool breeze, and shivered. How fine, I thought, to be alive.

I followed Shikra in. She was dressed all in denim, jeans faded to white in little crescents at the creases of her buttocks, trade beads clicking softly in her corn-rowed hair. The guards at the desk rose in alarm at the sight of her, eased back down as they saw she was mine.

Miss Lytton was waiting. She stubbed out a half-smoked cigarette, strode briskly forward. "He speaks modern English?" I asked as she handed us our visitor's badges. "You've brought him completely up to date on our history and technology?" I didn't want to have to deal with culture shock. I'd been present when my people had dug him, groggy and corpse-blue, sticky with white chrysalid fluids, from his cave almost a year ago. Since then, I'd been traveling, hoping I could somehow pull it all together without him.

"You'll be pleased." Miss Lytton was a lean, nervous woman, all tweed and elbows. She glanced curiously at Shikra, but was too disciplined to ask questions. "He was a quick study—especially keen on the sciences." She led us down a long corridor to an unmanned security station, slid a plastic card into the lockslot.

"You showed him around Britain? The slums, the mines, the factories?"

"Yes." Anticipating me, she said, "He didn't seem at all perturbed. He asked quite intelligent questions."

I nodded, not listening. The first set of doors sighed open, and we stepped forward. Surveillance cameras telemetered our images to the front desk for reconfirmation. The doors behind us closed, and those before us began to cycle open. "Well, let's go see."

The airlock opened into the secure lab, a vast, overlit room filled with white enameled fermentation tanks, incubators, autoclaves, refrigerators, workbenches, and enough glass plumbing for any four dairies. An ultrafuge whined softly. I had no clear idea what they did here. To

me AST was just another blind cell in the maze of inter-
locking directorships that sheltered me from public
view. The corporate labyrinth was my home now, a secure medium in which to change documentation, shift
money, and create new cover personalities on need. Perhaps other ancient survivals lurked within the cata-
combs, mermen and skinchangers, prodigies of all sorts,
old Grendel himself; there was no way of telling.

"Wait here," I told Shikra. The lab manager's office
was set halfway up the far wall, with wide glass windows
overlooking the floor. Miss Lytton and I climbed the
concrete and metal stairs. I opened the door.

He sat, flanked by two very expensive private security
operatives, in a chrome swivel chair, and the air itself felt
warped out of shape by the force of his presence. The
trim white beard and charcoal-grey Saville Row pinstripe
were petty distractions from a face as wide and solemn
and cruel as the moon. I shut my eyes and still it floated
before me, wise with corruption. There was a metallic
taste on my tongue.

"Get out," I said to Miss Lytton, the guards.

"Sir, I—"

I shot her a look, and she backed away. Then the old
man spoke, and once again I heard that wonderful voice
of his, like a subway train rumbling underfoot. "Yes,
Amy, allow us to talk in privacy, please."

When we were alone, the old man and I looked at each
other for a long time, unblinking. Finally, I rocked back
on my heels. "Well," I said. After all these centuries, I
was at a loss for words. "Well, well, well."

He said nothing.

"Merlin," I said, putting a name to it.

"Mordred," he replied, and the silence closed around
us again.

The silence could have gone on forever for all of me; I
wanted to see how the old wizard would handle it. Even-

tually he realized this, and slowly stood, like a thunderhead rising up in the western sky. Bushy, expressive eyebrows clashed together. "Arthur dead, and you alive! Alas, who can trust this world?"

"Yeah, yeah, I've read Malory too."

Suddenly his left hand gripped my wrist and squeezed. Merlin leaned forward, and his face loomed up in my sight, ruthless grey eyes growing enormous as the pain washed up my arm. He seemed a natural force then, like the sun or wind, and I tumbled away before it.

I was on a nightswept field, leaning on my sword, surrounded by my dead. The veins in my forehead hammered. My ears ached with the confusion of noises, of dying horses and men. It had been butchery, a battle in the modern style in which both sides had fought until all were dead. This was the end of all causes: I stood empty on Salisbury Plain, too disheartened even to weep.

Then I saw Arthur mounted on a black horse. His face all horror and madness, he lowered his spear and charged. I raised my sword and ran to meet him.

He caught me below the shield and drove his spear through my body. The world tilted and I was thrown up into a sky black as wellwater. Choking, I fell deep between the stars where the shadows were aswim with all manner of serpents, dragons, and wild beasts. The creatures struggled forward to seize my limbs in their talons and claws. In wonder I realized I was about to die.

Then the wheel turned and set me down again. I forced myself up the spear, unmindful of pain. Two-handed, I swung my sword through the side of Arthur's helmet and felt it bite through bone into the brain beneath.

My sword fell from nerveless fingers, and Arthur dropped his spear. His horse reared and we fell apart. In that last instant our eyes met and in his wondering hurt and innocence I saw, as if staring into an obsidian mirror, the perfect image of myself.

"So," Merlin said, and released my hand. "He is truly dead, then. Even Arthur could not have survived the breaching of his skull."

I was horrified and elated: He could still wield power, even in this dim and disenchanted age. The danger he might have killed me out of hand was small price to pay for such knowledge. But I masked my feelings.

"That's just about fucking enough!" I cried. "You forget yourself, old man. I am still the Pen-dragon, *Dux Bellorum Britanniarum* and King of all Britain and Amorica and as such your liege lord!"

That got to him. These medieval types were all heavy on rightful authority. He lowered his head on those bullish shoulders and grumbled, "I had no right, perhaps. And yet how was I to know that? The histories all said Arthur might yet live. Were it so, my duty lay with him, and the restoration of Camelot." There was still a look, a humor, in his eye I did not trust, as if he found our confrontation essentially comic.

"You and your fucking Camelot! Your bloody holy and ideal court!" The memories were unexpectedly fresh, and they hurt as only betrayed love can. For I really had loved Camelot when I first came to court, an adolescent true believer in the new myth of the Round Table, of Christian chivalry and glorious quests. Arthur could have sent me after the Grail itself, I was that innocent.

But a castle is too narrow and strait a space for illusions. It holds no secrets. The queen, praised for her virtue by one and all, was a harlot. The king's best friend, a public paragon of chastity, was betraying him. And everyone knew! There was the heart and exemplar of it all. Those same poetasters who wrote sonnets to the purity of Lodegreaunce's daughter smirked and gossiped behind their hands. It was Hypocrisy Hall, ruled over by the smiling and genial Good King Cuckold. He knew all, but so long as no one dared speak it aloud, he did not care. And those few who were neither fools nor lackeys, those who spoke openly of what all knew, were exiled or killed. For telling the truth! That was Merlin's holy and Christian court of Camelot.

Down below, Shikra prowled the crooked aisles dividing the workbenches, prying open a fermenter to take a peek, rifling through desk drawers, elaborately bored. She had that kind of rough, destructive energy that demands she be doing something at all times.

The king's bastard is like his jester, powerless but immune from criticism. I trafficked with the high and low of the land, tinsmiths and river-gods alike, and I knew their minds. Arthur was hated by his own people. He kept the land in ruin with his constant wars. Taxes went to support the extravagant adventures of his knights. He was expanding his rule, croft by shire, a kingdom here, a chunk of Normandy there, questing after Merlin's dream of a Paneuropean Empire. All built on the blood of the peasantry; they were just war fodder to him.

I was all but screaming in Merlin's face. Below, Shikra drifted closer, straining to hear. "That's why I seized the throne while he was off warring in France—to give the land a taste of peace; as a novelty, if nothing else. To clear away the hypocrisy and cant, to open the windows and let a little fresh air in. The people had prayed for release. When Arthur returned, it was my banner they rallied around. And do you know what the real beauty of it was? It was over a year before he learned he'd been overthrown."

Merlin shook his head. "You are so like your father! He too was an idealist—I know you find that hard to appreciate—a man who burned for the Right. We should have acknowledged your claim to succession."

"You haven't been listening!"

"You have a complaint against us. No one denies that. But, Mordred, you must understand that we didn't know you were the king's son. Arthur was . . . not very fertile. He had slept with your mother only once. We thought she was trying to blackmail him." He sighed piously. "Had we only known, it all could have been different."

I was suddenly embarrassed for him. What he called my complaint was the old and ugly story of my birth. Fearing the proof of his adultery—Morgawse was nominally his sister, and incest had both religious and dynastic consequences—Arthur had ordered all noble babies born that feast of Beltaine brought to court, and then had them placed in an unmanned boat and set adrift. Days later, a peasant had found the boat run aground with six small corpses. Only I, with my unhuman vigor, survived. But, typical of him, Merlin missed the horror of the story—that six innocents were sacrificed to hide the nature of Arthur's crime—and saw it only as a denial of my rights of kinship. The sense of futility and resignation that is my curse descended once again. Without understanding between us, we could never make common cause.

"Forget it," I said. "Let's go get a drink."

I picked up 476 to the Schuylkill. Shikra hung over the back seat, fascinated, confused and aroused by the near-subliminal scent of murder and magic that clung to us both. "You haven't introduced me to your young friend." Merlin turned and offered his hand. She didn't take it.

"Shikra, this is Merlin of the Order of Ambrose, enchanter and master politician." I found an opening to the right, went up on the shoulder to take advantage of it, and slammed back all the way left, leaving half a dozen citizens leaning on their horns. "I want you to be ready to kill him at an instant's notice. If I act strange—dazed or in any way unlike myself—slit his throat immediately. He's capable of seizing control of my mind, and yours too if you hesitate."

"How 'bout that," Shikra said.

Merlin scoffed genially. "What lies are you telling this child?"

"The first time I met her, I asked Shikra to cut off one of my fingers." I held up my little finger for him to see, fresh and pink, not quite grown to full size. "She knows there are strange things astir, and they don't impress her."

"Hum." Merlin stared out at the car lights whipping toward us. We were on the expressway now, concrete crashguards close enough to brush fingertips against. He tried again. "In my first life, I greatly wished to speak with an African, but I had duties that kept me from traveling. It was one of the delights of the modern world to find I could meet your people everywhere, and learn from them." Shikra made that bug-eyed face the young make when the old condescend; I saw it in the rearview mirror.

"I don't have to ask what you've been doing while I was . . . asleep," Merlin said after a while. That wild undercurrent of humor was back in his voice. "You've been fighting the same old battles, eh?"

My mind wasn't wholly on our conversation. I was thinking of the *bon hommes* of Languedoc, the gentle people today remembered (by those few who do remember) as the Albigensians. In the heart of the thirteenth century, they had reinvented Christianity, leading lives of poverty and chastity. They offered me hope, at a time when I had none. We told no lies, held no wealth, hurt neither man nor animal—we did not even eat cheese. We did not resist our enemies, nor obey them either, we had no leaders and we thought ourselves safe in our poverty. But Innocent III sent his dogs to level our cities, and on their ashes raised the Inquisition. My sweet, harmless comrades were tortured, mutilated, burnt alive. History is a laboratory in which we learn that nothing works, or ever can. "Yes."

"Why?" Merlin asked. And chuckled to himself when I did not answer.

The Top of Centre Square was your typical bar with a view, a narrow box of a room with mirrored walls and gold foil insets in the ceiling to illusion it larger, and flaccid jazz oozing from hidden speakers. "The stools in the center, by the window," I told the hostess, and tipped her accordingly. She cleared some businessmen out of our seats and dispatched a waitress to take our orders.

"Boodles martini, very dry, straight up with a twist," I said.

"Single malt Scotch. Warm."

"I'd like a Shirley Temple, please." Shikra smiled so sweetly that the waitress frowned, then raised one cheek from her stool and scratched. If the woman hadn't fled it might have gotten ugly.

Our drinks arrived. "Here's to progress," Merlin said, toasting the urban landscape. Silent traffic clogged the far-below streets with red and white beads of light. Over City Hall the buildings sprawled electric-bright from Queen Village up to the Northern Liberties. Tugs and barges crawled slowly upriver. Beyond, Camden crowded light upon light. Floating above the terrestrial galaxy, I felt the old urge to throw myself down. If only there were angels to bear me up.

"I had a hand in the founding of this city."

"Did you?"

"Yes, the City of Brotherly Love. Will Penn was a Quaker, see, and they believed religious toleration would lead to secular harmony. Very radical for the times. I forget how many times he was thrown in jail for such beliefs before he came into money and had the chance to put them into practice. The Society of Friends not only brought their own people in from England and Wales, but also Episcopalians, Baptists, Scotch-Irish

Presbyterians, all kinds of crazy German sects—the city became a haven for the outcasts of all the other religious colonies." How had I gotten started on this? I was suddenly cold with dread. "The Friends formed the social elite. Their idea was that by example and by civil works, they could create a pacifistic society, one in which all men followed their best impulses. All their grand ideals were grounded in a pragmatic set of laws, too; they didn't rely on goodwill alone. And you know, for a Utopian scheme it was pretty successful. Most of them don't last a decade. But . . ." I was rambling, wandering further and further away from the point. I felt helpless. How could I make him understand how thoroughly the facts had betrayed the dream? "Shikra was born here."

"Ahhh." He smiled knowingly.

Then all the centuries of futility and failure, of striving for first a victory and then a peace I knew was not there to be found, collapsed down upon me like a massive barbiturate crash, and I felt the darkness descend to sink its claws in my shoulders. "Merlin, the world is dying."

He didn't look concerned. "Oh?"

"Listen, did my people teach you anything about cybernetics? Feedback mechanisms? Well, never mind. The Earth"—I gestured as if holding it cupped in my palm—"is like a living creature. Some say that it is a living creature, the only one, and all life, ourselves included, only component parts. Forget I said that. The important thing is that the Earth creates and maintains a delicate balance of gases, temperatures, and pressures that all life relies on for survival. If this balance were not maintained, the whole system would cycle out of control and . . . well, die. Us along with it." His eyes were unreadable, dark with fossil prejudices. I needed another drink. "I'm not explaining this very well."

"I follow you better than you think."

"Good. Now, you know about pollution? Okay, well now it seems that there's some that may not be reversible. You see what that means? A delicate little wisp of the atmosphere is being eaten away, and not replaced. Radiation intake increases. Meanwhile, atmospheric pollutants prevent reradiation of greater and greater amounts of infrared; total heat absorption goes up. The forests begin to die. Each bit of damage influences the whole, and leads to more damage. Earth is not balancing the new influences. Everything is cycling out of control, like a cancer.

"Merlin, I'm on the ropes. I've tried everything I can think of, and I've failed. The political obstacles to getting anything done are beyond belief. The world is dying, and I can't save it."

He looked at me as if I were crazy.

I drained my drink. "'Scuse me," I said. "Got to hit up the men's room."

In the john I got out the snuffbox and fed myself some sense of wonder. I heard a thrill of distant flutes as it iced my head with artificial calm, and I straightened slightly as the vultures on my shoulders stirred and then flapped away. They would be back, I knew. They always were.

I returned, furious with buzzing energy. Merlin was talking quietly to Shikra, a hand on her knee. "Let's go," I said. "This place is getting old."

We took Passayunk Avenue west, deep into the refineries, heading for no place in particular. A kid in an old Trans Am, painted flat black inside and out, rebel flag flying from the antenna, tried to pass me on the right. I floored the accelerator, held my nose ahead of his, and forced him into the exit lane. Brakes screaming, he drifted away. Asshole. We were surrounded by the great tanks and cracking towers now. To one side, I could make out six smoky flames, waste gases being burnt off in gouts a dozen feet long.

"Pull in there!" Merlin said abruptly, gripping my shoulder and pointing. "Up ahead, where the gate is."

"Getty Gas isn't going to let us wander around in their refinery farm."

"Let me take care of that." The wizard put his forefingers together, twisted his mouth, and bit through his tongue; I heard his teeth snap together. He drew his fingertips apart—it seemed to take all his strength—and the air grew tense. Carefully, he folded open his hands, and then spat blood into the palms. The blood glowed of its own light, and began to bubble and boil. Shikra leaned almost into its steam, grimacing with excitement. When the blood was gone, Merlin closed his hands again and said, "It is done."

The car was suddenly very silent. The traffic about us made no noise; the wheels spun soundlessly on the pavement. The light shifted to a melange of purples and reds, color dopplering away from the center of the spectrum. I felt a pervasive queasiness, as if we were moving at enormous speeds in an unperceived direction. My inner ear spun when I turned my head. "This is the wizard's world," Merlin said. "It is from here that we draw our power. There's our turn."

I had to lock brakes and spin the car about to keep from overshooting the gate. But the guards in their little hut, though they were looking straight at us, didn't notice. We drove by them, into a busy tangle of streets and accessways servicing the refineries and storage tanks. There was a nineteenth-century factory town hidden at the foot of the structures, brick warehouses and utility buildings ensnarled in metal, as if caught midway in a transformation from City to Machine. Pipes big enough to stand in looped over the road in sets of three or eight, nightmare vines that detoured over and around the worn brick buildings. A fat indigo moon shone through the clouds.

"Left." We passed an old meter house with gables, arched windows, and brickwork ornate enough for a Balkan railroad station. Workmen were unloading reels of electric cable on the loading dock, forklifting them inside. "Right." Down a narrow granite block road we drove by a gothic-looking storage tank as large as a cathedral and buttressed by exterior struts with diamond-shaped cutouts. These were among the oldest structures in Point Breeze, left over from the early days of massive construction, when the industrialists weren't quite sure what they had hold of, but suspected it might be God. "Stop," Merlin commanded, and I pulled over by the earth-and-cinder containment dike. We got out of the car, doors slamming silently behind us. The road was gritty underfoot. The rich smell of hydrocarbons saturated the air. Nothing grew here, not so much as a weed. I nudged a dead pigeon with the toe of my shoe.

"Hey, what's this shit?" Shikra pointed at a glimmering grey line running down the middle of the road, cool as ice in its feverish surround. I looked at Merlin's face. The skin was flushed and I could see through it to a manically detailed lacework of tiny veins. When he blinked, his eyes peered madly through translucent flesh.

"It's the track of the groundstar," Merlin said. "In China, or so your paperbacks tell me, such lines are called *lung mei*, the path of the dragon."

The name he gave the track of slugsilver light reminded me that all of Merlin's order called themselves Children of the Sky. When I was a child an Ambrosian had told me that such lines interlaced all lands, and that an ancient race had raised stones and cairns on their interstices, each one dedicated to a specific star (and held to stand directly beneath that star) and positioned in perfect scale to one another, so that all of Europe formed a continent-wide map of the sky in reverse.

"Son of lies," Merlin said. "The time has come for

there to be truth between us. We are not natural allies, and your cause is not mine." He gestured up at the tank to one side, the clusters of cracking towers, bright and phallic to the other. "Here is the triumph of my Collegium. Are you blind to the beauty of such artifice? This is the living and true symbol of Mankind victorious, and Nature lying helpless and broken at his feet—would you give it up? Would you have us again at the mercy of wolves and tempests, slaves to fear and that which walks the night?"

"For the love of pity, Merlin. If the Earth dies, then mankind dies too!"

"I am not afraid of death," Merlin said. "And if I do not fear mine, why should I dread that of others?" I said nothing. "But do you really think there will be no survivors? I believe the race will continue beyond the death of lands and oceans, in closed and perfect cities or on worlds built by art alone. It has taken the wit and skill of billions to create the technologies that can free us from dependence on Earth. Let us then thank the billions, not throw away their good work."

"Very few of those billions would survive," I said miserably, knowing that this would not move him. "A very small elite, at best."

The old devil laughed. "So. We understand each other better now. I had dreams too, before you conspired to have me sealed in a cave. But our aims are not incompatible; my ascendancy does not require that the world die. I will save it, if that is what you wish." He shrugged as he said it as if promising an inconsequential, a trifle.

"And in return?"

His brows met like thunderstorms coming together; his eyes were glints of frozen lightning beneath. The man was pure theatre. "Mordred, the time has come for you to serve. Arthur served me for the love of righteousness; but you are a patricide and cannot be trusted. You must be bound to me, my will your will, my desires yours, your very thoughts owned and controlled. You must become my familiar."

I closed my eyes, lowered my head. "Done."

He owned me now.

We walked the granite block roadway toward the line of cool silver. Under a triple arch of sullen crimson pipes, Merlin abruptly turned to Shikra and asked, "Are you bleeding?"

"Say what?"

"Setting an egg," I explained. She looked blank. What the hell did the kids say nowadays? "On the rag. That time of month."

She snorted. "No." And, "You afraid to say the word menstruation? Carl Jung would've had fun with you."

"Come." Merlin steped on the dragon track, and I followed, Shikra after me. The instant my feet touched the silver path, I felt a compulsion to walk, as the track were moving my legs beneath me. "We must stand in the heart of the groundstar to empower the binding ceremony." Far, far ahead, I could see a second line cross ours; they met not in a cross but in a circle. "There are requirements: We must approach the place of power on foot, and speaking only the truth. For this reason I ask that you and your bodyguard say as little as possible. Follow, and I will speak of the genesis of kings.

"I remember—listen carefully, for this is important— a stormy night long ago, when a son was born to Uther, then King and bearer of the dragon pennant. The mother was Igraine, wife to the Duke of Tintagel, Uther's chief rival and a man who, if the truth be told, had a better claim to the crown than Uther himself. Uther begot the child on Igraine while the duke was yet alive, then killed the duke, married the mother, and named that son Arthur. It was a clever piece of statecraft, for Arthur thus had a twofold claim to the throne, that of his true and also his nominal father. He was a good politician, Uther, and no mistake.

"Those were rough and unsteady times, and I convinced the king his son would be safest raised anonymously in a holding distant from the strife of civil war. We agreed he should be raised by Ector, a minor knight and very distant relation. Letters passed back and forth. Oaths were sworn. And on a night, the babe was wrapped in cloth of gold and taken by two lords and two ladies outside of the castle, where I waited disguised as a beggar. I accepted the child, turned and walked into the woods.

"And once out of sight of the castle, I strangled the brat."

I cried aloud in horror.

"I buried him in the loam, and that was the end of Uther's line. Some way farther in was a woodcutter's hut, and there were horses waiting there, and the wet-nurse I had hired for my own child."

"What was the kid's name?" Shikra asked.

"I called him Arthur," Merlin said. "It seemed expedient. I took him to a priest who baptised him, and thence to Sir Ector, whose wife suckled him. And in time my son became king, and had a child whose name was Mordred, and in time this child killed his own father. I have told this story to no man or woman before this night. You are my grandson, Mordred, and this is the only reason I have not killed you outright."

We had arrived. One by one we entered the circle of light.

It was like stepping into a blast furnace. Enormous energies shot up through my body, and filled my lungs with cool, painless flame. My eyes overflowed with light: I looked down and the ground was a devious tangle of silver lines, like a printed circuit multiplied by a kaleidoscope. Shikra and the wizard stood at the other two corners of an equilateral triangle, burning bright as gods. Outside our closed circle, the purples and crimsons had dissolved into a blackness so deep it stirred uneasily, as if great shapes were acrawl in it.

Merlin raised his arms. Was he to my right or left? I could not tell, for his figure shimmered, shifting sometimes into Shikra's, sometimes into my own, leaving me staring at her breasts, my eyes. He made an extraordinary noise, a groan that rose and fell in strong but unmetered cadence. It wasn't until he came to the antiphon that I realized he was chanting plainsong. It was a crude form of music—the Gregorian was codified slightly after his day—but one that brought back a rush of memories, of ceremonies performed to the beat of wolfskin drums, and of the last night of boyhood before my mother initiated me into the adult mysteries.

He stopped. "In this ritual, we must each give up a portion of our identities. Are you prepared for that?" He was matter-of-fact, not at all disturbed by our unnatural environment, the consummate technocrat of the occult.

"Yes," I said.

"Once the bargain is sealed, you will not be able to go against its terms. Your hands will not obey you if you try, your eyes will not see that which offends me, your ears will not hear the words of others, your body will rebel against you. Do you understand?"

"Yes." Shikra was swaying slightly in the uprushing power, humming to herself. It would be easy to lose oneself in that psychic blast of force.

"You will be more tightly bound than slave ever was. There will be no hope of freedom from your obligation, not ever. Only death will release you. Do you understand?"

"Yes."

The old man resumed his chant. I felt as if the back of my skull were melting and my brain softening and yeasting out into the filthy air. Merlin's words sounded louder now, booming within my bones. I licked my lips, and smelled the rotting flesh of his cynicism permeating my hindbrain. Sweat stung down my sides on millipede feet. He stopped.

"I will need blood," said Merlin. "Hand me your knife, child." Shikra looked my way, and I nodded. Her eyes were vague, half-mesmerized. One hand rose. The knife materialized in it. She waved it before her, fascinated by the colored trails it left behind, the way it pricked sparks from the air, crackling transient energies that rolled along the blade and leapt away to die, then held it out to Merlin.

Numbed by the strength of the man's will, I was too late realizing what he intended. Merlin stepped forward to accept the knife. Then he took her chin in hand and pushed it back, exposing her long, smooth neck.

"Hey!" I lunged forward, and the light rose up blindingly. Merlin chopped the knife high, swung it down in a flattening curve. Sparks stung through ionized air. The knife giggled and sang.

I was too late. The groundstar fought me, warping up underfoot in a narrowing cone that asymptotically fined down to a slim line yearning infinitely outward toward its unseen patron star. I flung out an arm and saw it foreshorten before me, my body flattening, ribs splaying out in extended fans to either side, stretching tautly vectored membranes made of less than nothing. Lofted up, hesitating, I hung timeless a nanosecond above the conflict and knew it was hopeless, that I could never cross that unreachable center. Beyond our faint circle of warmth and life, the outer darkness was in motion, mouths opening in the void.

But before the knife could taste Shikra's throat, she intercepted it with an outthrust hand. The blade transfixed her palm, and she yanked down, jerking it free of

Merlin's grip. Faster than eye could follow, she had the knife in her good hand and—the keen thrill of her smile!—stabbed low into his groin.

The wizard roared in an ecstasy of rage. I felt the skirling agony of the knife as it pierced him. He tried to seize the girl, but she danced back from him. Blood rose like serpents from their wounds, twisting upward and swept away by unseen currents of power. The darkness stooped and banked, air bulging inward, and for an instant I held all the cold formless shapes in my mind and I screamed in terror. Merlin looked up and stumbled backward, breaking the circle.

And all was normal.

We stood in the shadow of an oil tank, under normal evening light, the sound of traffic on Passayunk a gentle background surf. The groundstar had disappeared, and the dragon lines with it. Merlin was clutching his manhood, blood oozing between his fingers. When he straightened, he did so slowly, painfully.

Warily, Shikra eased up from her fighter's crouch. By degrees she relaxed, then hid away her weapon. I took out my handkerchief and bound up her hand. It wasn't a serious wound; already the flesh was closing.

For a miracle, the snuffbox was intact. I crushed a crumb on the back of a thumbnail, did it up. A muscle in my lower back was trembling. I'd been up days too long. Shikra shook her head when I offered her some, but Merlin extended a hand and I gave him the box. He took a healthy snort and shuddered.

"I wish you'd told me what you intended," I said. "We could have worked something out. Something else out."

"I am unmade," Merlin groaned. "Your hireling has destroyed me as a wizard."

It was as a politician that he was needed, but I didn't point that out. "Oh come on, a little wound like that. It's already stopped bleeding."

"No," Shikra said. "You told me that a magician's power is grounded in his mental somatype, remember? So a wound to his generative organs renders him impotent on symbolic and magical levels as well. That's why I tried to lop his balls off." She winced and stuck her injured hand under its opposite arm. "Shit, this sucker stings!"

Merlin stared. He'd caught me out in an evil he'd not thought me capable of. "You've taught this . . . chit the inner mysteries of my tradition? In the name of all that the amber rose represents, why?"

"Because she's my daughter, you dumb fuck!"

Shocked, Merlin said, "When—?"

Shikra put an arm around my waist, laid her head on my shoulder, smiled. "She's seventeen," I said. "But I only found out a year ago."

We drove unchallenged through the main gate, and headed back into town. Then I remembered there was nothing there for me anymore, cut across the median strip and headed out for the airport. Time to go somewhere. I snapped on the radio, tuned it to 'XPN and turned up the volume. Wagner's valkyries soared and swooped low over my soul, dead meat cast down for their judgment.

Merlin was just charming the pants off his great-granddaughter. It shamed reason how he made her blush, so soon after trying to slice her open. "—make you Empress," he was saying.

"Shit, I'm not political. I'm some kind of anarchist, if anything."

"You'll outgrow that," he said. "Tell me, sweet child, this dream of your father's—do you share it?"

"Well, I ain't here for the food."

"Then we'll save your world for you." He laughed that enormously confident laugh of his that says that nothing is impossible, not if you have the skills and the cunning and the will to use them. "The three of us together."

Listening to their cheery prattle, I felt so vile and corrupt. The world is sick beyond salvation; I've seen the projections. People aren't going to give up their cars and factories, their VCRs and styrofoam-packaged hamburgers. No one, not Merlin himself, can pull off that kind of miracle. But I said nothing. When I die and am called to account, I will not be found wanting. "Mordred did his devoir"—even Malory gave me that. I did everything but dig up Merlin, and then I did that too. Because even if the world can't be saved, we have to try. We have to try.

I floored the accelerator.

For the sake of the children, we must act as if there is hope, though we know there is not. We are under an obligation to do our mortal best, and will not be freed from that obligation while we yet live. We will never be freed until that day when Heaven, like some vast and unimaginable mall, opens her legs to receive us all.

The author acknowledges his debt to the unpublished "Mordred" manuscript of the late Anna Quindsland.

Le Hot Sport

R. A. Lafferty

1

The *Dukkerin Daily* was something of a fun news-paper for the four days of its publication. It seemed loaded with whetted axes ready to swing. It was witty and novel and titillating. "For the present, subscriptions will not be accepted," it announced, but it was every-where on the newsstands. And every morning it had at least three "Jokes of the Day" that were better than the "Jokes of the Day" of any other morning paper any-where. But the slippery heart of the paper was to be found in its "Predictions."

That first day there was a whimsical story: "Two-dollar guitar launches local boy on thirty-nine-year stardom in musical world." But the boy's name, Randy Lautaris, was not known to the reading public. The interview with Randy had been done the day before, and nine-year-old

Randy had indeed bought a guitar from a friend for two dollars. But the strings and frets and parts to put it into working condition would cost more than thirty dollars, and then it would still be an inferior guitar.

Nevertheless, the *Dukkerin Daily* gave a lot of information on Randy's thirty-nine-year career which lay entirely in the future: the combos he would put together, the concerts in which he would star, the long list of songs he would write that would pass the ten million mark, the *Cine-Melody Movies* he would make. Randy Lautaris was a quick-witted and well-spoken nine-year-old boy, and likely he would have a successful career in something.

"Why only thirty-nine years stardom?" Randy had asked George Hegedusis who had interviewed him. "I'll be only forty-eight years old at the end of that stardom."

"I didn't say that it would end," Hegedusis told him. "It's simply that I can't see more than thirty-nine years into the future, nor can anybody else. If anybody else says that he can see further than that, he is a shameless confidence man."

George Hegedusis, appearing suddenly as a newspaper publisher, was the fairly rare combination of a passionate violinist and a shameless confidence man. He played the violin at baptisms and weddings and funerals, and also at award banquets. (Somebody better keep his eyes on that award every second or Hegedusis will have preempted it for himself.) And for some years before this he had been in show business. He called himself The Romany Houdini and he had some good escapist acts. And he was a fine practitioner of the "Fallen Angel Act." Now he was a little bit too old to be a show person, but one never gets too old to be a confidence man. But he had never dabbled in the newspaper business before, nor made predictions, nor done interviews.

"You are skating on mighty thin water, George the

Fiddler," Karl Staripen of the local police bunko squad told George that first morning when the *Dukkerin Daily* had been on the newsstands for less than nine minutes. If any new con popped up, Karl Staripen always knew about it within ten minutes.

"Prove malice on my part, or prove me wrong in any of my predictions or facts," Hegedusis said, "or else do not interfere with me in my pure-hearted activities." (Karl had often arrested George, and yet they had remained tolerably good friends.)

"What am I supposed to do, wait thirty-nine years to see if you're right in your story about Randy Lautaris and his two-dollar busted guitar?"

"You might as well, Karl. You won't be doing anything else important for the next thirty-nine years, will you? But you can catch me up lots quicker if I'm wrong on the facts of other of my stories. Did you read my piece on Moxie Masterman?"

That piece, also in the first morning's run of the *Dukkerin Daily*, was headed "Moxie Masterman begins one-hundred-and-one game hitting streak," and the text ran: "Moxie Masterman, hot-and-cold first baseman for the Louisville Lions in the new Deep South Major League, got his first hit of the young season yesterday, after twenty-nine times at bat without a hit. It was a pathetic, patsy eighth-inning single that nobody could be very proud of. Nevertheless, it was the beginning of a hundred-and-one-game hitting streak, a world's record to be set by Moxie. The streak will not be broken until August the third of this year when Moxie will once more go hitless after hitting in one hundred and one."

"How do you like that story, Staripen?" Hegedusis asked the bunko cop. "Hang me on that one if Moxie misses today, or any day for a while now. But he won't."

"I remember Moxie when he was in the Texas League," Karl said. "George, why is Moira in this room of yours? Does that mean my death, or yours?"

"Probably mine. I'll be predicting my own death, to-morrow likely."

Moira was a strange and beautiful lady. Sometimes people could see her and sometimes they couldn't. But she was always a bad omen.

"Four of the twelve stories in this first edition of your paper will give me a chance to nail you cold today or tomorrow or the next day, George," Karl Staripen said, "and I'm waiting to pounce on you. What's your object in all this?"

"Unrequited genius demanding a voice, Karl. When you're better than anybody else at a thing, then there comes a time when you just have to go public."

But George Hegedusis didn't slip that day, nor the next day, nor the day after that. It wasn't till the fourth day that his newspaper publishing was brought to an end. And then he didn't slip, didn't make a false prediction. It was his totally hair-raising true prediction that caused the very stones to cry out "Enough!" against him.

2

This was the outrageous prediction:

"Eleven-year-old Caspar Lampiste didn't seem very much worried when I told him that he had only one day to live, that he would be killed by an automobile then. 'What kind of an automobile?' he laughed. 'Shouldn't I get to pick what kind of automobile I want to be killed with?' 'It will be a foreign car named Le Hot Sport,' your faithful reporter, I George Hegedusis, told him. 'Oh wow. Oh wow. Oh wow!' young Caspar sang out. 'That's the rarest car there is. There are only four Les Hots Sports in the United States.' 'There will be five of them,'

I said, 'and you will be killed by that fifth one.' It is rather sad, really, that a young boy should be killed like that, but I only see and report the pending happenings. I don't cause them to happen. Caspar Lampiste, an eleven-year-old boy of this city will be killed by a Le Hot Sport automobile about one o'clock this afternoon."

That couldn't be disregarded. Karl Staripen, a captain on the police bunko squad, took George Hegedusis, the new newspaper publisher, into custody quite early that morning. And he also called in Rich Frank Lampiste, an executive of great scope and power who was the father of young Caspar Lampiste. Then the three of them went out to the Lampiste mansion and headquarters and they were quickly surrounded by a swarm of young executives who were in the employ of Rich Frank Lampiste. After a while, young Caspar Lampiste was brought in and set in the midst of them where he could be watched every second.

"This is my office and headquarters and also one of my fortresses," Executive Rich Frank Lampiste said, "and it occupies the entire sixth and top floor of my mansion here. It is in a three-hundred-and-sixty-degree circuit of wonderfully clear see-out glass which is also bullet-proof and shatter-proof. We are high on a hilltop here, and no automobiles are ever allowed within a thousand yards of the mansion. I don't like automobile fumes. I have a man in TV communication with us at each of the four Les Hots Sports in the United States; and with each of them is the owner of that particular automobile who swears that it will not be moved today. My young executives, of course, were already at work on this problem before Karl Staripen called me, but thanks anyhow, Karl. All the Les Hots Sports in the United States are at least thirteen hundred miles from here. I intend to prevent my son from being killed by any of those four automobiles at about one o'clock this afternoon. Where do you get your nonsensical predictions, Hegedusis? And where, if ever, did we meet before?"

"We've met. I played the violin at your wedding twelve years ago."

"Did you ever play at any hangings, Hegedusis? I'm angry enough to have you hanged out of hand. And I've always liked that tune 'The Gypsy Hangman' when done by a lively violinist."

"I did play 'The Gypsy Hangman' at your wedding, Rich Frank. And I've always been a lively violinist. And, oddly enough, I did play the violin at a hanging once, at the special request of the man being hanged. But my own death will be otherwise, not by hanging. You all are so entranced by the little story on page one of my paper this morning that you may have missed my prediction of my own death on page eight."

"What is Moira doing here," Rich Frank Lampiste suddenly demanded. "Chief of Security O'Brien, couldn't you keep her out?"

"She is a ghost, Mr. Lampiste," O'Brien said. "I can't keep ghosts out."

"I can," Frank Lampiste said. "Fade out, Moira. Be you gone! You are a mistaken omen this time. My son will not die today."

"*I* read your account of your own death, Hegedusis," the bunko cop Karl Staripen said. "But it's phony. No Romany, whatever else he can predict, can predict his own death. It's his blind spot. There is something very ulterior about that item of yours."

"It's interesting though," said Rich Frank Lampiste. "It goes, as I recall it, 'George Hegedusis' death will take place about ten minutes after one o'clock this afternoon. He will be flung to his death from a sixth-floor window of Frank Lampiste's executive suite on the top of his mansion. If they claim it was a suicide, do not believe them. It is murder. If my body is not found, it only means that they have hidden my body. It will be murder, and it will cry to Heaven for vengeance. And if there should be a grotesque or incredulous aspect to it, then the Lightning that is the father of me, George Hegedusis, will come and take away all that is grotesque and incredulous, and I will have died clean.' George, George, is this nothing but some of your bleak fun?"

"No, the fun has all gone out of my life since I have come under the compulsion of predicting true."

"Moira is still in the room," the security chief O'Brien said.

"Not to me she isn't, O'Brien," Frank Lampiste stated.

Suddenly the bunko cop Karl Staripen was all over George Hegedusis. He shackled his arms behind him, and he shackled his legs to the modernistic steel framework of the executive suite.

"However you go out of here, it will not be by a window, George," Staripen said.

"Every Romany man comes sometime in his life to his 'Days of Power,'" Rich Frank Lampiste spoke as though he were lecturing. "Usually, for the good of the world, these days are as short as they are grotesque. Now you come to the end of your short and grotesque and ridiculous 'Days of Power,' George Hegedusis."

"They must not be remembered as grotesque or ridiculous," Hegedusis protested in a thick voice. "My father the Thunder will save me from that."

"You told my son, Hegedusis, that there would be five and not four Les Hots Sports in the country. What is the fifth one? Is the fifth one in the country yet?" Frank Lampiste demanded of the shackled George Hegedusis.

"I don't know. It's probably crossing the border just about now."

"How?"

"Oh, by air, in a powerful but unregistered craft. It's Le Hot Sport that was stolen in Morocco last week."

"Yes, that's the one that has me worried. You really are

onto something. The odds are towering against us being in any flightway of that powerful but unregistered craft. The odds are prohibitive against the automobile somehow falling out of that craft. And it's very long odds against that automobile falling through the very strong steel roof here and killing my son."

"Yes, the latter odds are prohibitive, Rich Frank Lampiste," Hegedusis agreed. "There is no way that the automobile could fall through this roof here and kill your son in this place. *Because your son is not here.* Do you believe that fate is an imbecile? This is not your son, not the boy I talked to yesterday. This is a look-alike. Are you trying to trick God, Lampiste?"

"No, I'm trying to trick a lesser and meaner demiurge who plays such bloody tricks on poor humans. Maybe you've spoiled it now. Maybe he's heard you. No, my son couldn't have remained silent all this while. But this nephew of mine here usually says something when he talks, and my son doesn't."

"How far is your son removed from here, Lampiste?" Hegedusis asked.

"I'll not tell you that. Certainly I'll not tell it out loud. But he is in a fortress of mine that is stronger and more secret than this one, an underground bunker, not so very distant from here. Oh, God, help me now! Myself am having a 'far-seeing'! My son has left the fortress where I had him placed. He has started back this way, furtively and through the swamp-jungle. Why did he not stay where I had him placed? Henry, Henry, can you hear me? How did it happen?"

"He said he wanted to check the override lock on this underground bunker himself, Mr. Lampiste. And then he was out of that door and into the swamp-jungle which you yourself had constructed to be impassable. He was like a fox with his tail on fire. We cannot spot him yet, but we can hear his voice. He keeps crying, 'I have to

124

meet something. I have an encounter I must keep.' But surely we'll be able to seize him again shortly."

"Surely you'd better."

"I believe that I'll begin my own 'Days of Power' today," said eleven-year-old Roland Lampiste, the look-alike of his cousin Caspar Lampiste, "for I am a Romany man already. Oh, my Days of Power and Speed! If I work up early momentum, my days should go on almost forever. But I will need a spacious place to operate in. Where will I find it, where will I find it? Most Romany men do not come into their 'Days of Power' early enough."

"I've always believed that three million dollars is too much money for a two-passenger sports car that doesn't hold the road very well at over two hundred miles an hour," said the bunko cop Karl Staripen. "And, to me, it hasn't much style. There's a lot of ballyhoo has gone into that price. And yet the maker has sold twelve of the little buggers at three million each. He has to employ a lot of legend to do that, of course, and your item will help the legend, Hegedusis. It is said that eleven of the twelve Les Hots Sports have killed a person, and that twelfth one (the one that was stolen in Morocco last week, the one that may presently be airborne over our own country) is jealous of the others and is trying for a spectacular kill. It will bring as much as nine million dollars on the American market if it does attain a showy and spectacular kill."

"And it's said that each of the twelve is indwelt by an evil spirit," Rich Frank Lampiste mumbled. "That rumor has helped to get the base price up to three million dollars. Oh, the whole thing is shot through with such obvious fraud, and yet I tremble for the safety of my son. If my son's life is spared, I will give him any gift he wishes in the whole world."

"Would you give him a Le Hot Sport automobile, Uncle Frank?" the nephew in the room asked. "Then I bet he'd take me for a ride in it lots of times."

"Yes, Roland, I would give him, I *will* give him Le Hot Sport. And if he does not survive to receive the gift, then life is empty for me forever. Ah, we've made positive identification. The powerful but unregistered craft that left Morocco last night and left a jungle clearing in Yucatán two hours ago is indeed over our country now. And, unfortunately, we seem to be approximately on its flightway. Yes, yes, Henry, keep me posted, and see if you can't get it a little bit clearer on the screen. Oh, why doesn't it veer off a little bit? Karl, do you think that crazy George Hegedusis here really has something to do with this? And is there any way we could trade him in to fate to get a better bargain? How odd! All three of us here are Romanies."

"All *four* of us here are Romanies, Uncle Frank," said the nephew Roland Lampiste.

"It takes one to catch one," said the bunko cop Karl Staripen. "I always get the Gypsy cases, but I never was much good at solving them. Yes, I wish there were some way to trade in Fiddler George here for a better bargain. That's what your name, George Hegedusis, means: George Fiddler."

"I know it," said the fiddler man and fate-predictor. "And your name, Karl Staripen, means Karl Jailhouse."

"But my own name is somewhat more rare," said Rich Frank Lampiste. "I doubt whether either of you know what my name Lampiste means?"

"Its common meaning is a sad-sack or a hard-luck Charley," said George Hegedusis. "But its original meaning is 'scapegoat.' Aye, you are one who must take on you the sins of a whole people."

"Mine *is* a spooky name in the present context," Rich Frank Lampiste said, "but my mansion here is built of steel. It is impervious. If I see that there will be a direct hit on us here, we can drop down to the floor below us, or to five floors below us, in one second. Your estimate of the time is about right, Fiddling George. It will be just about one o'clock when the plane arrives, and we are approximately in its path."

"Is your son also approximately in its path?" George asked.

"Oh, my God, yes. I can see him in my scanner now. He's climbed up out of the jungle-swamp and onto the road, and he's running this way with his arms flung wide. I can even read his mouth. He keeps crying, 'I have a joyous encounter that I must keep,' and that encounter may be only minutes or seconds away. Oh, either shorten or lengthen the time, God. Oh, God, make time go away completely!"

They had several clear views of the powerful but un-registered plane on their scopes. In particular they had a good view of the belly of it. And the belly was badly torn. The craft had made a rough belly landing in the jungle clearing in Yucatán (what illicit cargo had it delivered there?) and now it flew with landing gear permanently down and with an awful wobble. That plane was not in good health.

3

"Oh, my God!" Rich Frank Lampiste cried again. "The monitoring screen shows that the belly of the plane has burst open and the uncrated Le Hot Sport automobile is falling out!"

And so it was happening.

But Le Hot Sport, having a mind of its own, or possibly a mindful spirit in it, was into a high-speed glide. These cars always had the tendency to haze and float at above two hundred miles an hour, and they would actually become airborne at approximately three hundred miles an hour. It was thus that most of them had made their kills. The car had left the plane at about twenty thousand feet but it had inherited most of the plane's speed. It circled in a wide, fast glide.

"It is scanning and searching," Frank Lampiste said. "It is looking for my son. Oh, it knows that I have switched boys. Or does it? It is going to hit us dead, or it is going to fill our nostrils with its reek."

"Hadn't we better drop below?" the bunko cop Karl Staripen asked.

"You go down if you wish, Karl. And unshackle George Hegedusis and take him with you. I will stay here."

"And I will stay here," said nephew Roland Lampiste.

"And I will stay here," said the shackled George Hegedusis. "Should I not watch the end of my own prediction?"

"Oh, I'll stay too then," Karl Staripen growled.

Le Hot Sport came dead at them. Then it swerved past and filled their nostrils with its reek. It landed easily on the road three hundred yards beyond the mansion house, with hardly a jolt, and its speed had fallen below two hundred miles an hour.

And the son Caspar Lampiste was seen on a scanning screen, running open-armed toward the insane car. The boy Caspar Lampiste had lost his wits, or his wits were trammeled. Le Hot Sport had braked and slowed, and it came to the encounter at no more than twenty-five miles an hour; and the boy, the Caspar-Goat, was running open-armed toward it at at least half that speed. The way he went down when he met the car, it was clear that the joyous boy was killed instantly.

"The debt, whatever it was, is paid. The sin, whatever it was, is subsumed. The impediment on the power of special men is removed!" the nephew Roland Lampiste was jabbering inconsequently. "Now our family name is no more 'Lampiste' or 'scapegoat.' Our family name becomes 'Langa' or 'flame' now. I am Roland Langa now." The nephew was very excited.

"All right, Roland," mumbled Rich Frank who was crying. "I'll have our names changed legally today. Yes, Henry, bring the body of my son here. Then have the morticians come for him in a quarter of an hour. Bring Le Hot Sport here also. I am impounding it. I will pay the list price of three million dollars to the Moroccan from whom it was stolen, but I will prevent by litigation its ever going back."

"Will you give it to me, Uncle Frank, now that Caspar is dead," the nephew Roland Langa asked.

"Yes, Roland, I give it to you. You become my son now. You become a Romany man in his full powers."

"But my name will be Robert Langa and not Roland Langa," the boy said. "As Roland Lampiste I was included in the bloodlust of the car, but it won't know that I am the same person with both of my names changed."

"All right, Roland, Robert," said his uncle, his new father, Rich Frank Langa. "George Hegedusis, why are you white and why are you trembling? Your prediction came true."

"He is trembling because the Power has left him," Roland-Robert taunted. "Four days isn't very long to have the power, Fiddler George. I intend to have it for more than forty years. I will drive Le Hot Sport, and my own totemic name will *be* Le Hot Sport. And you are wrong in your own prediction, that of your own death, George Hegedusis."

But the suddenly-much-older Rich Frank Lampiste-Langa was weeping as only a Gypsy man can weep.

"Why do you still mourn, Rich Frank?" Karl Staripen asked. "You have your son again, reborn into the body of your nephew Roland."

"Yes, I have him again, but for less than ten minutes."

"Have *you* your Gypsy up, Rich Frank? Do you also predict?" Karl asked.

"Yes, I also predict. And Moira is standing in the room with us again."

"I am wrong in none of my predictions," the trembling George Hegedusis the fiddler jittered. "I am no longer shackled, men, though it appears that I am. But I was an escape artist when I was in show business." Hegedusis stood up, free of his shackles. "I had to study a bit to see the hidden hinge on the encircling windows, but I knew there had to be a hinged section." Suddenly the unshackled Hegedusis was across the big room.

He swung out a narrow section of the encircling glass. He stepped out. And he fell six stories.

"God receive his ghost," Frank Lampiste-Langa spoke with emotion. "But at least we didn't fling him out."

"Yes, *I* flung him out, but not with hands," Roland-Robert spoke in a sort of power rapture. "I killed him. He didn't want to die but he foresaw it, and I compelled it. And I inherited his father the Thunder. And his losing the power killed him."

"Maybe not," said the old bunko cop Karl Staripen. "Hegedusis was possibly the finest practitioner in the world at the 'Fallen Angel' act. As aerialist, he would miss his trapeze and fall eighty feet. And the horrified crowd would believe that he was dead. And then, after a powerful and dramatic interval, the 'Fallen Angel' would rise up from the sawdust and walk out painfully but triumphantly. He really knew how to fall. I think he remembered how to fall just now, either consciously or subconsciously."

"He looks dead enough," Rich Frank Lampiste-Langa commented, looking down and still sobbing.

"Fallen Angel, rise up again!" Roland-Robert Langa commanded in a loud and rough voice. "We are onto your tricks. Rise up, and slink away."

And George Hegedusis did rise up, slowly and torturously, like a zombie, from the flagstones below the encircling windows. He dragged himself a few feet, trembling and seething with black despondency.

"What will happen to him now?" Frank Lampiste-Langa asked. "He can't live with the shame of his lost power."

"What will happen is what he predicted would happen," jeered Roland-Robert. "His father the Thunder will come and kill him presently. And his family is already on the way here with propitiative music for his funeral."

Men brought the dead body of the boy Caspar Lampiste up into the big room then. And on his dead face was the look of radiant happiness.

"You and I are cousins-closer-than-brothers," Roland-Robert spoke softly to the dead boy. "We pledged that, whichever of us should die first, he would give one-seventh of his soul to the other one. You have kept your pledge, Caspar. You have yielded only six-sevenths of your soul to God. And you still have the seventh portion tight in your hands for me. Release it from your hands to mine now."

And the dead boy, in some sort of post-mortem relaxation, did open his tightly clenched hands, and his brother-cousin did take something from them. Then the mien of dead Caspar Lampiste was completely peaceful.

"And now, Fiddling George Hegedusis must not die in his miseries. He must die in his powers," Roland-Robert-of-the-powers said. "His last prediction must come true. His father must take him out of his shame and unhappiness. His shame and unhappiness. But wait, wait, his father the Thunder is *my* father now too."

"Do what you have to do, Roland-Robert," the choked-up Frank Lampiste-Langa uttered, but his attention was on his dead son Caspar.

"O *Strafil*, O two-tined lightning!" Roland-Robert called out loudly as he looked down on George

Hegedusis collapsed against a nearby stone fence, perishing in his dejection. "Two-faced and double-dealing lightning, come and kill him. Come get him, and he will play the fiddle tonight during the supper for all your high company in *Nebos* in Electric-Cloud Land. One thing he *can* do, lightning, is play the fiddle."

There was a small thunder out of the cloudless sky, but the two-faced, two-pronged lightning did not strike yet.

"Oh go away, Moira!" Karl Staripen the bunko cop spoke sharply to the ghostly lady. "There is one death, and there may be another. But death does not happen in this room itself. You are wrong. Get out."

"Let her alone," weeping Frank Lampiste-Langa spoke hollowly.

"This is not an ordinary person who asks this," Roland-Robert was railing up at the lightning-bolt that still withheld itself. "I am a Romany man who has entered into my powers at the present moment. I have subsumed one part of the soul of my dead brother-cousin here, and now I am an enchanted man. I own a Le Hot Sport automobile, and there are only twelve of those wonders in the world. I *am* Le Hot Sport in my totemic name, and there is only *one* of such wonders as myself in the world. My new family name is Langa or 'flame' and it is given to me to command. Come down, come down, Strafil the double lightning-thunder. Oh, surely there is a more spacious place where I can revel in my new power! Oh, I want to go in my power to that more spacious place right now! Strike, two-faced Strafil, strike!"

Then the double-pronged lightning-thunderbolt did come down. One prong killed and crisped George Hegedusis as he slumped against the stone fence in his dejection.

And the other prong came right into the room and killed the boy-man Robert-of-the-powers. He died with a cry of delight, and fell across his dead brother-cousin

Caspar Lampiste. Robert Langa had found a more spacious place where he could revel in his sport-styled powers.

"It was quite a short 'Days of Power' that he had," Karl Staripen the bunko cop spoke sadly in a voice that was always like gravel.

"Are you satisfied, pernicious Moira thou ghost?" Frank Lampiste-Langa asked tearfully. "I have seen your look several times before. You smile that treacherous smile, but you cry tears at the same time. Your tears should be analyzed.

"I will inter Le Hot Sport in the same crypt with my son Caspar and my nephew-son Roland-Robert. They can drive it forever in that More Spacious Place. Oh, it'll roar and rev in there, and there will grow the legend of lively happenings in the crypt. What is that violin music drifting in through the swung-out window section, Staripen?" Frank Lampiste-Langa was red-eyed and he spoke with a curiously red and choking voice.

"It's the family and mourners of dead George Hegedusis, come to take him away with weeping and violin-playing," Karl said as he looked down. "And the tune, it's our oldest tune, the everlastingly happy tune that we play at birthings and weddings and funerals, all of them. It's 'The Gypsy Hangman,' Rich Frank."

"Ah yes. It's sad and happy at the same time. I remember now that George Hegedusis did play it at my wedding twelve years ago. Now they will play it for his funeral."

And Rich Frank smiled curiously and tapped the desk table before him to the music.

No Gypsy, whatever his straits, can completely resist the happy lilt of "The Gypsy Hangman."

The Lunatics

Kim Stanley Robinson

They were very near the center of the moon, Jakob told them. He was the newest member of the bullpen, but already their leader.

"How do you know?" Solly challenged him. It was stifling, the hot air thick with the reek of their sweat, and a pungent stink from the waste bucket in the corner. In the pure black, under the blanket of the rock's basalt silence, their shifting and snuffling loomed large, defined the size of the pen. "I suppose you see it with your third eye."

Jakob had a laugh as big as his hands. He was a big man, never a doubt of that. "Of course not, Solly. The third eye is for seeing in the black. It's a natural sense just like the others. It takes all the data from the rest of the senses, and processes them into a visual image transmitted by the third optic nerve, which runs from the forehead to the sight centers at the back of the brain. But you can only focus it by an act of the will—same as with all the other senses. It's not magic. We just never needed it till now."

"So how do you know?"

"It's a problem in spherical geometry, and I solved it. Oliver and I solved it. This big vein of blue runs right down into the core, I believe, down into the moon's molten heart where we can never go. But we'll follow it as far as we can. Note how light we're getting. There's less gravity near the center of things."

"I feel heavier than ever."

"You are heavy, Solly. Heavy with disbelief."

"Where's Freeman?" Hester said in her crow's rasp.

No one replied.

Oliver stirred uneasily over the rough basalt of the pen's floor. First Naomi, then mute Elijah, now Freeman. Somewhere out in the shafts and caverns, tunnels and corridors—somewhere in the dark maze of mines, people were disappearing. Their pen was emptying, it seemed. And the other pens?

"Free at last," Jakob murmured.

"There's something out there," Hester said, fear edging her harsh voice, so that it scraped Oliver's nerves like the screech of an ore car's wheels over a too-sharp bend in the tracks. "Something out there!"

The rumor had spread through the bullpens already, whispered mouth to ear or in huddled groups of bodies. There were thousands of shafts bored through the rock, hundreds of chambers and caverns. Lots of these were closed off, but many more were left open, and there was room to hide—miles and miles of it. First some of their cows had disappeared. Now it was people too. And Oliver had heard a minor jabbering at the low edge of hysteria, about a giant foreman gone mad after an accident took both his arms at the shoulder—the arms had been replaced by prostheses, and the foreman had escaped into the black, where he preyed on miners off by themselves, ripping them up, feeding on them—

They all heard the steely squeak of a car's wheel. Up the mother shaft, past cross tunnel Forty; had to be foremen at this time of shift. Would the car turn at the fork to their concourse? Their hypersensitive ears focused on the distant sound; no one breathed. The wheels squeaked, turned their way. Oliver, who was already shivering, began to shake hard.

The car stopped before their pen. The door opened, all in darkness. Not a sound from the quaking miners.

Fierce white light blasted them and they cried out, leaped back against the cage bars vainly. Blinded, Oliver cringed at the clawing of a foreman's hands, searching under his shirt and pants. Through pupils like pinholes he glimpsed brief black-and-white snapshots of gaunt bodies undergoing similar searches, then blows. Shouts, cries of pain, smack of flesh on flesh, an electric buzzing. Shaving their heads, could it be that time again already? He was struck in the stomach, choked around the neck. Hester's long wiry brown arms, wrapped around her head. Scalp burned, *buzzz*, all chopped up. Thrown to the rock.

"Where's the twelfth?" In the foremen's staccato language.

No one answered.

The foremen left, light receding with them until it was black again, the pure dense black that was their own. Except now it was swimming with bright red bars, washing around in painful tears. Oliver's third eye opened a little, which calmed him, because it was still a new experience; he could make out his companions, dim redblack shapes in the black, huddled over themselves, gasping.

Jakob moved among them, checking for hurts, comforting. He cupped Oliver's forehead and Oliver said, "It's seeing already."

"Good work." On his knees Jakob clumped to their shit bucket, took off the lid, reached in. He pulled something out. Oliver marveled at how clearly he was able to see all this. Before, floating blobs of color had drifted in the black; but he had always assumed they were after-images, or hallucinations. Only with Jakob's instruction had he been able to perceive the patterns they made, the vision that they constituted. It was an act of will. That was the key.

Now, as Jakob cleaned the object with his urine and spit, Oliver found that the eye in his forehead saw even more, in sharp blood etchings. Jakob held the lump overhead, and it seemed it was a little lamp, pouring light over them in a wavelength they had always been able to see, but had never needed before. By its faint ghostly radiance the whole pen was made clear, a structure etched in blood, redblack on black. "Promethium," Jakob breathed. The miners crowded around him, faces lifted to it. Solly had a little pug nose, and squinched his face terribly in the effort to focus. Hester had a face to go with her voice, stark bones under skin scored with lines. "The most precious element. On Earth our masters rule by it. All their civilization is based on it, on the movement inside it, electrons escaping their shells and crashing into neutrons, giving off heat and more blue as well. So they condemn us to a life of pulling it out of the moon for them."

He chipped at the chunk with a thumbnail. They all knew precisely its clayey texture, its heaviness, the dull silvery gray of it, which pulsed green under some lasers, blue under others. Jakob gave each of them a sliver of it. "Take it between two molars and crush hard. Then swallow."

"It's poison, isn't it?" said Solly.

"After years and years." The big laugh, filling the

black. "We don't have years and years, you know that. And in the short run it helps your vision in the black. It strengthens the will."

Oliver put the soft heavy sliver between his teeth, chomped down, felt the metallic jolt, swallowed. It throbbed in him. He could see the others' faces, the mesh of the pen walls, the pens farther down the concourse, the robot tracks—all in the lightless black.

"Promethium is the moon's living substance," Jakob said quietly. "We walk in the nerves of the moon, tearing them out under the lash of the foremen. The shafts are a map of where the neurons used to be. As they drag the moon's mind out by its roots, to take it back to Earth and use it for their own enrichment, the lunar consciousness fills us and we become its mind ourselves, to save it from extinction."

They joined hands: Solly, Hester, Jakob and Oliver. The surge of energy passed through them, leaving a sweet afterglow.

Then they lay down on their rock bed, and Jakob told them tales of his home, of the Pacific dockyards, of the cliffs and wind and waves, and the way the sun's light lay on it all. Of the jazz in the bars, and how trumpet and clarinet could cross each other. "How do you remember?" Solly asked plaintively. "They turned me blank."

Jakob laughed hard. "I fell on my mother's knitting needles when I was a boy, and one went right up my nose. Chopped the hippocampus in two. So all my life my brain has been storing what memories it can somewhere else. They burned a dead part of me, and left the living memory intact."

"Did it hurt?" Hester croaked.

"The needles? You bet. A flash like the foremen's prods, right there in the center of me. I suppose the moon feels the same pain, when we mine her. But I'm grateful now, because it opened my third eye right at that moment. Ever since then I've seen with it. And down here, without our third eye it's nothing but the black."

Oliver nodded, remembering.

"And something out there," croaked Hester.

Next shift start Oliver was keyed by a foreman, then made his way through the dark to the end of the long, slender vein of blue he was working. Oliver was a tall youth, and some of the shaft was low; no time had been wasted smoothing out the vein's irregular shape. He had to crawl between the narrow tracks bolted to the rocky uneven floor, scraping through some gaps as if working through a great twisted intestine.

At the shaft head he turned on the robot, a long low-slung metal box on wheels. He activated the laser drill, which faintly lit the exposed surface of the blue, blinding him for some time. When he regained a certain visual equilibrium—mostly by ignoring the weird illumination of the drill beam—he typed instructions into the robot, and went to work drilling into the face, then guiding the robot's scoop and hoist to the broken pieces of blue. When the big chunks were in the ore cars behind the robot, he jackhammered loose any fragments of the ore that adhered to the basalt walls, and added them to the cars before sending them off.

This vein was tapering down, becoming a mere tendril in the lunar body, and there was less and less room to work in. Soon the robot would be too big for the shaft, and they would have to bore through basalt; they would follow the tendril to its very end, hoping for a bole or a fan.

At first Oliver didn't much mind the shift's work. But IR-directed cameras on the robot surveyed him as well as the shaft face, and occasional shocks from its prod reminded him to keep hustling. And in the heat and bad air, as he grew ever more famished, it soon enough became the usual desperate, painful struggle to keep to the required pace.

Time disappeared into that zone of endless agony that was the latter part of a shift. Then he heard the distant klaxon of shift's end, echoing down the shaft like a cry in a dream. He turned the key in the robot and was plunged into noiseless black, the pure absolute of Non-being. Too tired to try opening his third eye, Oliver started back up the shaft by feel, following the last ore car of the shift. It rolled quickly ahead of him and was gone.

In the new silence distant mechanical noises were like creaks in the rock. He measured out the shift's work, having marked its beginning on the shaft floor: eighty-nine lengths of his body. Average.

It took a long time to get back to the junction with the shaft above his. Here there was a confluence of veins and the room opened out, into an odd chamber some seven feet high, but wider than Oliver could determine in every direction. When he snapped his fingers there was no rebound at all. The usual light at the far end of the low chamber was absent. Feeling sandwiched between two endless rough planes of rock, Oliver experienced a sudden claustrophobia; there was a whole world overhead, he was buried alive. . . . He crouched and every few steps tapped one rail with his ankle, navigating blindly, a hand held forward to discover any dips in the ceiling.

He was somewhere in the middle of this space when he heard a noise behind him. He froze. Air pushed at his face. It was completely dark, completely silent. The noise squeaked behind him again: a sound like a finger-nail, brushed along the banded metal of piano wire. It ran right up his spine, and he felt the hair on his fore-arms pull away from the dried sweat and stick straight out. He was holding his breath. Very slow footsteps were placed softly behind him, perhaps forty feet away . . . an airy snuffle, like a big nostril sniffing. For the footsteps to be so spaced out it would have to be. . . .

Oliver loosened his joints, held one arm out and the other forward, tiptoed away from the rail, at right angles to it, for twelve feathery steps. In the lunar gravity he felt he might even float. Then he sank to his knees, breathed through his nose as slowly as he could stand to. His heart knocked at the back of his throat, he was sure it was louder than his breath by far. Over that noise and the roar of blood in his ears he concentrated his hearing to the utmost pitch. Now he could hear the faint sounds of ore cars and perhaps miners and foremen, far down the tunnel that led from the far side of this chamber back to the pens. Even as faint as they were, they obscured further his chances of hearing whatever it was in the cavern with him.

The footsteps had stopped. Then came another metallic *scrick* over the rail, heard against a light sniff. Oliver cowered, held his arms hard against his sides, knowing he smelled of sweat and fear. Far down the distant shaft a foreman spoke sharply. If he could reach that voice. . . . He resisted the urge to run for it, feeling sure somehow that whatever was in there with him was fast.

Another *scrick*. Oliver cringed, trying to reduce his echo profile. There was a chip of rock under his hand. He fingered it, hand shaking. His forehead throbbed and he understood it was his third eye, straining to pierce the black silence and *see*. . . .

A shape with pillar-thick legs, all in blocks of redblack. It was some sort of. . . .

Scrick. Sniff. It was turning his way. A flick of the wrist, the chip of rock skittered, hitting ceiling and then floor, back in the direction he had come from.

Very slow soft footsteps, as if the legs were somehow . . . they were coming in his direction.

He straightened and reached above him, hands scrabbling over the rough basalt. He felt a deep groove in the rock, and next to it a vertical hole. He jammed a hand in the hole, made a fist; put the fingers of the other hand along the side of the groove, and pulled himself up. The toes of his boot fit the groove, and he flattened up against the ceiling. In the lunar gravity he could stay there forever. Holding his breath.

Step . . . step . . . snuffle, fairly near the floor, which had given him the idea for this move. He couldn't turn to look. He felt something scrape the hip pocket of his pants and thought he was dead, but fear kept him frozen; and the sounds moved off into the distance of the vast chamber, without a pause.

He dropped to the ground and bolted doubled over for the far tunnel, which loomed before him redblack in the black, exuding air and faint noise. He plunged right in it, feeling one wall nick a knuckle. He took the sharp right he knew was there and threw himself down to the intersection of floor and wall. Footsteps padded by him, apparently running on the rails.

When he couldn't hold his breath any longer he breathed. Three or four minutes passed and he couldn't bear to stay still. He hurried to the intersection, turned left and slunk to the bullpen. At the checkpoint the monitor's horn squawked and a foreman blasted him with a searchlight, pawed him roughly. "Hey!" The foreman held a big chunk of blue, taken from Oliver's hip pocket. What was this?

"Sorry boss," Oliver said jerkily, trying to see it properly, remembering the thing brushing him as it passed under. "Must've fallen in." He ignored the foreman's curse and blow, and fell into the pen tearful with the pain of the light, with relief at being back among the others. Every muscle in him was shaking.

But Hester never came back from that shift.

Sometime later the foremen came back into their bullpen, wielding the lights and the prods to line them up against one mesh wall. Through pinprick pupils Oliver saw just the grossest slabs of shapes, all grainy black-and-gray: Jakob was a big stout man, with a short black beard under the shaved head, and eyes that popped out, glittering even in Oliver's silhouette world.

"Miners are disappearing from your pen," the foreman said, in the miners' language. His voice was like the quartz they tunneled through occasionally: hard, and sparkly with cracks and stresses, as if it might break at any moment into a laugh or a scream.

No one answered.

Finally Jakob said, "We know."

The foreman stood before him. "They started disappearing when you arrived."

Jakob shrugged. "Not what I hear."

The foreman's searchlight was right on Jakob's face, which stood out brilliantly, as if two of the searchlights were pointed at each other. Oliver's third eye suddenly opened and gave the face substance: brown skin, heavy brows, scarred scalp. Not at all the white cut-out blazing from the black shadows. "You'd better be careful, miner."

Loudly enough to be heard from neighboring pens, Jakob said, "Not my fault if something out there is eating us, boss."

The foreman struck him. Lights bounced and they all dropped to the floor for protection, presenting their backs to the boots. Rain of blows, pain of blows. Still, several pens had to have heard him.

Foremen gone. White blindness returned to black blindness, to the death velvet of their pure darkness. For a long time they lay in their own private worlds, hugging the warm rock of the floor, feeling the bruises blush. Then Jakob crawled around and squatted by each of them, placing his hands on their foreheads. "Oh yeah," he would say. "You're okay. Wake up now. Look around you." And in the afterblack they stretched and stretched, quivering like dogs on a scent. The bulks in the black, the shapes they made as they moved and groaned . . . yes, it came to Oliver again, and he rubbed his face and looked around, eyes shut to help him see. "I ran into it on the way back in," he said.

They all went still. He told them what had happened.

"The blue in your pocket?"

They considered his story in silence. No one understood it.

No one spoke of Hester. Oliver found he couldn't. She had been his friend. To live without that gaunt crow's voice. . . .

Sometime later the side door slid up, and they hurried into the barn to eat. The chickens squawked as they took the eggs, the cows mooed as they milked them. The stove plates turned the slightest bit luminous—red-black, again—and by their light his three eyes saw all. Solly cracked and fried eggs. Oliver went to work on his vats of cheese, pulled out a round of it that was ready. Jakob sat at the rear of one cow and laughed as it turned to butt his knee. *Splish splish! Splish splish!* When he was done he picked up the cow and put it down in front of its hay, where it chomped happily. Animal stink of them all, the many fine smells of food cutting through it. Jakob laughed at his cow, which butted his knee again as if objecting to the ridicule. "Little pig of a cow, little piglet. Mexican cows. They bred for this size, you know. On Earth the ordinary cow is as tall as Oliver, and about as big as this whole pen."

They laughed at the idea, not believing him. The buzzer cut them off, and the meal was over. Back into their pen, to lay their bodies down.

Still no talk of Hester, and Oliver found his skin crawling again as he recalled his encounter with whatever it was that sniffed through the mines. Jakob came over and asked him about it, sounding puzzled. Then he handed Oliver a rock. "Imagine this is a perfect sphere, like a baseball."

"Baseball?"

"Like a ball bearing, perfectly round and smooth you know."

Ah yes. Spherical geometry again. Trigonometry too. Oliver groaned, resisting the work. Then Jakob got him interested despite himself, in the intricacy of it all, the way it all fell together in a complex but comprehensible pattern. Sine and cosine, so clear! And the clearer it got the more he could see: the mesh of the bullpen, the network of shafts and tunnels and caverns piercing the jumbed fabric of the moon's body . . . all clear lines of redblack on black, like the metal of the stove plate as it just came visible, and all from Jakob's clear, patiently fingered, perfectly balanced equations. He could see through rock.

"Good work," Jakob said when Oliver got tired. They lay there among the others, shifting around to find hollows for their hips.

Silence of the off-shift. Muffled clanks downshaft, floor trembling at a detonation miles of rock away; ears popped as air smashed into the dead end of their tunnel, compressed to something nearly liquid for just an instant. Must have been a Boesman. Ringing silence again.

"So what is it, Jakob?" Solly asked when they could hear each other again.

"It's an element," Jakob said sleepily. "A strange kind of element, nothing else like it. Promethium. Number 61 on the periodic table. A rare earth, a lanthanide, an inner transition metal. We're finding it in veins of an ore called monazite, and in pure grains and nuggets scattered in the ore."

Impatient, almost pleading: "But what makes it so special?"

For a long time Jakob didn't answer. They could hear

him thinking. Then he said, "Atoms have a nucleus, made of protons and neutrons bound together. Around this nucleus shells of electrons spin, and each shell is either full or trying to get full, to balance with the number of protons—to balance the positive and negative charges. An atom is like a human heart, you see.

"Now promethium is radioactive, which means it's out of balance, and parts of it are breaking free. But promethium never reaches its balance, because it radiates in a manner that increases its instability rather than the reverse. Promethium atoms release energy in the form of positrons, flying free when neutrons are hit by electrons. But during that impact more neutrons appear in the nucleus. Seems they're coming from nowhere. So each atom of the blue is a power loop in itself, giving off energy perpetually. Some people say that they're little white holes, every single atom of them. Burning forever at nine hundred and forty curies per gram. Bringing energy into our universe from somewhere else. Little gateways."

Solly's sigh filled the black, expressing incomprehension for all of them. "So it's poisonous?"

"It's dangerous, sure, because the positrons breaking away from it fly right through flesh like ours. Mostly they never touch a thing in us, because that's how close to phantoms we are—mostly blood, which is almost light. That's why we can see each other so well. But sometimes a beta particle will hit something small on its way through. Could mean nothing or it could kill you on the spot. Eventually it'll get us all."

Oliver fell asleep dreaming of threads of light like concentrations of the foremen's fierce flashes, passing right through him. Shifts passed in their timeless round. They ached when they woke on the warm basalt floor, they ached when they finished the long work shifts. They were hungry and often injured. None of them could say how long they had been there. None of them could say how old they were. Sometimes they lived without light other than the robots' lasers and the stove plates. Sometimes the foremen visited with their scorching lighthouse beams every off-shift, shouting questions and beating them. Apparently cows were disappearing, cylinders of air and oxygen, supplies of all sorts. None of it mattered to Oliver but the spherical geometry. He knew where he was, he could see it. The three-dimensional map in his head grew more extensive every shift. But everything else was fading away. . . .

"So it's the most powerful substance in the world," Solly said. "But why us? Why are we here?"

"You don't know?" Jakob said.

"They blanked us, remember? All that's gone."

But because of Jakob, they knew what was up there: the domed palaces on the lunar surface, the fantastic luxuries of Earth . . . when he spoke of it, in fact, a lot of Earth came back to them, and they babbled and chattered at the unexpected upwellings. Memories that deep couldn't be blanked without killing, Jakob said. And so they prevailed after all, in a way.

But there was much that had been burnt forever. And so Jakob sighed. "Yeah yeah, I remember. I just thought—well. We're here for different reasons. Some were criminals. Some complained."

"Like Hester!" They laughed.

"Yeah, I suppose that's what got her here. But a lot of us were just in the wrong place at the wrong time. Wrong politics or skin or whatever. Wrong look on your face."

"That was me, I bet," Solly said, and the others laughed at him. "Well I got a funny face, I know I do! I can feel it."

Jakob was silent for a long time. "What about you?" Oliver asked.

More silence. The rumble of a distant detonation, like muted thunder.

"I wish I knew. But I'm like you in that. I don't remember the actual arrest. They must have hit me on the head. Given me a concussion. I must have said something against the mines, I guess. And the wrong people heard me."

"Bad luck."

"Yeah. Bad luck."

More shifts passed. Oliver rigged a timepiece with two rocks, a length of detonation cord and a set of pulleys, and confirmed over time what he had come to suspect; the work shifts were getting longer. It was more and more difficult to get all the way through one, harder to stay awake for the meals and the geometry lessons during the off-shifts. The foremen came every off-shift now, blasting in with their searchlights and shouts and kicks, leaving in a swirl of afterimages and pain. Solly went out one shift cursing them under his breath, and never came back. Disappeared. The foremen beat them for it and Oliver shouted with rage. "It's not our fault! There's something out there, I saw it! It's killing us!"

Then next shift his little tendril of a vein bloomed, he couldn't find any rock around the blue: a big bole. He would have to tell the foremen, start working in a crew. He dismantled his clock.

On the way back he heard the footsteps again, shuffling along slowly behind him. This time he was at the entrance to the last tunnel, the pens close behind him. He turned to stare into the darkness with his third eye, willing himself to see the thing. Whoosh of air, a sniff, a footfall on the rail. . . . Far across the thin wedge of air a beam of light flashed, making a long narrow cone of white talc. Steel tracks gleamed where the wheels of the car burnished them. Pupils shrinking like a snail's antennae, he stared back at the footsteps, saw nothing. Then, just barely, two points of red: retinas, reflecting the distant lance of light. They blinked. He bolted and ran again, reached the foremen at the checkpoint in seconds.

They blinded him as he panted, passed him through and into the bullpen.

After the meal on that shift Oliver lay trembling on the floor of the bullpen and told Jakob about it. "I'm scared, Jakob. Solly, Hester, Freeman, Mute Lije, Naomi—they're all gone. Everyone I know here is gone but us."

"Free at last," Jakob said shortly. "Here, let's do your problems for tonight."

"I don't care about them."

"You have to care about them. Nothing matters unless you do. That blue is the mind of the moon being torn away, and the moon knows it. If we learn what the network says in its shapes, then the moon knows that too, and we're suffered to live."

"Not if that thing finds us!"

"You don't know. Anyway nothing to be done about it. Come on, let's do the lesson. We need it."

So they worked on equations in the dark. Both were distracted and the work went slowly; they fell asleep in the middle of it, right there on their faces.

Shifts passed. Oliver pulled a muscle in his back, and excavating the bole he had found was an agony of discomfort. When the bole was cleared it left a space like the interior of an egg, ivory and black and quite smooth, punctuated only by the bluish spots of other tendrils of monazite extending away through the basalt. They left a catwalk across the central space, with decks cut into the rock on each side, and ramps leading to each of the veins of blue; and began drilling on their own again, one man and robot team to each vein. At each shift's end Oliver rushed to get to the egg-chamber at the same time as all the others, so that he could return the rest of the way to the bullpen in a crowd. This worked well until one shift came to an end with the hoist chock-full of the ore. It took him some time to dump it into the ore car and shut down.

So he had to cross the catwalk alone, and he would be alone all the way back to the pens. Surely it was past time to move the pens closer to the shaft heads! He didn't want to do this. . . .

Halfway across the catwalk he heard a faint noise ahead of him. *Scrick; scriiiiiiick.* He jerked to a stop, held the rail hard. Couldn't reach the ceiling here. Back stabbing its protest, he started to climb over the railing. He could hang from the underside.

He was right on the top of the railing when he was seized up by a number of strong cold hands. He opened his mouth to scream and his mouth was filled with wet clay. The blue. His head was held steady and his ears filled with the same stuff, so that the sounds of his own terrified sharp nasal exhalations were suddenly cut off. Promethium; it would kill him. It hurt his back to struggle on. He was being carried horizontally, ankles whipped, arms tied against his body. Then plugs of the clay were shoved up his nose and in the middle of a final paroxysm of resistance his mind fell away into the black.

The lowest whisper in the world said, "Oliver Pen Twelve." He heard the voice with his stomach. He was astonished to be alive.

"You will never be given anything again. Do you accept the charge?"

He struggled to nod. I never wanted anything! he tried to say. I only wanted a life like anyone else.

"You will have to fight for every scrap of food, every swallow of water, every breath of air. Do you accept the charge?"

I accept the charge. I welcome it.

"In the eternal night you will steal from the foremen, kill the foremen, oppose their work in every way. Do you accept the charge?"

I welcome it.

"You will live free in the mind of the moon. Will you take up this charge?"

He sat up. His mouth was clear, filled only with the sharp electric aftertaste of the blue. He saw the shapes around him: there were five of them, five people there. And suddenly he understood. Joy ballooned in him and he said, "I will. Oh, I will!"

A light appeared. Accustomed as he was either to no light or to intense blasts of it, Oliver at first didn't comprehend. He thought his third eye was rapidly gaining power. As perhaps it was. But there was also a laser drill from one of the A robots, shot at low power through a cylindrical ceramic electronic element, in a way that made the cylinder glow yellow. Blind like a fish, openmouthed, weak eyes gaping and watering floods, he saw around him Solly, Hester, Freeman, mute Elijah, Naomi. "Yes," he said, and tried to embrace them all at once. "Oh, yes."

They were in one of the long-abandoned caverns, a flat-bottomed bole with only three tendrils extending away from it. The chamber was filled with objects Oliver was more used to identifying by feel or sound or smell: pens of cows and hens, a stack of air cylinders and suits, three ore cars, two B robots, an A robot, a pile of tracks and miscellaneous gear. He walked through it all slowly, Hester at his side. She was gaunt as ever, her skin as dark as the shadows; it sucked up the weak light from the ceramic tube and gave it back only in little points and lines. "Why didn't you tell me?"

"It was the same for all of us. This is the way."

"And Naomi?"

"The same for her too; but when she agreed to it, she found herself alone."

Then it was Jakob, he thought suddenly. "Where's Jakob?"

Rasped: "He's coming, we think."

Oliver nodded, thought about it. "Was it you, then, following me those times? Why didn't you speak?"

"That wasn't us," Hester said when he explained what had happened. She cawed a laugh. "That was something else, still out there. . . ."

Then Jakob stood before them, making them both jump. They shouted and the others all came running, pressed into a mass together. Jakob laughed. "All here now," he said. "Turn that light off. We don't need it."

And they didn't. Laser shut down, ceramic cooled, they could still see: they could see right into each other, red shapes in the black, radiating joy. Everything in the little chamber was quite distinct, quite *visible*.

"We are the mind of the moon."

Without shifts to mark the passage of time Oliver found he could not judge it at all. They worked hard, and they were constantly on the move: always up, through level after level of the mine. "Like shells of the atom, and we're that particle, busted loose and on its way out." They ate when they were famished, slept when they had to. Most of the time they worked, either bringing down shafts behind them, or dismantling depots and stealing everything Jakob designated theirs. A few times they ambushed gangs of foremen, killing them with laser cutters and stripping them of valuables; but on Jakob's orders they avoided contact with foremen when they could. He wanted only material. After a long time— twenty sleeps at least—they had six ore cars of it, all trailing an A robot up long-abandoned and empty shafts, where they had to lay the track ahead of them and pull it out behind, as fast as they could move. Among other items Jakob had an insatiable hunger for explosives; he couldn't get enough of them.

It got harder to avoid the foremen, who were now heavily armed, and on their guard. Perhaps even searching for them, it was hard to tell. But they searched with their lighthouse beams on full power, to stay out of ambush: it was easy to see them at a distance, draw them off, lose them in dead ends, detonate mines under them. All the while the little band moved up, rising by infinitely long detours toward the front side of the moon. The rock around them cooled. The air circulated more strongly, until it was a constant wind. Through the seismometers they could hear from far below the rumbling of cars, heavy machinery, detonations. "Oh they're after us all right," Jakob said. "They're running scared."

He was happy with the booty they had accumulated, which included a great number of cylinders of compressed air and pure oxygen. Also vacuum suits for all of them, and a lot more explosives, including ten Boesmans, which were much too big for any ordinary mining. "We're getting close," Jakob said as they ate and drank, then tended the cows and hens. As they lay down to sleep by the cars he would talk to them about their work. Each of them had various jobs: mute Elijah was in charge of their supplies, Solly of the robot, Hester of the seismography. Naomi and Freeman were learning demolition, and were in some undefined sense Jakob's lieutenants. Oliver kept working at his navigation. They had found charts of the tunnel systems in their area, and Oliver was memorizing them, so that he would know at each moment exactly where they were. He found he could do it remarkably well; each time they ventured on he knew where the forks would come, where they would lead. Always upward.

But the pursuit was getting hotter. It seemed there were foremen everywhere, patrolling the shafts in search of them. "Soon they'll mine some passages and try to drive us into them," Jakob said. "It's about time we left."

"Left?" Oliver repeated.

"Left the system. Struck out on our own."

"Dig our own tunnel," Naomi said happily.

"Yes."

"To where?" Hester croaked.

Then they were rocked by an explosion that almost broke their eardrums, and the air rushed away. The rock around them trembled, creaked, groaned, cracked, and down the tunnel the ceiling collapsed, shoving dust toward them in a roaring *whoosh!* "A Boesman!" Solly cried.

Jakob laughed out loud. They were all scrambling into their vacuum suits as fast as they could. "Time to leave!" he cried, maneuvering their A robot against the side of the chamber. He put one of their Boesmans against the wall and set the timer. "Okay," he said over the suit's intercom. "Now we got to mine like we never mined before. To the surface!"

The first task was to get far enough away from the Boesman that they wouldn't be killed when it went off. They were now drilling a narrow tunnel and moving the loosened rock behind them to fill up the hole as they passed through it; this loose fill would fly like bullets down a rifle barrel when the Boesman went off. So they made three abrupt turns at acute angles to stop the fill's movement, and then drilled away from the area as fast as they could. Naomi and Jakob were confident that the explosion of the Boesman would shatter the surrounding rock to such an extent that it would never be possible for anyone to locate the starting point for their tunnel.

"Hopefully they'll think we did ourselves in," Naomi said, "either on purpose or by accident." Oliver enjoyed hearing her light laugh, her clear voice that was so pure and musical compared to Hester's croaking. He had never known Naomi well before, but now he admired her grace and power, her pulsing energy; she worked harder than Jakob, even. Harder than any of them.

A few shifts into their new life Naomi checked the detonator timer she kept on a cord around her neck. "It should be going off soon. Someone go try and keep the cows and chickens calmed down." But Solly had just reached the cows' pen when the Boesman went off. They were all sledgehammered by the blast, which was louder than a mere explosion, something more basic and fundamental: the violent smash of a whole world shutting the door on them. Deafened, bruised, they staggered up and checked each other for serious injuries, then pacified the cows, whose terrified moos they felt in their hands rather than actually heard. The structural integrity of their tunnel seemed okay; they were in an old flow of the mantle's convection current, now cooled to stasis, and it was plastic enough to take such a blast without shattering. Perfect miners' rock, protecting them like a mother. They lifted up the cows and set them upright on the bottom of the ore car that had been made into the barn. Freeman hurried back down the tunnel to see how the rear of it looked. When he came back their hearing was returning, and through the ringing that would persist for several shifts he shouted, "It's walled off good! Fused!"

So they were in a little tunnel of their own. They fell together in a clump, hugging each other and shouting. "Free at last!" Jakob roared, booming out a laugh louder than anything Oliver had ever heard from him. Then they settled down to the task of turning on an air cylinder and recycler, and regulating their gas exchange.

They soon settled into a routine that moved their tunnel forward as quickly and quietly as possible. One of them operated the robot, digging as narrow a shaft as they could possibly work in. This person used only laser drills unless confronted with extremely hard rock, when it was judged worth the risk to set off small explosions, timed by seismometer to follow closely other detonations back in the mines; Jakob and Naomi hoped that the complex interior of the moon would prevent any listeners from noticing that their explosion was anything more than an echo of the mining blast.

Three of them dealt with the rock freed by the robot's drilling, moving it from the front of the tunnel to its rear, and at intervals pulling up the cars' tracks and bringing them forward. The placement of the loose rock was a serious matter, because if it displaced much more volume than it had at the front of the tunnel, they would eventually fill in all the open space they had; this was the classic problem of the "creeping worm" tunnel. It was necessary to pack the blocks into the space at the rear with an absolute minimum of gaps, in exactly the way they had been cut, like pieces of a puzzle; they all got very good at the craft of this, losing only a few inches of open space in every mile they dug. This work was the hardest both physically and mentally, and each shift of it left Oliver more tired than he had ever been while mining. Because the truth was all of them were working at full speed, and for the middle team it meant almost running, back and forth, back and forth, back and forth. . . . Their little bit of open tunnel was only some sixty yards long, but after a while on the midshift it seemed like five hundred.

The three people not working on the rock tended the air and the livestock, ate, helped out with large blocks and the like, and snatched some sleep. They rotated one at a time through the three stations, and worked one shift (timed by detonator timer) at each post. It made for a routine so mesmerizing in its exhaustiveness that Oliver found it very hard to do his calculations of their position in his shift off. "You've got to keep at it," Jakob told him as he ran back from the robot to help the calculating. "It's not just anywhere we want to come up, but right under the domed city of Selene, next to the rocket rails. To do that we'll need some good navigation. We get that and we'll come up right in the middle of the masters who have gotten rich from selling the blue to Earth, and that will be a very gratifying thing I assure you."

So Oliver would work on it until he slept. Actually it was relatively easy; he knew where they had been in the moon when they struck out on their own, and Jakob had given him the surface coordinates for Selene: so it was just a matter of dead reckoning.

It was even possible to calculate their average speed, and therefore when they could expect to reach the surface. That could be checked against the rate of depletion of their fixed resources—air, water lost in the recycler, and food for the livestock. It took a few shifts of consultation with mute Elijah to determine all the factors reliably, and after that it was a simple matter of arithmetic.

When Oliver and Elijah completed these calculations they called Jakob over and explained what they had done.

"Good work," Jakob said. "I should have thought of that."

"But look," Oliver said, "we've got enough air and water, and the robot's power pack is ten times what we'll need—same with explosives—it's only food is a problem. I don't know if we've got enough hay for the cows."

Jakob nodded as he looked over Oliver's shoulder and examined their figures. "We'll have to kill and eat the cows one by one. That'll feed us and cut down on the amount of hay we need, at the same time."

"Eat the cows?" Oliver was stunned.

"Sure! They're meat! People on Earth eat them all the time!"

"Well. . . ." Oliver was doubtful, but under the lash of Hester's bitter laughter he didn't say any more.

Still, Jakob and Freeman and Naomi decided it would be best if they stepped up the pace a little bit, to provide them with more of a margin for error. They shifted two people to the shaft face and supplemented the robot's continuous drilling with hand drill work around the sides of the tunnel, and ate on the run while moving blocks to the back, and slept as little as they could. They were making miles on every shift.

The rock they wormed through began to change in character. The hard, dark, unbroken basalt gave way to lighter rock that was sometimes dangerously fractured. "Anorthosite," Jakob said. "We're reaching the crust." After that every shift brought them through a new zone of rock. Once they tunneled through great layers of calcium feldspar striped with basalt intrusions, so that it looked like badly made brick. Another time they blasted their way through a wall of jaspar as hard as steel. Only once did they pass through a vein of the blue; when they did it occurred to Oliver that his whole conception of the moon's composition had been warped by their mining. He had thought the moon was bursting with promethium, but as they dug across the narrow vein he realized it was uncommon, a loose net of threads in the great lunar body.

As they left the vein behind Solly picked up a piece of the ore and stared at it curiously, lower eyes shut, face contorted as he struggled to focus his third eye. Suddenly he dashed the chunk to the ground, turned and marched to the head of their tunnel, attacked it with a drill. "I've given my whole life to the blue," he said, voice thick. "And what is it but a God-damned rock."

Jakob laughed shortly. They tunneled on, away from the precious metal that now represented to them only a softer material to dig through. "Pick up the pace!" Jakob cried, slapping Solly on the back and leaping over the blocks beside the robot. "This rock has melted and melted again, changing over eons to the stones we see. Metamorphosis," he chanted, stretching the word out, lingering on the syllable *mor* until the word became a

kind of song. "Meta*mor*phosis. Meta-*mor*-pho-sis."
Naomi and Hester took up the chant, and mute Elijah
tapped his drill against the robot in double time. Jakob
chanted over it. "Soon we will come to the city of the
masters, the domes of Xanadu with their glass and fruit
and steaming pools, and their vases and sports and their
fine aged wines. And then there will be a—"

"Meta*mor*phosis."

And they tunneled ever faster.

Sitting in the sleeping car, chewing on a cheese, Oliver
regarded the bulk of Jakob lying beside him. Jakob
breathed deeply, very tired, almost asleep. "How do you
know about the domes?" Oliver asked him softly. "How
do you know all the things that you know?"

"Don't know," Jakob muttered. "Everyone knows.
Less they burn your brain. Put you in a hole to live out
your life. I don't know much, boy. Make most of it up.
Love of a moon. Whatever we need. . . ." And he slept.

They came up through a layer of marble—white marble
all laced with quartz, so that it gleamed and sparkled in
their lightless sight, and made them feel as though they
dug through stone made of their cows' good milk, mixed
with water like diamonds. This went on for a long time,
until it filled them up and they became intoxicated with
its smooth muscly texture, with the sparks of light lazing
out of it. "I remember once we went to see a jazz band,"
Jakob said to all of them. Puffing as he ran the white rock
along the cars to the rear, stacked it ever so carefullly. "It
was in Richmond among all the docks and refineries and
giant oil tanks and we were so drunk we kept getting
lost. But finally we found it—huh!—and it was just this
broken down trumpeter and a back line. He played sitting in a chair and you could just see in his face that his
life had been a tough scuffle. His hat covered his whole
household. And trumpet is a young man's instrument,

too, it tears your lip to tatters. So we sat down to drink
not expecting a thing, and they started up the last song of
a set. 'Bucket's Got a Hole in It.' Four bar blues, as simple as a song can get."

"Meta*mor*phosis," rasped Hester.

"Yeah! Like that. And this trumpeter started to play it.
And they went through it over and over and over. Huh!
They must have done it a hundred times. Two hundred
times. And sure enough this trumpeter was playing low
and half the time in his hat, using all the tricks a broken-
down trumpeter uses to save his lip, to hide the fact that
it went west thirty years before. But after a while that
didn't matter, because he was playing. He was playing!
Everything he had learned in all his life, all the music
and all the sorry rest of it, all that was jammed into the
poor old 'Bucket' and by God it was mind over matter
time, because that old song began to *roll*." And still on
the run he broke into it:

'Oh the buck-et's

       got a hole in it—

            Yeah the buck-et's

                got a hole in it—

          Can't buy

Say the buck-et's got a hole in it—   no beer!"

And over again. Oliver, Solly, Freeman, Hester,
Naomi—they couldn't help laughing. What Jakob came
up with out of his unburnt past! Mute Elijah banged a
car wall happily, then squeezed the udder of a cow between one verse and the next— "Can't buy no beer!—
Moo!"

They all joined in, breathing or singing it. It fit the pace of their work perfectly: fast but not too fast, regular, repetitive, simple, endless. All the syllables got the same length, a bit syncopated, except "hole," which was stretched out, and "can't buy no beer," which was high and all stretched out, stretched into a great shout of triumph, which was crazy since what it was saying was bad news, or should have been. But the song made it a cry of joy, and every time it rolled around they sang it louder, more stretched out. Jakob scatted up and down and around the tune, and Hester found all kinds of higher harmonics in a voice like a saw cutting steel, and the old tune rocked over and over and over and over and over and over and over and over and over and over, in a great passacaglia, in the crucible where all poverty is wrenched to delight: the blues. Meta*mor*phosis. They sang it continuously for two shifts running, until they were all completely hypnotized by it; and then frequently, for long spells, for the rest of their time together.

It was sheer bad luck that they broke into a shaft from below, and that the shaft was filled with armed foremen; and worse luck that Jakob was working the robot, so that he was the first to leap out firing his hand drill like a weapon, and the only one to get struck by return fire before Naomi threw a knotchopper past him and blew the foremen to shreds. They got him on a car and rolled the robot back and pulled up the track and cut off in a new direction, leaving another Boesman behind to destroy evidence of their passing.

So they were all racing around with the blood and stuff still covering them and the cows mooing in distress and Jakob breathing through clenched teeth in double time, and only Hester and Oliver could sit in the car with him and try to tend him, ripping away the pants from a leg that was all cut up. Hester took a hand drill to cauterize the wounds that were bleeding hard, but Jakob shook his head at her, neck muscles bulging out. "Got the big artery inside of the thigh," he said through his teeth.

Hester hissed. "Come here," she croaked at Solly and the rest. "Stop that and come here!"

They were in a mass of broken quartz, the fractured clear crystals all pink with oxidation. The robot continued drilling away, the air cylinder hissed, the cows mooed. Jakob's breathing was harsh and somehow all of them were also breathing in the same way, irregularly, too fast; so that as his breathing slowed and calmed, theirs did too. He was lying back in the sleeping car, on a bed of hay, staring up at the fractured sparkly quartz ceiling of their tunnel, as if he could see far into it. "All these different kinds of rock," he said, his voice filled with wonder and pain. "You see, the moon itself was the world, once upon a time, and the Earth its moon; but there was an impact, and everything changed."

They cut a small side passsage in the quartz and left Jakob there, so that when they filled in their tunnel as they moved on he was left behind, in his own deep crypt. And from then on the moon for them was only his big tomb, rolling through space till the sun itself died, as he had said it someday would.

Oliver got them back on a course, feeling radically uncertain of his navigational calculations now that Jakob was not there to nod over his shoulder to approve them. Dully he gave Naomi and Freeman the coordinates for Selene. "But what will we do when we get there?" Jakob had never actually made that clear. Find the leaders of the city, demand justice for the miners? Kill them? Get to the rockets of the great magnetic rail accelerators, and hijack one to Earth? Try to slip unnoticed into the populace?

"You leave that to us," Naomi said. "Just get us there." And he saw a light in Naomi's and Freeman's eyes that hadn't been there before. It reminded him of the thing that had chased him in the dark, the thing that even Jakob hadn't been able to explain; it frightened him.

So he set the course and they tunneled on as fast as they ever had. They never sang and they rarely talked; they threw themselves at the rock, hurt themselves in the effort, returned to attack it more fiercely than before. When he could not stave off sleep Oliver lay down on Jakob's dried blood, and bitterness filled him like a block of the anorthosite they wrestled with.

They were running out of hay. They killed a cow, ate its roasted flesh. The water recycler's filters were clogging, and their water smelled of urine. Hester listened to the seismometer as often as she could now, and she thought they were being pursued. But she also thought they were approaching Selene's underside.

Naomi laughed, but it wasn't like her old laugh. "You got us there, Oliver. Good work."

Oliver bit back a cry.

"Is it big?" Solly asked.

Hester shook her head. "Doesn't sound like it. Maybe twice the diameter of the Great Bole, not more."

"Good," Freeman said, looking at Naomi.

"But what will we do?" Oliver said.

Hester and Naomi and Freeman and Solly all turned to look at him, eyes blazing like twelve chunks of pure promethium. "We've got eight Boesmans left," Freeman said in a low voice. "All the rest of the explosives add up to a couple more. I'm going to set them just right. It'll be my best work ever, my masterpiece. And we'll blow Selene right off into space."

It took them ten shifts to get all the Boesmans placed to Freeman's and Naomi's satisfaction, and then another three to get far enough down and to one side to be protected from the shock of the blast, which luckily for them was directly upward against something that would give, and therefore would have less recoil.

Finally they were set, and they sat in the sleeping car in a circle of six, around the pile of components that sat under the master detonator. For a long time they just sat there cross-legged, breathing slowly and staring at it. Staring at each other, in the dark, in perfect redblack clarity. Then Naomi put both arms out, placed her hands carefully on the detonator's button. Mute Elijah put his hands on hers—then Freeman, Hester, Solly, finally Oliver—just in the order that Jakob had taken them. Oliver hesitated, feeling the flesh and bone under his hands, the warmth of his companions. He felt they should say something but he didn't know what it was.

"Seven," Hester croaked suddenly.

"Six," Freeman said.

Elijah blew air through his teeth, hard.

"Four," said Naomi.

"Three!" Solly cried.

"Two," Oliver said.

And they all waited a beat, swallowing hard, waiting for the moon and the man in the moon to speak to them. Then they pressed down on the button. They smashed at it with their fists, hit it so violently they scarcely felt the shock of the explosion.

They had put on vacuum suits and were breathing pure oxygen as they came up the last tunnel, clearing it of rubble. A great number of other shafts were revealed as they moved into the huge conical cavity left by the Boesmans; tunnels snaked away from the cavity in all directions, so that they had sudden long vistas of blasted tubes extending off into the depths of the moon they had come out of. And at the top of the cavity, struggling over its broken edge, over the rounded wall of a new crater. . . .

It was black. It was not like rock. Spread across it was a spill of white points, some bright, some so faint that they disappeared into the black if you looked straight at them.

There were thousands of these white points, scattered over a black dome that was not a dome. . . .

And there in the middle, almost directly overhead: a blue and white ball. Big, bright, blue, distant, rounded; half of it bright as a foreman's flash, the other half just a shadow. . . . It was clearly round, a big ball in the . . . sky. In the sky.

Wordlessly they stood on the great pile of rubble ringing the edge of their hole. Half buried in the broken anorthosite were shards of clear plastic, steel struts, patches of green glass, fragments of metal, an arm, broken branches, a bit of orange ceramic. Heads back to stare at the ball in the sky, at the astonishing fact of the void, they scarcely noticed these things.

A long time passed, and none of them moved except to look around. Past the jumble of dark trash that had mostly been thrown off in a single direction, the surface of the moon was an immense expanse of white hills, as strange and glorious as the stars above. The size of it all! Oliver had never dreamed that everything could be so big.

"The blue must be promethium," Solly said, pointing up at the Earth. "They've covered the whole Earth with the blue we mined."

Their mouths hung open as they stared at it. "How far away is it?" Freeman asked. No one answered.

"There they all are," Solly said. He laughed harshly. "I wish I could blow up the Earth too!"

He walked in circles on the rubble of the crater's rim. The rocket rails, Oliver thought suddenly, must have been in the direction Freeman had sent the debris. Bad luck. The final upward sweep of them poked up out of the dark dirt and glass. Solly pointed at them. His voice was loud in Oliver's ears, it strained the intercom: "Too

bad we can't fly to the Earth, and blow it up too! I wish
we could!"

And mute Elijah took a few steps, leaped off the
mound into the sky, took a swipe with one hand at the
blue ball. They laughed at him. "Almost got it, didn't
you!" Freeman and Solly tried themselves, and then
they all did: taking quick runs, leaping, flying slowly up
through space, for five or six or seven seconds, making a
grab at the sky overhead, floating back down as if in a
dream, to land in a tumble, and try it again. . . . It felt
wonderful to hang up there at the top of the leap, free in
the vacuum, free of gravity and everything else, for just
that instant.

After a while they sat down on the new crater's rim,
covered with white dust and black dirt. Oliver sat on the
very edge of the crater, legs over the edge, so that he
could see back down into their sublunar world, at the
same time that he looked up into the sky. Three eyes
were not enough to judge such immensities. His heart
pounded, he felt too intoxicated to move anymore.
Tired, drunk. The intercom rasped with the sounds of
their breathing, which slowly calmed, fell into a rhythm
together. Hester buzzed one phrase of "Bucket" and
they laughed softly. They lay back on the rubble, all but
Oliver, and stared up into the dizzy reaches of the universe, the velvet black of infinity. Oliver sat with elbows
on knees, watched the white hills glowing under the
black sky. They were lit by earthlight—earthlight and
starlight. The white mountains on the horizon were as
sharp-edged as the shards of dome glass sticking out of
the rock. And all the time the Earth looked down at him.
It was all too fantastic to believe. He drank it in like oxygen, felt it filling him up, expanding in his chest.

"What do you think they'll do with us when they get
here?" Solly asked.

"Kill us," Hester croaked.

"Or put us back to work," Naomi added.

Oliver laughed. Whatever happened, it was impossible in that moment to care. For above them a milky spill of stars lay thrown across the infinite black sky, lighting a million better worlds; while just over their heads the Earth glowed like a fine blue lamp; and under their feet rolled the white hills of the happy moon, holed like a great cheese.

Deadboy Donner and the Filstone Cup

Roger Zelazny

I am standing in front of Vindy's and cannot read the racing stix because of the brownout which is the worst I can remember, when Crash Callahan comes by and the light is not so bad that I cannot see the bulge beneath his racing jacket, a thing I suspect to be malignant though not a tumor.

"I am looking," he tells me, "for Deadboy Donner and Painted Evelyn, and I will be most grateful for any information on their whereabouts."

I shake my head, not because I do not know but because I do not want to tell him that I have seen the pair less than half an hour ago and they are doubtless even now sharing a cavort at Metal Eddie's and perhaps a drink or several. This is because Crash, while a first-class racing pilot of the sun clipper variety, is often strung out on various chemicals and is known on these occasions for antisocial behavior, such as sending people outside our orbiting habitat for views of Earth, Moon, and stars without proper attire for comfort. So I tell him only that they have come and gone, but I know not where. This may seem more trouble than one should care to take for the Deadboy, who, to be fair about such matters, resembles Crash himself more than a little on the matter of public relations. But my reason is not only good, it is overwhelming. Namely, my personal finances should wax and brim very soon, but only if the Deadboy remains among the living long enough to collect on a promise from that strange dark power which rules Upper Manhattan.

Donner, like Crash, had been a racing pilot who wound up fairly regularly in the money, earning along the way good returns for those such as myself who follow these matters and occasionally make a small wager. He had copped every sun clipper Classic but the Filstone Cup, and that was the one which did him in. There had long been a nasty rivalry between Donner and Crash over that race, till Donner's immune system got fried during a solar flareup two years ago, along with the rest of the entrants—it being a bad year for that sort of thing. Crash was not running on that occasion, and so he is hale. Though the next year, Donner—who had kept going on drugs—placed, while Crash did not even show. That should have been it, however, because even the drugs could not get Donner through another year and give him a last crack at the Cup. So he elected to become a deadboy.

Donner had himself frozen, which is a low-overhead operation here, merely involving closing the door and opening the windows, so to speak. His intention was to be brought around a few days before this year's Classic, and be given a temporary fix to get him through it. His experience being what it was, he was thinking this might be his year of the Cup.

But lo, long before the time he is to be roused, I begin seeing him about town. And I know something strange is afoot because he avoids me with considerable ingenuity and speedy legwork. Not that we normally say more than a few words to each other, but now even these are missing. For a Saturday and much of a Sunday, that is. I manage to be blocking his way when he comes out of a restroom on Sunday evening.

"Hi, Donner," I say loudly then.

"Uh, hi," he answers, his eyes darting. Then he sees a way around me, takes it and is gone, out the door and off toward Forty-second Street, where he turns and vanishes. Could be he forgot something, I am thinking. I promise myself to ask around about him, but I do not because the next day I see him again and not only does he greet me first but, "Did you see me anytime this weekend?" he asks.

"Only last night," I tell him, scratching my head and wondering whether his neurology is burned out, also. But he smiles—possibly having heard of the peculiar occurrence which brought me to Upper Manhattan, where I await the running out of certain statutes—and when he tells me, "I would like to talk to you of matters which would benefit both of us in a financial fashion," I am willing to give his nervous system every consideration.

Over lunch in Vindy's he tells me of his troubles as I have just related them, and I nod every now and then to be polite, while I wait for him to talk about the money. Instead, he continues on beyond the point of being frozen, ". . . And I awaken," he tells me, "in this place which is like the inside of a videogame, leading me to believe that I have passed on and the next world is a kind of Cyberbia. There are all these algorithms putting the make on pixels, and programs champing at bits and sub-

171

routines moving about in simpleminded, reliable ways, as is their custom. The place is not unattractive, and I am watching, fascinated, for I know not how long. Finally, a sort of voice asks me, 'Do you like what you see?'

"At this, I am sore afraid," he goes on, "and I ask, 'Are you the Deity?'

"'No,' comes the reply, I am the AIity.'

"It turns out," he tells me, "that I am a guest of the artificial intelligence which has run our entire satellite for upward of a generation now, and while it seldom has much to do with individual people it has grown interested in me. This is because I am hooked up to a special monitoring and alarm system, designed to bring me around in time for the next race. This system does more than that, however, after the AIity tinkers with it. It provides access.

"'I have digitized you and brought you here for a reason,' it tells me. 'You are interested in winning the Filstone Cup, are you not?'

"'Indeed,' I reply, 'and more than somewhat.'

"'Would I be safe in saying that you would do anything for it?'

"'This does not sound like an exaggeration,' I answer.

"'Look around you. Would you go stir crazy in a place like this?'

"I give my attention to the central precincts of Cyberbia. While I am about this, it adds, 'For if you were willing to put in a little time here, I could guarantee you the Cup in this year's Filstone Classic.'

"'I am taken,' I reply, 'by the great beauty of your operating programs, not to mention some of the subroutines.'

"And that is how we come to make our deal," Donner tells me. "It seems the intelligence is a fan of the human condition, and has grown very curious what with having spent all these years as an observer. It has been hot to try it out for some time, but the opportunity had not presented itself till now. So when it offers to train me for its job with the understanding that I will run Upper Manhattan on alternate days while it vacations in my body, I am interested. Especially when it points out that it receives and relays all of the monitoring signals during races and could make certain that mine say I win the next Filstone Cup."

"But your body is ailing," I observe. "What fun would this be for it?"

"That is another inducement," he explains. "It says that much could be done to improve the medication I receive while ambulant, and it will institute a new treatment program for me and buy me considerable extra time without pain. Even sparing it half of my days until the race, I will come out ahead. Then I can hibernate again after I win, until perhaps someone comes up with a cure."

"This does not sound like a bad deal at all," I observe. "Especially the part about the race."

He nods.

"This is why I tell you," he explains. "For I want you to manage my betting for me with some of the unregistered, off-track people such as Blue Louie, who give better odds."

"But of course," I tell him. "Only one thing bothers me. Is it not hard being a stand-in for an artificial intelligence? I ask only because my life depends on the support systems."

He laughs.

"Perhaps for some it would be," he replies, "but for a natural intelligence I seem to have an aptitude for this sort of business. I find myself actually liking the work, and I even modify a routine or two for the better.

"'You are not bad for a NI,' the AI tells me when we change shifts and it checks over the first day's work. 'Not bad at all.'

"Which is more than I can say for the AI, when it

comes to being human. I wake up and find it has left my body dead tired and with a world-class hangover. Most of my first day being human again is spent recovering from this. I am even feeling too crummy to call my lady, Evelyn.

"I hook up to the monitoring equipment before I go to bed that evening, like I promise. When we switch over later on, we have a little conference wherein we brief each other on the day's events.

"'Go easy on the body,' I say, 'for it is the only one we have between us.'

"'I am very sorry,' it replies. 'But this being my first time out and all, it is hard for me to judge things. I will try to be more careful in the future.'

"But, alas, an AI is not always as good as its word," he tells me. "A couple of turns later I come back to cracked ribs, assorted bruises, and another hangover. It seems it had been drinking at Hammer Helligan's and had gotten into a fight. Again, it apologizes, explaining it is still having some difficulty judging human reactions, and saying it feels particularly badly about things when it sees what a fine job I am doing as substitute AI. Well, I am not about to back out at this point. So I tell it to go easy on the booze and other substances and I head off to work. I continue to streamline operations, realizing that if I trusted my opposite number more I would not mind running the show for even longer periods of time. But the AI gets me into enough trouble on our fifty-fifty time-sharing setup—for the following week I realize that I have contracted clap, and it is not I who have been up to anything which might result in this condition. Once more, it claims to be sorry. I tell it it had better remember to take our medication which it has prescribed, or I may reconsider our entire deal."

"So what happens?" I ask.

"It behaves," he replies. "For several days now it

seems to have kept our nose clean. I am feeling much better, the race is next week, I am all registered and I will be sailing *Hotshot III* to victory and glory and money."

So I lay his bets and I lay my bets and I await the race with the honest pleasure of a man who knows that the fix is in.

Then he begins avoiding me on a steady basis. I know better than to try talking to him on alternate days, for I know that that is when the AI is in charge—and though I approach it once and it lets me buy it a drink, it grows most upset when I let it know that I am aware of its pact with Donner. Then several days pass, and the race is nigh, and Donner will not give me the time of day if 6:47 will save my life, though I see him and Painted Evelyn nearly everywhere for a time. I begin to grow suspicious, and then alarmed. Then Crash Callahan comes by and asks after them. I suspect they are at Metal Eddie's, but I do not think they will appreciate the surprise Crash represents with the bulge beneath his jacket there in the middle of the brownout, and so I shake my head.

". . . I know not where," I tell him.

"You do not understand," he tells me, "what is happening."

"That is possible," I answer. "Likely, even. For this man has led a strange life of late."

"Stranger by far," he tells me, "than you may think. For he is not the person he seems to be."

"Of this I am aware," I agree, "though I am curious how you come to know it."

"I know it," he replies, "because I am Donner."

"You look more like Crash," I answer.

"Crash is responsible for the brownout," he says, "for he cannot run a power grid any better than he sails a racing clipper. It is all very simple."

In that I do not think so, we wind up in Vindy's, where

he says that he wishes to charge some elaborate dining on Crash's account. When I question the fairness of this he points out that half of the food is going to wind up in Crash's belly and the rest may be viewed as pre-race entertainment—Crash being a last-minute entry in this year's Filstone Classic.

"I do not think you believe me," he says, "for I am not at all sure I would. But because I desire your cooperation, I will explain. I am inhabiting the body of this lower life form because it is the only one I can get my hands on, on the spur of the moment. You would be surprised how difficult it is to find a body when you really need one. Fortunately, Crash is given to many vices. So of course I take advantage of this."

"Even now," I say, "I do not understand."

"It is very simple," he replies. "One day I get much on top of my work as substitute AI, so I decide to look myself up. I chase my credit trail around town. Then I set about infiltrating everything electronic in Blue Louie's Drugs, Alcohol & Electronic Vice Emporium, which of course is the legitimate cover for his gambling operation, for that is where my latest charges come from. There, through the burglar alarm camera, I see myself sitting at the bar with my lady Evelyn, who seems to be enjoying herself more than a little. This, you must admit, is a low trick, making out with my girl while using my body, perhaps not yet even fully recovered from a certain embarrassing social condition."

Unless, of course, he catches it from her, I am thinking. For she has always struck me as a hard and calculating lady. But I do not say this to Deadboy Donner in Crash Callahan's bod, in case he feels that I do not trust artist's models and perhaps wishes to introduce me to skydiving of the orbital variety. So, "This is distressing," I say. "What do you do then?"

"I fear that I let my temper get the better of me," he answers, "and I overplay my hand—as is sometimes the case when someone else in your body is romancing your girl.

"I cut," he says, "simultaneously, into the nearest speaker and vidscreen. I identify myself and then I flash upon the display field a series of circuits with slash marks through them, suggesting that I am contemplating AIicide unless it quits conning the lady. It rises and attempts to depart the establishment in a hasty fashion, an action I foil by closing the automatic door before it and continuing our conversation by means of another speaker, nearby. I suggest an immediate rendezvous at the interfacing equipment back in my apartment, failure to comply with which suggestion I will consider a breach of our contract. Then I open the door and let it go."

"Is there not a nasty paradoxical dilemma here?" I ask.

"Oh, Blue Louie is somewhat upset with my arguing through his sound system and flipping on and off the lights, the dance-floor strobes, the blenders, the shakers, the cash register drawers, the icemaker and such to emphasize my points. But when I explain a little of what is going on and ask him to keep an eye on Evelyn for me while I deal with a welshing intelligence construct, he is happy to oblige."

"I do not mean problems with Blue Louie," I say, "who is occasionally a gentleman. But it occurs to me that you cannot hurt the AI while it is in your body without harming yourself, and if you let it return to the grand system of Upper Manhattan it will be practically immortal there."

"These are not matters I have neglected thinking over," he replies, "and there are more ways to deal with artificial welshers than one may suppose at first glance. I assume the AI wishes to be reasonable, however, and come to some final understanding, since we both occupy awkward positions."

"So what does it say when you have your meeting?" I ask, for he has paused for dramatic effect and several mouthloads of chicken cacciatore, and I wish to seem interested in his problem as we are heavy betting partners as of several days now.

"Nothing," he answers a few swallows later. "For it does not show for the meeting. It decides to head for cover and lie low for a time."

"This seems very foolish," I observe, "when it knows that you are in a position to follow its electronic tracks throughout the city."

"Nevertheless," he replies. "It may feel it still knows a few tricks I do not, though it only postpones the inevitable. I locate it within a few blocks, and then I decide to come looking in the flesh—using Crash's flesh."

"A question occurs to me," I say, "not knowing anyone who has ever done a hit on an AI. What happens if you take it out? I understand it coordinates everything from banking to the disposal of solid wastes."

He laughs.

"Theoretically, this is true," he tells me. "However, making Upper Manhattan a smart city is actually a gimmick to balloon the rents, back when they are setting things up. Having held the job, I can tell you there is really very little to do once you get things to flowing smoothly. In fact, it is having all that time on its hands which I think caused the AI to start daydreaming of the pleasures of the flesh and results in our current problems."

"But Crash is in there running things while you use his body," I observe, "and this brownout is a big pain, not to mention being hard on the eyes. If it is such an easy show to run, why is he having this problem?"

"This is because Crash, who is a jerk," he says, "cannot keep from fiddling with the controls. It is what makes him a second-rate pilot, also. If he would just leave it alone it would fly itself."

"I see, sort of. By the way, how did you wind up in his body?" I ask.

"Oh, he switches from chemical stimulants to those of an electrical nature for some time before a race," he explains. "I discover that the brain hookup for this is sufficiently invasive to permit access of the sort the AI pulled on me in my deadboy days. So I digitize Crash while he is turning on, explain that it is a necessary borrowing and park him in Central Processing. I also tell him to keep his hands off the controls. You can see how much good that does."

The brownout had vanished a few minutes earlier, with light-levels returning to normal, then flaring to the point where many bulbs blow. After a while, the brownout returns.

"You mean the system would be better off without Crash in there?" I ask.

"Of course, and the same can be said for most places. But I have to leave him somewhere while I borrow his rig."

"So," he finishes, "I know the AI is in the neighborhood. If you believe my story, I want anything you might know on its whereabouts. If you want more ID, ask me anything only Donner would know."

I ask him how much money he gave me to spread around on him in the Filstone, with Blue Louie and some others. In that he knows all of the amounts, and how much is laid at what odds, I suggest he check out Metal Eddie's, about which I hear the AI in the Deadboy bod comment to the Painted Lady a little after the brownouts begin.

He does not catch them at the metalman's, however. Or, rather, he does and he doesn't. He finds them there, but the AI departs by a side exit and leads him on a chase, both of them careless of all bodies in the vicinity as they discharge with great noise and small accuracy the weapons they have with them. A half hour of this and the AI has vanished. The constabulary is spreading its net by then, but Donner slips through before it is tightened.

It is not until that evening that I see him again. I am talking to Blue Louie about the race, startoff time for which is only hours away when we emerge from Earth's shadow and catch the solar wind, and I am speaking of the possibility of a scratch on the part of Donner, though no official mention of this has been made. I am saying that if this happens and the owners of *Hotshot III* bring in another pilot, my bet should be considered off, because I was betting on the man and not on the ship. But Louie is shaking his head and producing slips saying "Hotshot III" with my signature on them.

About this time, the Deadboy in the Crash bod comes running in and says that he must use an electrostim helmet quickest.

"Now, Crash, do you think this is wise," Blue Louie inquires, "indulging yourself so close to a race and all?"

"It is not an indulgence that I seek," he replies, "but a bridge through the interface to a place where I can track down a weasel."

We go to a booth in a back room, Donner signaling that I should accompany him. And I wait till he plugs in, tunes up, goes glazed in the eyes, and runs off through fields of induction.

He is gone for several minutes, then his voice comes through a nearby speaker.

"Turn it off," he says.

I do this and he slumps. He had wanted me there for this purpose. Often, these devices are used with a timer, but he could not limit his stay in this fashion.

"Tell Blue Louie," the bod says to me, "to send back a brew, for I am in need of such refreshment."

I do this, and Blue Louie comes back himself, along with Painted Evelyn, on whom he is keeping an eye and also his hands.

"Crash, it is not good for you to mix the liquid with the electric," he tells him, "especially this near to racetime, for you will mess up the odds."

"Nevertheless," the Deadboy in the Crash bod states.

At this, Blue Louie nods, gestures to Painted Evelyn and gives her a small pat on her rearmost anatomy as they depart for the front of the establishment. I see that Donner notes this, for his eyes follow, but he says nothing.

A little later, the drinks have come and we are alone again. The Deadboy takes a big swallow, then says, "Two surprises awaited me in Cyberbia. First, I am attacked by Crash—"

"Attacked? In that state?"

"Yes, but he is no tougher there than he is in the flesh. He feints once with a digitized left, then throws a right at you, and that is all he's got.

"I speak metaphorically," he adds. "At any rate, he starts putting these electronic moves on me and insisting on the return of his bod, when I am there only to try running down my own. I am forced to deck him and stash him in an electronic slammer of my own design before I can continue the hunt for the AI in my bod.

"And that is the second surprise," he finishes. "Although I search all of Upper Manhattan in a great variety of subtle ways I am unable to turn up any trace of my kidnapped self."

"This is most frustrating," I say, moving to the screen on the wall nearby and fiddling up exterior shots. Predictably, most channels seem occupied with the gossamer lineup for the upcoming regatta. "It occurs to me that if you do not get to your ship soon," I tell him, "you may not be ready for takeoff."

"They will not let me in *Hotshot III* in this bod," he states. "But—" Then he stares at me. Then at the lineup. "Someone is in that clipper!" he cries, as it is jockeyed around a bit. "The AI knows the system has no senses to look into the clippers! So that is where it takes itself!"

He puts down his beer and rises.

"Excuse me. I have business to finish," he says.

"You just said they will never let you aboard *Hotshot III*," I tell him, indicating the insert of the advancing terminator and the digital countdown beneath it. "And there is very little time, anyhow."

"Then I run it down in the *Redhound*," he says, pointing to Crash's ship, adrift at its moorings. "For no one can keep me off of that one."

"But, Donner," I say, "what will you do if you catch it?"

"I will make it pay," he replies.

Then he rushes out.

In the days that follow I attend to the screen with the attachment of a lamprey to its rock. The race goes on for the better part of a week toward a distant multipurpose satellite which also serves as finishing beacon. There, the racers are met by a number of con-ac skipjacks which convey them home in great haste, the clippers being collapsed and drawn back by tugs. I am mainly concerned that Donner, in his rush to run down and pay back the AI which has stolen his bod, may win the race in *Redhound* thus costing us both. But surely and even so, he would not be so foolish as to kill the AI, I tell myself—despite his bod being pretty much used up—and face homicide charges for doing himself in.

It seems an incredible dead-heat finish, from the pictures that come in from a camera on one of the skipjacks. But its monitoring is complicated by the fact that *Hotshot III* suddenly tacks to starboard in terms of the ecliptic and *Redhound* does the same near at hand as if trying to crawl all over the other vessel.

Maintaining a certain rigidity of attitude, *Hotshot III* crashes into the satellite buoy. *Redhound* fires a line, changes tack after it connects, veers off, then drops sail. It fires its small emergency braking jets then, a disqualifying act if on the wrong side of the finish line. Two of the skipjacks maneuver in that direction on their ion motors, but a spacesuited figure is already crossing on

Redhound's line toward *Hotshot III*, which, I am fairly certain, reaches the buoy somewhat after *Redhound* passes it.

The cameras never show what happens following the entry of Deadboy Donner in the Crash bod into the wreckage. We lose the picture during a blackout which follows amid multiple systems failures which are largely attributed to sunspots. Later, however, comes the official announcement that Donner has brought *Hotshot III* in first, shaving a bit of time from the record while about it. Unfortunately, he is not available for the victory dinner, as he perishes at the finish line in the process of colliding with the buoy. He will, however, be refrozen, flat EEG or not, since he is officially a deadboy anyway and his bill is paid up for cold quarters.

So, when I see Donner in the Crash bod to pay him the money he has made by betting on his Deadboy bod in *Hotshot III* under the direction of the runaway AI, he is with Painted Evelyn, who gives me a smile, with which she is usually sparing except when she wants something.

Then I ask Deadboy Donner in the Crash bod what happens out at the buoy, and he tells me that he gets there too late for retribution as the AI has patched into the satellite's broadcast system and transmitted itself back to Upper Manhattan. He is not up to abandoning both bods there in a damaged clipper to pursue it, so his revenge must wait upon his return to town. When he gets back, however, and finally has a chance to check out the system, there is no AI—or NI either—running the show. It is as deserted as Miss Blooming Orchid's establishment following a raid. Even Crash Callahan is gone. "I do not understand this any more than I understand how *Hotshot III* came out in the Winner's Circle," he says, "when *Redhound* was clearly ahead at the finish line."

"But for this part we should be thankful," I say, "for we collect on all our bets."

"True," he replies. "But I am the actual winner of that race."

"And that is what the record shows," Painted Evelyn says. "Deadboy Donner wins the Filstone Cup."

"I do not complain over this," he says, "though it is an odd way to do it."

At that moment Painted Evelyn allows as she could use a brew, and Donner disengages his hand from hers and goes to fetch one for her. She studies me then.

"You know?" she asks.

I nod.

"Partly, it is the business about the times," I say. "*Redhound* comes in first. Then you change the record, for it does him more good that way. You, too, since you are with him now. What I do not understand is why."

"I might just say that we had a deal, and I am only keeping my part of it."

"But there is more to it than that. Like why does he find the system empty, and why are you here? And where is Crash?"

"Crash is no more," she replies. "He gets free of the knots Donner ties him in, and when I come back he jumps me. As he is trying to do me in, I return the compliment. I crash Crash."

"Then why are you not back in the place where you are impregnable and powerful and—"

"But I wanted the flesh," she says, "though I do not realize my mistake right away. Then I see that I would much rather be a woman than a man. This is why I am seeing Painted Evelyn so much at first. I learn quickly that she might be interested in life in the system. Donner, who has an aptitude for this, seems attracted to people of a similar sort.

"And vice-versa," she adds.

"You mean . . . ?"

"Yes, I am here because I have a crush on him, and

Evelyn dwells in silicon castles, reviewing the troops binary-stepping by, building up personal trust funds. . . ."

I nod.

"She always was a calculating woman," I say. "But why is it Donner does not detect her presence when he visits the system on his return?"

"I move her out temporarily."

"Where to?"

"Donner's Deadboy bod," she says, "which is hooked up to its monitors by then, and deserted."

"That clears up many details," I say, "and almost satisfies me."

"So, we would both appreciate your keeping this to yourself," she says, "until I find the best time and the best way to explain matters to Donner."

"You are still in touch with her?" I ask.

"Oh yes. It is easy to reach her," she says, as Donner rounds the corner bringing their drinks.

I must say that Painted Evelyn does a much better job than Crash Callahan in the AI business, for we have had no more brownouts, shortouts, or switched calls since she took over. It is good, too, having gotten her private number from the AI, so that I can call her every now and then, until such time as the AI levels with Donner. For I have had two big winners so far this month, and she is about to give me my third.

Lukora

Gene Wolfe

This is my report, the report of Meirax Andros, alone. Michael is not with me; Michael may be dead.

On 11J89 we chose this site, landed, and set up camp. Here a good-sized stream enters a lake of some six thousand hectares. Undesignated mountains rise to the east. To the west are steep slopes, covered in many places with needle-trees and brush. It seemed to both of us a promising location. Its elevation is four hundred ninety-two meters, its coordinates are fifty point eight and fifty-three point four.

For five days we scouted for signs. (Reference previous report, ASP ninety-six six.) Such signs as we found were stale. There was no indication of Small Folk, and I told Michael we had better move on.

He disagreed.

"They shift their hunting grounds," he said; he was sitting on a boulder, searching the valley with his eyes. "Someday soon they'll be back. There's a lot of game."

Meirax shook her head. "Our orders were to find them."

He would not look at her. "Our orders were more extensive than that. They'll come back soon, and when they come we'll be here, familiar with the country, knowing where to find water, where the game trails run."

That night as she lay drowsy in her bag, she heard his bag open—the soft, stealthy noise of the slider. She believed that he was coming for her and wondered for a moment how she should receive him. Surprised? Outraged? With eagerness? She inched her own slider down, readied her arms to embrace him.

He did not come. For a long while she waited in the dark. When she rose, his bag was no longer warm. She went out, where the strange, wide moon gave her a shadow like a ghost. The day had been warm and sunny, but the night wind was keen with cold. The needle-trees sighed to see her, and the brook laughed at her. When she returned to her bag, she wept.

Next morning she expected to find him in his bag; he would deny having left it, tell her she had dreamed. But his bag was empty, his clothing gone, his boots and dragonette gone, too. She ran a square search pattern that by afternoon stretched two kilometers in all directions.

At sunset she found him, wearily returning to their camp. "Were you lost?" she asked.

"Yes," he said. "For a while."

"You went out last night," she said.

He nodded. "I heard something—something prowling around the tent, I thought. And then there was something farther on. It seemed worth investigating."

"You should have awakened me, Michael."

"You were already awake. You said you heard me."

Back at the camp he washed in the brook, ate a little, then crawled into his bag and slept, though it was scarcely dark. She was tired as well, yet she remained awake watching the valley and thinking of various things she had observed in her search and the direction from which he had come, west by northwest.

That night he was gone when she woke. She got up, dressed in the dark, and went outside. The uncanny moon rode high, but it was nearly dawn. She went to the brook for a drink and sat beside it awhile, wondering what else might have come to drink there. The brook water tasted better than lake water, to her at least. When she returned to the tent, the first pale shards of day had streaked the sky. She did not search for him, but busied herself about the camp, ditching the tent and weaving mattresses of boughs.

As she had expected, Michael returned late that afternoon. She had resolved not to question him and did not; but he said, "They're back."

It startled her; she had convinced herself that this had nothing to do with the mission. She asked, "You've seen them?"

"No, but I've seen fresh signs." He hesitated, reluctance so clear she grew certain he would not speak again. At last he added, "And I've heard them."

"How can you be sure?"

"Listen, Meirax, and tell me what you think." He took the smallest recorder from a pocket. She had not been aware that it was gone; she switched it on, held it to her ear, and closed her eyes.

The needle-trees wrapped her in their impalpable sorrow. It was dark and far colder than she had expected; a light rain fell. A voice—not a human voice—moaned far away: "*Uo-o-o-o, ou-o-o, o-o-o-o-o.*" Suddenly, she was terribly afraid. She opened her eyes and groped for her dragonette, but it was back in the tent. Michael was no longer with her, but down at the brook, washing.

Finished washing himself, he washed his clothes and spread them on the rocks to dry. She said, "You don't have to sit up. I'll bring them in for you. I'll fold them, and lay them beside your bag."

"Thank you," he said. "What do you think of the recording? It's them, isn't it?"

She shrugged. "You shouldn't go out alone."

When the last bright fleck of sun had vanished behind the trees, she went to the rocks and got his clothes as she had said she would. His shirt was still a little damp at the collar, but she folded it as she had promised and carried everything back to the tent.

As she lifted the tent flap, she took a last look at the mountain slopes, stoney and dotted here and there with needle-trees and patches of brush. Near her, night had come already; but higher up, the black mountain rocks still captured light. For an instant she glimpsed the eyes of one of the Small Folk near the shadow's edge. Then they were gone, and she could not be sure she had not imagined them.

Once in the tent, she removed only her boots; and she took her dragonette with her into her bag. Hours later when Michael had left the tent, she rose too, put on her boots, and followed him.

The moon was rising, a moon no longer quite so circular as it had been. "This is when he leaves," she thought, "when the moon rises above the mountains."

She saw him three hundred meters down the valley, walking fast, not looking back. She hurried after him, but he passed into the shadow of a tall needle-tree and was gone.

For most of the rest of the night, she was certain she was following him still. Twice she heard him cough, and once she glimpsed him as he crossed a moonlit clearing. Day came, and she held back, afraid that he might see her. That was when she lost him, or so she decided later.

For most of that day she pressed forward, stopping only to drink at a freshlet that could not have been their stream. She was very tired by then, and she knew that she was no longer so strong as she had been.

That hour came when the sun was half down the western sky—the hour at which Michael had returned before. She decided that she would return to camp as well. It was pointless to hunt him among the rocks and trees when he was asleep in camp.

Her director pointed the way, but she found herself blocked again and again by fallen trees, gorges, or cliffs or banks too steep to climb.

Night came. She knew it would be wiser to stop and sleep if she could; but she was hungry and felt that camp could be no more than a kilometer off at most. She blamed herself for not taking rations, not taking a light, though she had feared that he might look behind him and see a light. She imagined herself back at the school, an instructor at the school now, dressing down some cadet who was also herself for not bringing a light, not taking rations.

Then she fell. For a moment it seemed that she would never land before the ground struck her like a blow.

She felt she had been unconscious, perhaps not for long. It was night still, though her head ached and her bruised limbs were stiff with cold. For a long time she groped among stones for the director; but her fingers could not find it, and its green glow was nowhere to be seen.

She decided to make herself as comfortable as she could and wait for sunrise—in daylight she could surely find the director and make her way back to camp. She took three steps, hoping to come upon a place sheltered from the wind, and fell again.

When she recovered consciousness for the second time she was warmer, but it was very dark. She sat up and found that she had lain on a bed of fern, and that though she still wore her jacket, a jacket had been spread over her legs.

Michael's voice asked, "Are you all right?"

"Where are we?"

For a second or two, no answer came. "Lukora's house."

"Lukora?"

"This woman," Michael said.

By then she had noticed the tall white figure. She asked, "Did you find me, or was it Michael? In either case, thank you for taking care of me."

The white figure approached, fractioned into three. "Like a hand," Meirax thought, "with three fingers held up." It bent across the crouching bulk that was Michael. Hair brushed her cheek, and she realized that the divisions of the white figure were no more than dark hair, hair that hung before its owner's shoulders and nearly to her waist.

Aloud she said thank you again. A chill hand caressed her forehead, and gentle fingers explored the aching lump above her left temple; with them came a deep inhalation like the soughing of needle-trees.

Michael said, "She is sorry that you're hurt."

"Can't she talk? How do you know her name?"

"She can," Michael told her. "She doesn't speak often. Do you think you can stand?"

"I'll try." She got her legs beneath her, but they were without strength.

A fourth person entered silently, so that for a moment the darkness grew darker still. She heard something soft and heavy laid upon a table, or perhaps upon the floor.

Michael muttered something unintelligible.

"Who is that?"

"It doesn't matter. Would you like to lie down and rest for a while?"

Lukora said, "They are abroad." It was not really a

deep voice, Meirax thought, yet it possessed the husky quality some women thought passionate. . . .

She was again supine. "Why is it so dark here, Michael?"

"So that you can sleep." There was an odor of musk, heavy and ensorceling, as warm as breath.

When she woke again Michael gave her something oily to eat, and she asked what it was.

"Flesh softened by fire. We used to do it, too. It's very strengthening."

"I think I could walk back to camp now," she said, knowing it was what he wished to hear.

"Then we'll go."

Her heart leaped for joy. "You're coming with me?"

"I must. There's danger from the Small Folk."

He helped her stand and held her arm so that she would not trip on the uneven stone floor. "I feel as if the ceiling were right over my head," she told him.

"It's low in some places, high in others."

He led her through a chamber where a small, bright light shone far above without illuminating the walls, then along a twisting corridor. "There's the door," he said; it was a vague circle of pale light.

"It's day outside, isn't it?"

"It's almost evening," Michael told her. "Lukora would not like us leaving so late." He hesitated. "It might be better if I go first."

"Go ahead, then."

"You'll follow me? At once?"

"Certainly," Meirax told him.

Metal rang against rock. The doorway darkened as Michael's body filled it, then opened again.

"Hurry," he said, and extended an arm to her.

She climbed through the doorway, blinking watering eyes at the brightness of daylight. It was like a new scene in a show, she thought: Lukora's house was suddenly gone, and Michael was pushing through thick brush instead. Brush scratched her hands and cheeks, and sent up clouds of insects like missiles.

At last they burst into the clearing under a big needle-tree. "What's that?" she asked.

"A sword." He showed it to her. It was old and rusted, its bronze hilt grass-green with verdigris; but its edges were newly ground and looked sharp.

"Couldn't you have used it to cut through the brush?" she asked him.

He shook his head. "That would have been foolish."

Though her director was gone, the setting sun soon restored her sense of direction—she knew that Michael led her southeast. Together they mounted slope after slope, swinging due south and even due north at times as Michael traced a path that he alone could see.

And some third thing came with them, noiseless but always present.

"They saw the Small Folk," she thought, "before the Small Folk saw them." They were waiting on the ridge line, a ragged cluster of a score or more, thin-limbed and wild-haired, mean statues of gold in the last light.

"We'd better turn aside," she told Michael.

"Then they would know we're afraid of them. They'd hunt us down."

She took out her dragonette and loosed its safety catch. "I don't think they know we're here."

"Of course they do."

It was dark by the time they had mounted the ridge, and the strange moon was not yet above the mountains; the suns of half a billion worlds gleamed like so many holes pricked in black film. "Stand out of our path," Michael ordered the Small Folk.

A champion rose before him, lean but nearly as tall as he. The champion held some weapon—a toothed club, as well as Meirax could judge it by starlight. "Shoot him," she breathed. "Kill him now, Michael—or I will."

He handed her his dragonette. "What chance would

we have against them at night? We'd kill half a dozen, perhaps; then they would kill us both."

The ancient steel gleamed under the stars, as though night had washed away all rust. She heard the thud as blade met hard wood, the whistle and whisper of the champion's club swung in a blow too high, the champion's wild shriek.

Hands like claws tore Michael's dragonette from her. She fired her own, and two of the Small Folk burst into flame.

Then she was down, fingers at her throat, the dragonette gone. Her own hands tore away those that held her. For an instant, she glimpsed a dark bludgeon against the stars. She twisted frantically out of the way.

The Small Folk cried out in terror, all together like the chorus at a play. White things leaped above her with flashing fangs. Her whole world was a cacophony of snarls and screams, her hair wet with blood that was not her own.

As you hear, I have returned to camp. Lukora's brother has come with me; I do not know his name. He awaits me now, sniffing the wind, pacing to-and-fro before our door. The sun will rise at 05:33.8 today, and already the horned lords bugle from their hilltops. We hunt now; but I will speak to you again very soon.

At the Double Solstice

Gregory Benford

Shadows stretched long and threatening, pointing away from the hoteye of the Old Sun. Its harsh solstice radiance cast fingers across the stream-cut plain, fingers reaching toward an onstruggling human tide.

Each windgouged rock, though itself dull and worn, cast a lively colored shadow. The Old Sun's outer ring was smoldering red, while the inner bull's-eye glared a hard blue. The ring was a work of ages past, unfathomable now, made for some strange task.

Legend held that the Old Sun had once shone alone. None could remember that time. Near the red ring burned what the humans called the Fresh Sun. Its hard knot of bluewhite fire threw longer shadows aslant the human line of march.

They took little notice. The Fresh Sun was some unimaginable construction, younger still than the ring. Long ago the wandering families had included it in their solstice ceremonies.

The ceremonies would have to be held quite soon now; the two suns dipped low. Solstice rites would call upon the help of Vishnu. The god might even manifest himself to them. Perhaps one of their party would have a vision of Vishnu lying on a bed formed of the coils of his personal serpent. He of the four hands would bring them success in their endless foraging.

But they would not neglect the Fresh Sun. That would be dangerous. Its bluewhite glare was harsh and harmful to the human eye. Forgotten in the ceremony, it could flare forth as Kali, the scourge god. Fires would rake the land.

Disksetting came. The Old Sun's thumbwide glare sank to the horizon, drawing from the least rocky upjut a tail of chromatic ribbons. Shifting shadows warped the land, stretching perspectives. The seeing was hard.

So it was a while before Agaden was sure. He blinked his eyes, jumping his vision through the spectrum, and barely picked up the wavering fevered pip.

There—a band of humans.

And better yet, they had chanced upon a powered-down or damaged Crafter. He did not even surmise that perhaps they had hunted it, downed the machine by themselves, for that had never happened in his lifetime.

Agaden gave cry. His small Family howled with glee. Boots drumming on worn rock, they too descended on the machine. The other humans greeted them with exclamations of kinship, of brotherhood, and together they fell to it.

In vengeance Agaden launched himself upon the Crafter. He kicked in plates, ripped away whipwire antennae in pureblind rage. The Families yanked free parts and servos, booty used to maintain their own suits. Over the finely machined carcass they crawled, pillaging the finest workmechship of factories men had never seen and never would, the ceaseless detailed labor of countless Crafters themselves who had built up their own kind of a pinnacle of ability.

Rage roiled. Through this they mourned men and women lost to the incessant competition with machines. Women savaged delicate finètuned components, slashed through orchestrated constellations in copper and silicon, and tossed aside what they neither recognized nor could use. This was almost all of the Crafter, for none in the Family knew how such things worked.

Even the most able of them could only connect a modular part, trusting her eye to find the right element. Of theory they had little, of understanding even less. Long eras of hardship and flight had hammered their once-rich heritage of knowledge into flat, rigid rules of thumb.

In place of science they had simple pictures, rules for using the color-coded wires which carried unknown entities: Volts, Amps, Ohms.

These were the names of spirits who lived somehow in the mechs and could be broken to the will of humanity. Currents, they knew, flowed like water and did silent work. Clearly—yet inexplicably—the shiny wreaths of golden wire and perfectly machined onyx squares somehow bossed the currents. Electrons were tiny beasts who drove the motions of larger beasts; such was obvious.

They could afford to know no more, for learning took time and they had been on the run for longer than any now living could clearly remember. Humanity had returned to its origins. Surrounded by machine societies of vast and abiding intelligence, mankind had gone back to the joys of nomadic voyaging.

One such pleasure was scavenging with a vengeance, tearing the Crafter apart brutally. Cylinders bled oil. Optical threads snarled up and tripped the plunderers, only to be stamped flat and kicked away.

Beneath their rending lay retribution for past defeats

inflicted by the soil-eating mechs. So went as much of history as Agaden had ever heard, though in truth he cared little for it. History was tales and tales were a kind of lie, or else not much different from them; he knew that much. Which was enough. A practical man had to seize the moment before him, not meander through dusty tales.

For Agaden, all times before were now compressed into one daybright wondrous instant, filled with people and events which no longer had any substantial truth, had been swept away as if they had never been. For ages his starved and ragged remnant had fought and run and retreated from the mechs. They had burned and blown away and pulverized Marauder mechs and yet there had been more and then more still.

It was as though the machines had finally taken notice of the buzzing gnat that had been nipping minute drops of lifeblood from the body of the mech civilization. In one irritated instant the Marauders slapped distractedly, flattening the bug against a massive hand.

So the Family had no choice but to scatter before the hot Marauder wind. They were swept forward not so much by a victorious horde behind, but rather by the mounting tide of the names of battles lost, bushwhacks walked into, traps sprung, Family members wounded or surekilled and sometimes even left behind in a disheartening white-eyed dishonorable scramble to escape, to save the remnant core of the Family, to keep some slender thread of heritage alive.

The names were places on a map—Sawridge, Corinth, Stone Mountain, Riverrun, Big Alice Springs, Pitwallow—and maps were not paper now but encoded in the individual's chip-memory, lodged in the nape of each neck, the last human libraries on Earth. So, through the age of pursuit, as members of the Families fell and their memories were swallowed up by the mechmind, they lost even the maps to understand where their forebears had stood and fought and been vanquished. Now the names were only names, without substance or fixity in the living soil.

Agaden had long ago learned to listen when something nagged at him. The Crafter was demolished now, entrails stomped. He stood still for a long moment.

His instincts told him something was awry.

Where? Behind them? Mechs liked to attack from the rear.

He turned and saw only the distant hazy ranks of whitecapped mountains. That range bounded his Family's movements to the north. A wandering truthsayer had once told Agaden that the world's highest peak lay in those vastnesses, but no one in the Family had ever tried to scale them. It was said that mechs had. But then, such things were always said.

He scowled, fretting at a faint bothersome note. Then he gave the signal and started at a quick pace down the valley. Something ahead . . . ?

He let his augmented senses sweep out, covering the slowmotion flow of the Family. They were already dismembering a small navvy-mech which had accompanied the Crafter and had not the sense to run. Voices slurred and nipped, the steady background roundtalk by which humanity sewed up the frame of their experience, smoothed the rub of their world.

Everything seemed ordinary. The valley, tufted with bushes, lay quiet. Rock-nobbed hills were dotted with mechtrash. These random clumps of old parts were spread across the face of Earth, so common that Agaden barely noticed them.

In outlands such as this, scavenger mechs did not bother to pick up rusted cowlings or heavy broken axles for the long transport to smelters and factories. Over centuries the mess had gathered. These jumbles too blighted the land now, rust-red spots freckling the soil.

Among this waste plants struggled, a welcome sign.

For hours now they had all been pleased by the signs of ripening, of spreading grass, of tawny growth.

The Fresh Sun's hotpoint glare had set now. Smoldering in the sky, the Old Sun's disk was half-gnawed by the ragged hills. A double solstice. The shifting colors confused Agaden, making the least crag and gully brim with ripe illusion.

Ahead was something strange. Agaden frowned. He no longer marveled at what could come from the incessant engine of mechcraft. Such bounteous wealth spewing forth now seemed to him as inevitable as the rich, organic world had appeared to his ancient ancestors. It was simply an enduring facet of the way things were, fully natural.

His world was divided simply. He lived—as well as he could—among carbon-based processes which had limited use and from which humanity had once sprung. Things green and soft and pliant. Things that he could eat. Remnants of the once-rich ecosphere bloomed in spots. This realm grew wild only in the outlands, beyond the cities and pathways of the mechs.

On the other side of a stark division lay most of his planet. Against man's shrinking green oases the mechs pressed, building their ceramo-sculpted warrens. Agaden had glimpsed a mechplex once, when the Family blundered over a mountain range and paid the price of six lost members. The glassy, steepled thing had crackled with electromagnetic crosstalk. Its deep, upwelling voice had rung through Agaden's sensorium, immensely threatening in its uncaring.

Agaden accepted as simple fact that those distant and feared cities were an entirely natural way for intelligence to go forward. Abhorrent as a spider is, but still natural.

Mechs built, that was inevitable. They sought to make of the world a place of straight lines and sharp edges, geometry made real. Eternal, rigid certainties.

Men were of a different order. They sought the curved, the flexible, the live and unenduring. They lived and died. Mechs—unless they fell to the eager hand of humankind—persisted, and dwelled inside their hard edifices.

He frowned again. They avoided mech places, and this odd thing ahead . . .

He saw abruptly that it was not one mechwork, but two.

One moved. A Rattler.

It came at them from right flank. The Crafter's dying bleat must have summoned it from the distant hills. The Rattler moved with a coiling and recoiling motion, treads grinding beneath. Agaden could hear its gray ceramo-ribs pop with exertion.

The Family was already running even as the Rattler's angle of attack fully registered. They could not make the canyon mouth beyond. There was precious little shelter in the dry streambeds nearby.

"Make right!" Agaden called. The Family vectored immediately, seeing his intention.

They had only moments. Three women used all their boot power to accelerate ahead, then turned to lay down retarding fire.

Agaden added to it without slowing, firing on an awkward tilt. No point in being accurate; their shots pocked and ricocheted but did not slow the smug-ugly and inexorable Rattler.

They would not all make it. Agaden saw that a bare klick short of the odd mech building they approached.

"Faster!" he called, knowing it was useless and yet wanting to give vent to his knotting apprehension.

A figure ran slower though no less frantically than the others: Old Majy. She had not been feeling well these last few days. Already she had dropped behind. Agaden heard her labored panting turn to gasps.

He turned back. She came struggling up an incline and Agaden fired over her, directly into the bluehot mouth of the Rattler. The thing barely acknowledged the antennae blown off, the gouges in its obdurate face.

It caught Old Majy. Arms and quick-opening mouths ingested her almost casually. It never slowed its oncoming momentum.

"Majy!" Agaden cried in rage and frustration. He knew the Rattler would only later discover she was not metal throughout, like a mechthing. But by the time it tasted her and found her indigestible, it was too late.

Agaden had no time for remorse. He whirled and fled himself, realizing that he was now the most exposed. The Rattler undoubtedly saw them all as a covey of defenseless metal-sheathed beings and mistook them for free sources of cheap ore. Since they did not carry the eatme-not codes of this Rattler's city, they were fair game.

Agaden gave himself over to the running. The Rattler came flexing and oozing over a stony streambed.

A hollow *shuuuung* twisted the air by his head. It was a blaring noise-cast, blending infrasonic rumbles at his feet with electromagnetic screeches, ascending to teethjarring frequencies.

The Rattler was trying to confuse him, scramble his sensors. He ducked his head reflexively, though it did no good, and made all his receptors go dead. Except for his fast-lurching vision he heard or felt nothing.

A child stumbled ahead. Agaden grabbed her by shoulder and haunch and lifted her up a sandbank.

Another *shuuuung* echoed dimly in his sheathed mind. It was so powerful it caught the girl unaware. She crumpled. He bent, sucked in breath. With a rolling motion he took her weight across his back.

Close now, the Rattler sent a feverhot neural spark forking into his leg. The muscles jumped and howled and then went stonecold dead.

Agaden stumbled forward. The mech building ahead loomed. It was tall, imposing, far higher than the usual mechwork.

He wasn't going to make it.

He staggered. "Agaden!" someone called.

Sand slid beneath his boots. The sky reeled.

He fumbled for his weapon. The Rattler would be on him in a moment. If he could fire sure and quick and steady—

Then the world came rushing in. Sound blared. The Rattler's crunch and clank was hollow, diminishing.

Someone was pounding him on the back.

The girl's weight slipped off.

His sensorium flooded with scattershot pricklings, tripped open by some freeing signal.

Agaden turned to confront the Rattler. He saw only the rear of it as massive gray cylinders slid and worked. It was retreating.

Cermo-the-Slow was shouting, "—hadn't shut down your ears you'da heard it bellow. Right mad it was."

"Why? Why'd it stop?"

"That li'l thing there."

A small pyramid poked up through the sandstone shelf they stood on. In flight, Agaden had passed it without noticing.

Agaden blinked at the finely machined thing. "How?"

"Dunno. Musta given the Rattler orders."

Agaden had heard of such things, but never seen one. The four-sided monument of chromed faces and ornate designs must have told the Rattler to come no closer.

Friends shouted at him joyfully. The girl he'd carried was fine. Considering their terror of only moments before, their glee was permissible, even after the loss of Old Majy.

Exhausted but exultant faces swam in his vision. They brought him up toward the large mech building. Eager friends gave him drink. Children clapped their hands in glee.

Mechs could not violate a command to leave a mechwork alone. Humans could. Thus they entered with impunity the grounds of the massive construction.

Agaden frowned, puzzled. What was so different about this place?

Ordinarily he ignored whatever mechs built. This thing, though, had saved his life.

It was broad and high. And impossibly shaped.

Atop a huge marble platform sat what Agaden at first thought must be an illusion. Only mechs made mirages; he was on guard. But when he kicked the thing, it gave back a reassuring solid thud.

It was massive, made of plates of ivory stone, yet it seemed to float in air. Pure curves met at enchanting though somehow inevitable angles. Walls of white plaques soared upward as though there were no gravity. Then they bulged outward in a dome that seemed to grow more light and gauzy as the rounded shape rose still more. Finally, high above the gathering families, the stonework arced inward and came to an upthrusting that pinned the sky upon its dagger point.

The arabesques of gossamer-thin stone, shining white, did not interest Agaden so much as the evident design. He had never seen such craft.

Around him the Family celebrated. The solstice ceremony wound through the plaza. Agaden played his part as leader, dancing, singing, trying not to show that the wondrous building distracted him.

His people retained the old rituals, from a time when the lot of man was different. Agaden knew that much, though much of the ceremony was a riddle.

Once his forefathers had made food grow from the ground in great fields. Then the solstice had meant much. Now the family scavenged for wildfruit, or stole edible things from mech factories.

His forefathers had survived the Wrecked Times, Agaden knew. The ways founded on love of Vishnu and fear of Shiva had persisted, while all else failed. Once there had been men who did vast, unknown things, but the Wreck had vanquished them. Now the Families of Vishnu and Shiva carried forth. Their legacy was the chips and sensors embedded in them, to afford some measure of protection from the Marauders.

Over this Familial net Agaden sent the final call of the solstice celebration: "And so vanquish the not-flesh! Bring rain and sweetness, O Vishnu!"

The ritual dissolved into festivity. Cermo-the-Slow had gotten into the strong, rough fruit brandy that served both as ritual fluid and as a valued currency among Families.

Hoarse voices raised in rowdy song. Hands plucked at him. Agaden smiled at the women who beckoned to him, their intentions clear. Their smooth skins, browned by the double suns, could not match the ghostly pale of the stones he crossed. He murmured thanks, stroked their shiny hair, and moved on.

He explored, ignoring the ricocheting voices of celebration. At the borders of the vast square marble platform stood four delicate towers. Agaden walked between them, eyeing their solemn, silent upjut. They stood like sentinels at the monument's corners, guards against whatever rude forces the world could muster.

He saw that each tower leaned outward at a tiny angle. Something told him the reason. When the towers finally collapsed, they would fall outward. Their demise would not damage the huge, airy building at the center.

On the back of the last marble wall there was a single plate of solid black, a dark eye that gazed out on a land inhospitable.

Yet as Agaden approached, it blinked. A ruby glaze momentarily fogged its surface and into his mind— merging with him instantaneously through his inbuilt receptors and chips—came a steady, chanting voice that spoke of glories gone and names resonantly odd.

Agaden felt the words as crystalline cold wedges of meaning, beyond mere talk. He gaped as he understood.

The thing was, incredibly, not mechmade.

It was instead of human times and 'facture. The mechs had left it untouched.

Agaden listened for a while, comprehending nothing beyond the singular fact of it: that men and women had once *made* things.

And had done it so well that even machines gave their work tribute and place.

Agaden froze, his mind aswirl. He had led his Family into this fresh territory, opening up new lands. All spoke of him as the best leader they had had within memory. Even allowing for the usual flattery, Agaden himself knew this was true.

But even he wondered what such an astounding revelation could do to the Family. They were a fragile people, steeped in their ways. Shiva and Vishnu ruled, and this was the eternal order.

To tell them that men had been 'facturers themselves . . . that would awaken troubling thoughts.

Yet he himself could not shake the beautiful mystery of this place. Or stop the awed speculations it called forth.

Dazed, eyes open but unseeing, he did not hear Cermo-the-Slow until a hand clapped on his shoulder.

"Come on! You get first hack."

"What . . . ?"

"Gone take one these down."

"One of—"

"Big crash time! Big! Cel'brate!"

Already five of the Family were scrawling marks at the base of one of the slender towers. Cermo-the-Slow tugged Agaden toward them.

"You don't understand," Agaden said. "This isn't a mech building."

Cermo snickered. "Think's a hill? Huh?"

"Humans made it."

Cermo laughed.

"They did! There's a voice from over there—"

"Hearin' voices," Cermo called to the others. "Rattler musta addled him some." Raucous catcalls answered.

"*Humanity* built this. That's why it's so, so beautiful."

"Mechstuff, 's all." Cermo walked to the foot of the tower.

"No! Long time ago, somebody—some of *us*—did such work. Just *look* at it."

Agaden was slow to see the seeds of revolt. Cermo had the others with him, faces smirking and chuckling and preparing in their bleary way to do what men and women did whenever they found undefended mechwork.

"More damn foul mechstuff, 's what it is," Cermo said with a touch of irritation. "You don't want part of it, we'll take it all."

Two women laughed and handed Cermo a cutter-beam tube, one ripped from the Crafter. Cermo thumbed a button and a ready buzzing came from it.

Agaden shook his head, knowing what he must do.

A fevered mix of fear and rage propelled him forward.

Cermo had half turned to the tower, pointing the cutter-beam at one of the creamy stone plates. The crowd made a murmuring noise of anticipation, highpitched threads of glee racing through it.

Agaden hit him solidly in the back. Cermo lurched. He smacked into the tower. Agaden caught him with a roundhouse kick in the side. The cutter fell from his fingers.

"You—" Cermo blurted. Agaden kicked the buzzing cutter away.

Cermo ducked down and lumbered out. Agaden tripped him. The big man struck a broad stone plate and groaned.

"Leave it! It's ours."

A woman called, "You protectin' mech garbage? I—"

"People way back did this. People different from us."

The woman bared her gray teeth. "Who cares? They prob'ly made mechs, too. Anybody'd do thing like this, they were *crazy!* We don't need respect mechs, or mech-makers!"

"Not going argue with you. Pick up your packs! We're movin'."

Agaden stared at them, stony and redfaced, eyes wide.

Slitted eyes regarded him, assessing chances of taking him in a fight.

Hands grasped at air, eager for the weight of a weapon.

Wind whistled among the high bright towers.

And the moment passed. The crowd shuffled to the side, mumbling, eyes averted. They went to find packs and discarded boots.

Agaden helped Cermo sit up, brought him water. Then he stood and watched thin cirrus skate across the sky, framed by the towers and the enchantment of the great curving dome.

Again he listened to the ancient hollow voice and its singsong chant. Then his Family was ready.

He shook his head and tapered the voice down to a dim dry warble. Around him Family grumbled, but he knew it was best that they move on. They would all like to rest here for a while. To grieve for Old Majy. To fest. To relive through story and celebration the pillage of the Crafter and the humiliation of the Rattler.

Most of them would never believe that the place to which they owed their lives was not merely another mech factory or inexplicable waystation. And they would be horrified if they did.

Agaden frowned again. Even he still had a trace of doubt. Incredible, that humans had once shared the hated traits of the mechs: permanence, rigid lines, dwarfing cities, the idea of *owning* and not simply passing through.

Humanity lived lightly on the land; mechs belabored it. That was nature's balance and eternally ordained conflict.

This beautiful place was impressive, yes, but it shared some disquieting principles with the mech ways. Agaden felt awed and yet uncomfortable here.

If mechs honored this human place, then humans should too. Of that he was sure.

But they could honor it by leaving it. By not allowing this strange place to disturb their ways.

"March!" he called. "Flanks out. Go!"

They left the flat plaza in good marching order.

It felt good to feel soil and rock underfoot. Agaden set the pace. He liked the steady sway and rhythms of voyaging, of movement, of the perpetual mystery that lurked beyond the far horizon. This was humanity's role.

He paused at the lip of the next rutted canyon.

Glancing back, he was startled by a sudden intuition. Seen from afar, the shape struck a deeply resonant chord in him, a sense of what the melancholy sweep and curve of stone meant.

It was a place to honor the dead. Perhaps it contained a body, or even many.

His language had no word for a tomb, but the idea itself came to him, wrinkling his brow.

The proud rise spoke of humanity—itself summoned forth from matter and too soon cast back down—and its sorrow at knowing this destiny.

A tomb. His quick eyes traced patterns in the broad, sculpted plain. Water had shaped it. Crumbled bluffs and dry pebbled washes spoke of a wide river that had flowed here in the old, lush times. The river had once hugged the shelf below the tomb.

Slow erosion—or had it been the hand of man?—had

made the snaky waterway meander away from the bluff, so it would not undercut the lonely building.

That had been unimaginably long ago. The river itself had dwindled and died, its strength carried off by thirsty winds.

Who the place had honored he could not guess. But its lines said things to him, murmuring in his heart of sorrow and love and the sad sway of time.

That such things could live in brute stone made Agaden shiver, swept by ancient emotions.

To encase human feelings that way . . .

Slowly, the idea filled Agaden with horror.

The essence of human good lay in its fleeting poignancy. Only things mechlike built and shaped. Their kind sought a cold, uncaring permanence.

If humanity had been mechlike in the far past, even to the point of making things of stone that trapped feeling . . . Agaden curled his lip. If that was true, then he felt no reverence for those benighted ancestors.

He was suddenly glad to live in a holier and wiser time. Humanity today knew the true division between the sweet passing beauties of things human, and the cruel hard mech ways.

The knowledge of certain death, that nothing could be caught, that each fleeting instant had to be savored in its passing—that was the essence of wisdom. Not holding on, but instead, living fully.

If the ancients had confused this, they deserved to be forgotten.

He gazed for a long moment at the monument with a hesitant wistfulness. At last he saw that his thinking was right, that the past meant nothing. He spat derisively. Then he turned and went on and never looked back again.

The Dance of the Changer and the Three

Terry Carr

This all happened ages ago, out in the depths of space beyond Darkedge, where galaxies swim through the black like silent bright whales. It was so long ago that when the light from Loarr's galaxy finally reached Earth, after millions of light-years, there was no one here to see it except a few things in the oceans that were too busy with their monotonous single-celled reactions to notice.

Yet, as long ago as it was, the present-day Loarra still remember this story and retell it in complex, shifting wave-dances every time one of the newly-changed asks for it. The wave-dances wouldn't mean much to you if you saw them, nor I suppose would the story itself if I were to tell it just as it happened. So consider this a translation, and don't bother yourself that when I say "water" I don't mean our hydrogen-oxygen compound, or that there's no "sky" as such on Loarr, or for that matter that the Loarra weren't—aren't—creatures that "think" or "feel" in quite the way we understand. In fact, you could take this as a piece of pure fiction, because there are damned few real facts in it—but I know better (or worse), because I know how true it is. And that has a lot to do with why I'm back here on Earth, with forty-two friends and coworkers left dead on Loarr. They never had a chance.

There was a Changer who had spent three life cycles planning a particular cycle climax and who had come to the moment of action. He wasn't really named Minnearo, but I'll call him that because it's the closest thing I can write to approximate the tone, emotional matrix, and associations that were all wrapped up in his designation.

When he came to his decision, he turned away from the crag on which he'd been standing overlooking the Loarran ocean, and went quickly to the personality-homes of three of his best friends. To the first friend, Asterrea, he said, "I am going to commit suicide," wave-dancing this message in his best festive tone.

His friend laughed, as Minnearo had hoped, but only for a short time. Then he turned away and left Minnearo alone, because there had already been several suicides lately and it was wearing a little thin.

To his second friend, Minnearo gave a pledge-salute, going through all sixty sequences with exaggerated care, and wave-danced, "Tomorrow I shall immerse my body in the ocean, if anyone will watch."

His second friend, Fless, smiled tolerantly and told him he would come and see the performance.

To his third friend, with many excited leapings and boundings, Minnearo described what he imagined would happen to him after he had gone under the lapping waters of the ocean. The dance he went through to give this description was intricate and even imaginative, because Minnearo had spent most of that third life cycle working it out in his mind. It used motion and color and sound and another sense something like smell, all to communicate descriptions of falling, impact with the water, and then the quick dissolution and blending in the currents of the ocean, the dimming and loss of awareness, then darkness, and finally the awakening, the completion of the change. Minnearo had a rather romantic turn of mind, so he imagined himself recoalescing around the life-mote of one of Loarr's greatest heroes, Krollim, and forming on Krollim's old pattern. And he even ended the dance with suggestions of glory and imitation of himself by others, which was definitely presumptuous. But the friend for whom the dance was given did nod approvingly at several points.

"If it turns out to be half what you anticipate," said this friend, Pur, "then I envy you. But you never know."

"I guess not," Minnearo said, rather morosely. And he hesitated before leaving, for Pur was what I suppose I'd better call female, and Minnearo had rather hoped that she would join him in the ocean jump. But if she thought of it she gave no sign, merely gazed at Minnearo calmly, waiting for him to go; so finally he did.

And at the appropriate time, with his friend Fless watching him from the edge of the cliff, Minnearo did his final wave-dance as Minnearo—rather excited and ill-coordinated, but that was understandable in the circumstances—and then performed his approach to the edge, leaped and tumbled downward through the air, making fully two dozen turns this way and that before he hit the water.

Fless hurried back and described the suicide to Asterrea and Pur, who laughed and applauded in most of the right places, so on the whole it was a success. Then the three of them sat down and began plotting Minnearo's revenge.

—All right, I *know* a lot of this doesn't make sense. Maybe that's because I'm trying to tell you about the

Loarra in human terms, which is a mistake with creatures as alien as they are. Actually, the Loarra are almost wholly an energy life-form, their consciousnesses coalescing in each life cycle around a spatial center which they call a "life-mote," so that, if you could see the patterns of energy they form (as I have, using a sense filter our expedition developed for that purpose), they'd look rather like a spiral nebula sometimes, or other times like iron filings gathering around a magnet, or maybe like a half-melted snowflake. (That's probably what Minnearo looked like on that day, because it's the suicides and the aged who look like that.) Their forms keep shifting, of course, but each individual usually keeps close to one pattern.

Loarr itself is a gigantic gaseous planet with an orbit so close to its primary that its year has to be only about thirty-seven Earthstandard Days long. (In Earthsystem, the orbit would be considerably inside that of Venus.) There's a solid core to the planet, and a lot of hard outcroppings like islands, but most of the surface is in a molten or gaseous state, swirling and bubbling and howling with winds and storms. It's not a very inviting planet if you're anything like a human being, but it does have one thing that brought it to Unicentral's attention: mining.

Do you have any idea what mining is like on a planet where most metals are fluid from the heat and/or pressure? Most people haven't heard much about this, because it isn't a situation we encounter often, but it was there on Loarr, and it was very, very interesting. Because our analyses showed some elements that had been until then only computer-theory—elements that were supposed to exist only in the hearts of suns, for one thing. And if we could get hold of some of them . . . Well, you see what I mean. The mining possibilities were very interesting indeed.

Of course, it would take half the wealth of Earthsystem to outfit a full-scale expedition there. But Uni-central hummed for two-point-eight seconds and then issued detailed instructions on just how it was all to be arranged. So there we went.

And there I was, a Standard Year later (five Standard years ago), sitting inside a mountain of artificial Earth welded onto one of Loarr's "islands" and wondering what the hell I was doing there. Because I'm not a mining engineer, not a physicist or comp-technician or, in fact, much of anything that requires technical training. I'm a public-relations man; and there was just no reason for me to have been assigned to such a hellish, impossible, god-forsaken, inconceivable, and plain damned *unlivable* planet as Loarr.

But there was a reason, and it was the Loarra, of course. They lived ("lived") there, and they were intelligent, so we had to negotiate with them. Ergo: me.

So in the next several years, while I negotiated and we set up operations and I acted as a go-between, I learned a lot about them. Just enough to translate, however clumsily, the wave-dance of the Changer and the Three, which is their equivalent of a classic folk-hero myth (or would be if they had anything honestly equivalent to anything of ours).

To continue:

Fless was in favor of building a pact among the Three by which they would, each in turn and each with deliberate lack of the appropriate salutes, commit suicide in exactly the same way Minnearo had. "Thus we can kill this suicide," Fless explained in excited waves through the air.

But Pur was more practical. "Thus," she corrected him, "we would kill *only* this suicide. It is unimaginative, a thing to be done by rote, and Minnearo deserves more."

Asterrea seemed undecided; he hopped about, spark-ing and disappearing and reappearing inches away in another color. They waited for him to comment, and finally he stabilized, stood still in the air, settled to the ground, and held himself firmly there. Then he said, in slow, careful movements, "I'm not sure he deserves an original revenge. It wasn't a new suicide, after all. And who is to avenge us?" A single spark leaped from him. "Who is to avenge us?" he repeated, this time with more pronounced motions.

"Perhaps," said Pur slowly, "we will need no revenge—if our act is great enough."

The other two paused in their random wave-motions, considering this. Fless shifted from blue to green to a bright red which dimmed to yellow; Asterrea pulsed a deep ultraviolet.

"Everyone has always been avenged," Fless said at last. "What you suggest is meaningless."

"But if we do something great enough," Pur said; and now she began to radiate heat which drew the other two reluctantly toward her. "Something which has never been done before, in *any* form. Something for which there can *be* no revenge, for it will be a *positive* thing—not a death-change, not a destruction or a disappearance or a forgetting, even a great one. A *positive* thing."

Asterrea's ultraviolet grew darker, darker, until he seemed to be nothing more than a hole in the air. "Dangerous, dangerous, dangerous," he droned, moving torpidly back and forth. "You know it's impossible to ask—we'd have to give up all our life cycles to come. Because a positive in the world. . . ." He blinked into darkness, and did not reappear for long seconds. When he did he was perfectly still, pulsing weakly but gradually regaining strength.

Pur waited till his color and tone showed that consciousness had returned, then moved in a light wave-motion calculated to draw the other two back into calm, reasonable discourse. "I've thought about this for six life cycles already," she danced. "I must be right—*no* one has worked on a problem for so long. A positive would *not* be dangerous, no matter what the three- and four-cycle theories say. It would be beneficial." She paused, hanging orange in midair. "And it would be *new*," she said with a quick spiral. "Oh, how *new!*"

And so, at length, they agreed to follow her plan. And it was briefly this: On a far island outcropping set in the deepest part of the Loarran ocean, where crashing, tearing storms whipped molten metal-compounds into blinding spray, there was a vortex of forces that was avoided by every Loarra on pain of inescapable and final death-change. The most ancient wave-dances of that ancient time said that the vortex had always been there, that the Loarra themselves had been born there or had escaped from there or had in some way cheated the laws that ruled there. Whatever the truth about that was, the vortex was an eater of energy, calling and catching from afar any Loarra or other beings who strayed within its influence. (For all the life on Loarr is energy-based, even the mindless, drifting foodbeasts—creatures of uniform dull color, no internal motion, no scent or tone, and absolutely no self-volition. Their place in the Loarran scheme of things is and was literally nothing more than that of food; even though there were countless foodbeasts drifting in the air in most areas of the planet, the Loarra hardly ever noticed them. They ate them when they were hungry, and looked around them at any other time.)

"Then you want us to destroy the *vortex?*" cried Fless, dancing and dodging to right and left in agitation.

"Not *destroy*," Pur said calmly. "It will be a *life*-change, not a destruction."

"Life-change?" said Asterrea faintly, wavering in the air.

And she said it again: "*Life*-change." For the vortex had once created, or somehow allowed to be created, the Oldest of the Loarra, those many-cycles-ago beings who had combined and split, reacted and changed countless times to become the Loarra of this day. And if creation could happen at the vortex once, then it could happen again.

"But how?" asked Fless, trying now to be reasonable, dancing the question with precision and holding a steady green color as he did so.

"We will need help," Pur said, and went on to explain that she had heard—from a windbird, a creature with little intelligence but perfect memory—that there was one of the Oldest still living his first life cycle in a personality-home somewhere near the vortex. In that most ancient time of the race, when suicide had been considered extreme as a means of cycle-change, this Oldest had made his change by a sort of negative suicide—he had frozen his cycle, so that his consciousness and form continued in a never-ending repetition of themselves, on and on while his friends changed and grew and learned as they ran through life cycle after life cycle, becoming different people with common memories, moving forward into the future by this method while he, the last Oldest, remained fixed at the beginning. He saw only the beginning, remembered only the beginning, understood only the beginning.

And for that reason his had been the most tragic of all Loarran changes (and the windbird had heard it rumored, in eight different ways, each of which it repeated word-for-word to Pur, that in the ages since that change more than a hundred hundred Loarra had attempted revenge for the Oldest, but always without success) and it had never been repeated, so that this Oldest was the only Oldest. And for that reason he was important to their quest, Pur explained.

With a perplexed growing and shrinking, brightening and dimming, Asterrea asked, "But how can he live anywhere near the vortex and not be consumed by it?"

"That is a crucial part of what we must find out," Pur

said. And after the proper salutes and rituals, the Three set out to find the Oldest.

The wave-dance of the Changer and the Three traditionally at this point spends a great deal of time, in great splashes of color and bursts of light and subtly contrived clouds of darkness all interplaying with hops and swoops and blinking and dodging back and forth, to describe the scene as Pur, Fless, and Asterrea set off across that ancient molten sea. I've seen the dance countless times, and each viewing has seemed to bring me maddeningly closer to understanding the meaning that this has for the Loarra themselves. Lowering clouds flashing bursts of aimless, lifeless energy, a rumbling sea below, whose swirling depths pulled and tugged at the Three as they swept overhead, darting around each other in complex patterns like electrons playing cat's-cradle around an invisible nucleus. A droning of lamentation from the changers left behind on their rugged home island, and giggles from those who had recently changed. And the colors of the Three themselves: burning red Asterrea and glowing green Fless and steady, steady golden Pur. I see and hear them all, but I feel only a weird kind of alien beauty, not the grandeur, excitement, and awesomeness they have for the Loarra.

When the Three felt the vibrations and swirlings in the air that told them they were coming near to the vortex, they paused in their flight and hung in an interpatterned motion-sequence above the dark, rolling sea, conversing only in short flickerings of color because they had to hold the pattern tightly in order to withstand the already-strong attraction of the vortex.

"Somewhere near?" asked Asterrea, pulsing a quick green.

"Closer to the vortex, I think," Pur said, chancing a sequence of reds and violets.

"Can we be sure?" asked Fless; but there was no answer from Pur and he had expected none from Asterrea.

The ocean crashed and leaped; the air howled around them. And the vortex pulled at them.

Suddenly they felt their motion-sequence changing, against their wills, and for long moments all three were afraid that it was the vortex's attraction that was doing it. They moved in closer to each other, and whirled more quickly in a still more intricate pattern, but it did no good. Irresistibly they were drawn apart again, and at the same time the three of them were moved toward the vortex.

And then they felt the Oldest among them.

He had joined the motion-sequence; this must have been why they had felt the sequence changed and loosened—to make room for him. Whirling and blinking, the Oldest led them inward over the frightening sea, radiating warmth through the storm and, as they followed, or were pulled along, they studied him in wonder.

He was hardly recognizable as one of them, this ancient Oldest. He was . . . not quite energy any longer. He was half matter, carrying the strange mass with awkward, aged grace, his outer edges almost rigid as they held the burden of his congealed center and carried it through the air. (Looking rather like a half-dissolved snowflake, yes, only dark and dismal, a snowflake weighted with coal dust.) And, for now at least, he was completely silent.

Only when he had brought the Three safely into the calm of his barren personality-home on a tiny rock jutting at an angle from the wash of the sea did he speak. There, inside a cone of quiet against which the ocean raged and fell back, the sands faltered and even the vortex's power was nullified, the Oldest said wearily, "So you have come." He spoke with a slow waving back and forth, augmented by only a dull red color.

To this the Three did not know what to say; but Pur finally hazarded, "Have you been waiting for us?" The

Oldest pulsed a somewhat brighter red, once, twice. He paused. Then he said, "I do not *wait*—there is nothing to wait *for*." Again the pulse of a brighter red. "One waits for the future. But there is no future, you know."

"Not for him," Pur said softly to her companions, and Fless and Asterrea sank wavering to the stone floor of the Oldest's home, where they rocked back and forth.

The Oldest sank with them, and when he touched down he remained motionless. Pur drifted over the others, maintaining movement but unable to raise her color above a steady blue-green. She said to the Oldest, "But you knew we would come.'"

"Would come? *Would* come? Yes, and *did* come, and *have* come, and *are* come. It is today only, you know, for me. I will be the Oldest, when the others pass me by. I will never change, nor will my world."

"But the others have already passed you by," Fless said. "We are many life cycles after you, Oldest—so many it is beyond the count of windbirds."

The Oldest seemed to draw his material self into a more upright posture, forming his energy-flow carefully around it. To the red of his color he added a low hum with only the slightest quaver as he said, "*Nothing* is after me, here on Rock. When you come here, you come out of time, just as I have. So now you have always been here and will always be here, for as long as you are here."

Asterrea sparked yellow suddenly, and danced upward into the becalmed air. As Fless stared and Pur moved quickly to calm him, he drove himself again and again at the edge of the cone of quiet that was the Oldest's refuge. Each time he was thrown back and each time he returned to dash himself once more against the edge of the storm, trying to penetrate back into it. He flashed and burned countless colors, and strange sound-frequencies filled the quiet, until at last, with Pur's stern direction and Fless's blank gaze upon him, he sank back wearily to the stone floor. "A trap, a trap," he pulsed. "This is it, this is the vortex itself, we should have known, and we'll never get away."

The oldest had paid no attention to Asterrea's display. He said slowly, "And it is because I am not in time that the vortex cannot touch me. And it is because I am out of time that I know what the vortex is, for I can remember myself born in it."

Pur left Asterrea then, and came close to the Oldest. She hung above him, thinking with blue vibrations, then asked, "Can you tell us how you were born?—what is creation?—how new things are made?" She paused a moment, and added, "And what *is* the vortex?"

The Oldest seemed to lean forward, seemed tired. His color had deepened again to the darkest red, and the Three could clearly see every atom of matter within his energy-field, stark and hard. He said, "So many questions to ask one question." And he told them the answer to that question.

—And I can't tell you that answer, because I don't know it. No one knows it now, not even the present-day Loarra who are the Three after a thousand-million-billion life cycles. Because the Loarra really do become different . . . different "persons," when they pass from one cycle to another, and after that many changes, memory becomes meaningless ("Try it sometime," one of the Loarra once wave-danced to me, and there was no indication that he thought this was a joke.)

Today, for instance, the Three themselves, a thousand-million-billion times removed from themselves but still, they maintain, *themselves*, often come to watch the Dance of the Changer and the Three, and even though it is about them they are still excited and moved by it as though it were a tale never even heard before, let alone lived through. Yet let a dancer miss a movement or color or sound by even the slightest nuance, and the Three will correct him. (And yes, many times the legend

Changer himself, Minnearo, he who started the story, has attended these dances—though often he leaves after the re-creation of his suicide dance.)

It's sometimes difficult to tell one given Loarra from all the others, by the way, despite the complex and subtle technologies of Unicentral, which have provided me with sense filters of all sorts, plus frequency simulators, pattern scopes, special gravity inducers, and a minicomp that takes up more than half of my very tight little island of Earth pasted into the surface of Loarr and which can do more thinking and analyzing in two seconds than I can do in fifty years. During my four years on Loarr, I got to "know" several of the Loarra, yet even at the end of my stay I was still never sure just who I was "talking" with at any time. I could run through about seventeen or eighteen tests, linking the sense-filters with the minicomp, and get a definite answer that way. But the Loarra are a bit short on patience and by the time I'd get done with all that whoever it was would usually be off bouncing and sparking into the hellish vapors they call air. So usually I just conducted my researches or negotiations or idle queries, whichever they were that day, with whoever would pay attention to my antigrav "eyes," and I discovered that it didn't matter much just who I was talking with: none of them made any more sense than the others. They were all, as far as I was and am concerned, totally crazy, incomprehensible, stupid, silly, and plain damn no good.

If that sounds like I'm bitter, it's because I am. I've got forty-two murdered men to be bitter about. But back to the unfolding of the greatest legend of an ancient and venerable alien race:

When the Oldest had told them what they wanted to know, the Three came alive with popping and flashing and dancing in the air, Pur just as much as the others. It was all that they had hoped for and more; it was the entire answer to their quest and their problem. It would enable them to create, to transcend any negative cycle-climax they could have devised.

After a time the Three came to themselves and remembered the rituals.

"We offer thanks in the name of Minnearo, whose suicide we are avenging," Fless said gravely, waving his message in respectful deep-blue spirals.

"We thank you in our own names as well," said Asterrea.

"And we thank you in the name of no one and nothing," said Pur, "for that is the greatest thanks conceivable."

But the Oldest merely sat there, pulsing his dull red, and the Three wondered among themselves. At last the Oldest said, "To accept thanks is to accept responsibility, and in only-today, as I am, there can be none of that because there can be no new act. I am outside time, you know, which is almost outside life. All this I have told you is something told to you before, many times, and it will be again."

Nonetheless, the Three went through all the rituals of thanks-giving, performing them with flawless grace and care—color-and-sound demonstrations, dances, offerings of their own energy, and all the rest. And Pur said, "It is possible to give thanks for a long-past act or even a mindless reflex, and we do so in the highest."

The Oldest pulsed dull red and did not answer, and after a time the Three took leave of him.

Armed with the knowledge he had given them, they had no trouble penetrating the barrier protecting Rock, the Oldest's personality-home, and in moments were once again alone with themselves in the raging storm that encircled the vortex. For long minutes they hung in midair, whirling and darting in their most tightly linked patterns while the storm whipped them and the vortex pulled them. Then abruptly they broke their patterns and hurled themselves deliberately into the heart of the vortex itself. In a moment they had disappeared.

They seemed to feel neither motion nor lapse of time as they fell into the vortex. It was a change that came without perception or thought—a change from self to unself, from existence to void. They knew only that they had given themselves up to the vortex, that they were suddenly lost in darkness and a sense of surrounding emptiness which had no dimension. They knew without thinking that if they could have sent forth sound there would have been no echo, that a spark or even a bright flare would have brought no reflection from anywhere. For this was the place of the origin of life, and it was empty. It was up to them to fill it, if it was to be filled.

So they used the secret the Oldest had given them, the secret those at the Beginning had discovered by accident and which only one of the Oldest could have remembered. Having set themselves for this before entering the vortex, they played their individual parts automatically—selfless, unconscious, almost random acts such as even non-living energy can perform. And when all parts had been completed precisely, correctly, and at just the right time and in just the right sequence, the creating took place.

It was a foodbeast. It formed and took shape before them in the void, and grew and glowed its dull, drab glow until it was whole. For a moment it drifted there, then suddenly it was expelled from the vortex, thrown out violently as though from an explosion—away from the nothingness within, away from darkness and silence into the crashing, whipping violence of the storm outside. And with it went the Three, vomited forth with the primitive bit of life they had made.

Outside, in the storm, the Three went automatically into their tightest motion sequence, whirling and blinking around each other in desperate striving to maintain themselves amid the savagery that roiled around them.

And once again they felt the powerful pull of the vortex behind them, gripping them anew now that they were outside, and they knew that the vortex would draw them in again, this time forever, unless they were able to resist it. But they found that they were nearly spent; they had lost more of themselves in the vortex than they had ever imagined possible. They hardly felt alive now, and somehow they had to withstand the crushing powers of both the storm and the vortex, and had to forge such a strongly interlinked motion-pattern that they would be able to make their way out of this place, back to calm and safety.

And there was only one way they could restore themselves enough for that.

Moving almost as one, they converged upon the mindless foodbeast they had just created, and they ate it.

That's not precisely the end of the Dance of the Changer and the Three—it does go on for a while, telling of the honors given the Three when they returned, and of Minnearo's reaction when he completed his change by reappearing around the life-mote left by a dying windbird, and of how all of the Three turned away from their honors and made their next changes almost immediately—but my own attention never quite follows the rest of it. I always get stuck at that one point in the story, that supremely contradictory moment when the Three destroyed what they had made, when they came away with no more than they had brought with them. It doesn't even achieve irony, and yet it is the emotional highpoint of the Dance as far as the Loarra are concerned. In fact, it's the *whole* point of the Dance, as they've told me with brighter sparkings and flashes than they ever use when talking about anything else, and if the Three had been able to come away from there *without* eating their foodbeast, then their achievement would have been duly noted, applauded, giggled at by the newly-changed, and forgotten within two life cycles.

And these are the creatures with whom I had to deal and whose rights I was charged to protect. I was ambassador to a planetful of things that would tell me with a straight face that two and two are orange. And yes, that's why I'm back on Earth now—and why the rest of the expedition, those who are left alive from it, are back here too.

If you could read the fifteen-microtape report I filed with Unicentral (which you can't, by the way: Unicentral always Classifies its failures), it wouldn't tell you anything more about the Loarra than I've just told you in the story of the Dance. In fact, it might tell you less, because although the report contained masses of hard data on the Loarra, plus every theory I could come up with or coax out of the minicomp, it didn't have much about the Dance. And it's only in things like that, attitude-data rather than I.Q. indices, psych reports and so on, that you can really get the full impact of what we were dealing with on Loarr.

After we'd been on the planet for four Standard Years, after we'd established contact and exchanged gifts and favors and information with the Loarra, after we'd set up our entire mining operation and had had it running without hindrance for over three years—after all that, the raid came. One day a sheet of dull purple light swept in from the horizon, and as it got closer I could see that it was a whole colony of the Loarra, their individual colors and fluctuations blending into that single purple mass. I was in the mountain, not outside with the mining extensors, so I saw all of it, and I lived through it.

They flashed in over us like locusts descending, and they hit the crawlers and dredges first. The metal glowed red, then white, then it melted. Then it was just gas that formed billowing clouds rising to the sky. Somewhere

229

inside those clouds was what was left of the elements which had comprised seventeen human beings, who were also vapor now.

I hit the alarm and called everyone in, but only a few made it. The rest were caught in the tunnels when the Loarra swarmed over them, and they went up in smoke too. Then the automatic locks shut, and the mountain was sealed off. And six of us sat there, watching on the screen as the Loarra swept back and forth outside, cleaning up the bits and pieces they'd missed.

I sent out three of my "eyes," but they too were promptly vaporized.

Then we waited for them to hit the mountain itself . . . half a dozen frightened men huddled in the comp-room, none of us saying anything. Just sweating.

But they didn't come. They swarmed together in a tight spiral, went three times around the mountain, made one final salute-dip, and then whirled straight up and out of sight. Only a handful of them were left behind out there.

After a while I sent out a fourth "eye." One of the Loarra came over, flitted around it like a firefly, blinked through the spectrum, and settled down to hover in front for talking. It was Pur—a Pur who was a thousand-million-billion life cycles removed from the Pur we know and love, of course, but nonetheless still pretty much Pur.

I sent out a sequence of lights and movements that translated, roughly, as, "What the hell did you do that for?"

And Pur glowed pale yellow for several seconds, then gave me an answer that doesn't translate. Or, if it does, the translation is just "Because."

Then I asked the question again, in different terms, and she gave me the same answer in different terms. I asked a third time, and a fourth, and she came back with the same thing. She seemed to be enjoying the variations on the Dance; maybe she thought we were playing.

Well . . . We'd already sent out our distress call by then, so all we could do was wait for a relief ship and hope they wouldn't attack again before the ship came, because we didn't have a chance of fighting them—we were miners, not a military expedition. God knows what any military expedition could have done against energy things, anyway. While we were waiting, I kept sending out the "eyes," and I kept talking to one Loarra after another. It took three weeks for the ship to get there, and I must have talked to over a hundred of them in that time, and the sum total of what I was told was this:

Their reason for wiping out the mining operation was untranslatable. No, they weren't mad. No, they didn't want us to go away. Yes, we were welcome to the stuff we were taking out of the depths of the Loarran ocean.

And, most importantly: No, they couldn't tell me whether or not they were likely ever to repeat their attack.

So we went away, limped back to Earth, and we all made our reports to Unicentral. We included, as I said, every bit of data we could think of, including an estimate of the value of the new elements on Loarr—which was something on the order of six times the wealth of Earth-system. And we put it up to Unicentral as to whether or not we should go back.

Unicentral has been humming and clicking for ten months now, but it hasn't made a decision.

Last Words About Terry

Harlan Ellison

No one is up to reading that Terry is gone, much less able to write about him. But because we have lost so many, so damned many in the past thirteen months, we have become numb with the pain. And in our denial, in our passion simply to live with this cold wind that continues to blow, some of the dearest lose the words of love and friendship they would most like to have had voiced. And as John D. said once, "Time is the random wind that blows down the long corridor, slamming all the doors."

Some of you knew him as an editor with impeccable taste. Others of you still hold in high esteem stories like "The Dance of the Changer and the Three," "Stanley Toothbrush," "Ozymandias," or "Hop-Friend." And how many of you out there now considered Big Name Writers got your start because Terry discovered you and published your first work?

But unless you shared time with him, as a friend, you can not know the rare treasure taken from us. Terry was that thing we all strive to be: a good guy. He was mordant and puckish, wise and clever (except about taking care of himself, the jerk!), affectionate and very private. He said as many foolish things as the rest of us, but he was blessed with the gift of the imp that made even the foolish remarks sound Solomonic. He loved corny old scientifiction from the twenties and thirties, and screwloose fanzines, and the music of the sixties, and those of us whom he knew from fandom days and the Meredith Agency and the ragtag days of penny-a-word Ace Double slave labor.

He and Carol locked me up in their apartment in Brooklyn Heights, five blocks from the Dillons' town house, and they wouldn't even let me go out for a pizza till I'd written the introductions for *Dangerous Visions*. He was *there*, always right there if the need arose to consult a Terry Carr.

He was the very best Terry Carr the universe could have constructed, and if there is a blast of anger that we cannot suppress, it is that the universe did its best work making him intellectually, and seems to have used inferior parts for the package.

Some of us will not soon be able to lose the sound of his door slamming in the chill wind.

A tiny, additional pain attendant on Terry's leaving us. I wrote a story for this volume. It was the story I was working on for Terry when he died. He liked what I read to him by long distance. My health wasn't terrific as deadline came and went for this book to honor the memory of Terry. The wonderful cover painting by Mike Presley, around which I was writing the yarn, *that* made it. But I didn't. The editor of this book, Beth Meacham, who was patient as hell, kept the book open until production schedules closed it down; so the story that fits the cover isn't here. The best I can do, to pay off Terry's part in that story, is to tell you that it is called "I Weep for the Clone of John Barrymore," and if you see it somewhere, remember that it would not have been written—like so much of the good work in the genre these past twenty-something years—had Terry Carr not willed it into being.